T0147129

Charmed at First Sight

Books by Sharla Lovelace

Charmed in Texas Novels
A Charmed Little Lie
Lucky Charmed
Once a Charmer

"Enchanted by You," a novella included in *The Cottage on Pumpkin and Vine*

Charmed at First Sight

Sharla Lovelace

LYRICAL SHINE
Kensington Publishing Corp.
www.kensingtonbooks.com

LYRICAL SHINE BOOKS are published by

Kensington Publishing Corp.
119 West 40th Street
New York, NY 10018

All Kensington titles, imprints, and distributed lines are available at special quantity discounts for bulk purchases for sales promotion, premiums, fundraising, educational, or institutional use.

Special book excerpts or customized printings can also be created to fit specific needs. For details, write or phone the office of the Kensington Sales Manager: Kensington Publishing Corp., 119 West 40th Street, New York, NY 10018. Attn. Sales Department. Phone: 1-800-221-2647.

Lyrical Shine and Lyrical Shine logo Reg. U.S. Pat. & TM Off.

First Electronic Edition: July 2018
eISBN-13: 978-1-5161-0701-8
eISBN-10: 1-5161-0701-2

First Print Edition: July 2018
ISBN-13: 978-1-5161-0702-5
ISBN-10: 1-5161-0702-0

Printed in the United States of America

To my beloved Southeast Texas:
This story was finished during Hurricane Harvey, while rain and tears
flooded our world. I've never in my life been so proud to be a Texan
than I was in the midst of that, watching all the kindness and love of
so many selfless people coming together, banding together, helping
each other, and being stronger because of it. To my family and friends,
my neighborhood, my town, my county, and my state—being "Texas
Strong...Come Hell or High Water" has never meant more. Here's to
healing, recovering, and rebuilding, and dry, sunny days.

Acknowledgments

Hello lovely Readers!

I know it's been a bit since we've gotten to hang out in Charmed, and I LOVE you all for waiting for CHARMED AT FIRST SIGHT! I'm so excited to revisit Lanie and Nick and Carmen and Sully and Allie and Bash (whew), and bring in a few new faces! In this book, we get to know one of Bash's clients, the owners of Cherrydale Flower Farm…and boy, do we! A runaway bride and a mysterious hot motorcycle man land in Charmed, and stir up ALL kinds of chaos. But don't worry! All your favorites are right up in the thick of all the shenanigans with the new kids, because you know they can't stay out of trouble.

As usual, this book wouldn't have happened without the TLC from my agent, Jessica Faust, and my editor, Wendy McCurdy, as well as all the Kensington Lyrical team that made it shine. My eternal thanks to them all.

My family deserves awards for putting up with me when I'm writing, even the members who don't live here anymore. Family knows no limits when there is unlimited texting, so whether in the other room or out of state, no one is exempt from the gripey mama-on-deadline. Troy, Ethan, and Amanda, I love y'all bunches.

This was my first book written, by the way, in my brand-spanking-new author cottage that my amazing hubby built for me. I've been writing in the kids' room, the living room, and my bedroom for years, and he finally said enough was enough. He was tired of turning down the TV. LOL. No, seriously, he built me a dream office that I couldn't have imagined possible, and this book baby was the first result! If you want to see pictures, go to www.sharlalovelace.com and click on the Extras tab.

I hope you enjoy falling in love with Micah and Leo as much as I did! And please feel free to message me on Facebook or Twitter or any of the social places at @sharlalovelace and/or e-mail me at sharla@sharlalovelace. com to let me know what you think!

Okay, now go see what Micah's about to do, because I'm telling you, she's a hot mess. ☺

xoxo
Sharla

CHAPTER ONE

Why the hell didn't I go with the flats?

That thought would kick my ass later.

Shoes? Really? At a moment like that, my heart pounding in my ears, sweating through fifteen miles of lace, silk, and guilt, and picturing everyone's appalled faces right about now—I was just wishing for good running shoes?

I was a selfish, horrible troll.

A troll who they'd be looking for any minute.

"Shit!" I huffed, weaving through the cars parked along the street, holding up a dress that cost more than my car—"My car!" I gasped, stopping short and spinning around. It was in the back of the church, waiting to take Jeremy and me to the reception…but no, my keys were in Jeremy's pants pocket, on his body, at the altar, waiting on the selfish horrible troll. *Don't think about that.* "Damn it!"

I whirled back around and jogged into the street on my four-inch heels to make better time, knowing that at any minute someone would figure it out. Jeremy, my brothers, my friends—no, *Jeremy's* friends. Someone would come to see why the big heavy music that shook the floor so hard I felt it in my hoo-hah didn't come accompanied with a girl in a big white dress. My window was narrow at best.

I just had to make it to the signal light at the corner. Then I could— what? Call a cab? In Cherrydale, Texas? Right. And on what, my special holographic phone? Unlike my actual one still back in the dressing room.

*Breathe…run…breathe…run…*I chanted in my head to the rhythm of my feet hitting the pavement. Hopping really, like I was on stilts. *Breathe…*

run...At the light, I could duck into the old Smith's Drugstore, and pray that Mr. Dan, the pharmacist, would let me use his phone to call an Uber. Breathlessly, I reached the drugstore door, the glass etched with time and dust and grimy fingers, and pulled. Nothing.

It was—

"It's two o'clock," I huffed. "Who closes at—" I shut my eyes, willing back the tears of panic I felt welling up in my eyes and throat. Mr. Dan was at the wedding, too. Of course he was. Because Jeremy's mother invited the whole damn town...

Plan B—what the hell was plan B when there was never really a plan A? I glanced upward. Really to drive back the tears, but I'd take any help at that moment.

What are you doing, Micah?

The unmistakable rumble of a Harley preceded an all-black machine straddled by an equally unmistakable male in jeans stretched to love him and a black T-shirt, his head and face completely covered in a black helmet as he rolled up to the light and set boots on the ground to balance the bike.

He turned his head my way and goose bumps went down my back. I swear there was a question there. I couldn't see his face, but—no. *No. That's not plan B*, little voices said in my head. *You're a responsible person now. You own—well, you sort of own a business. You have bills. Obligations. You're a Roman.*

Yeah. That one right there should have slapped me back down the street. But being a respectable Roman, always held to some invisible standard that only my oldest brother could pull off, wasn't working for me today.

Harley-guy's right hand reached up, sliding the mirrored visor open, revealing dark eyes that even from twenty feet away made my breath catch. In a good way.

Shit, double fuckwaffles! *No!* I didn't need breath-catching in *any* way. I just ran my dumb ass away from one man. But what the hell were my feet doing? I took two steps toward him, and I definitely saw the question that time. Curiosity. Puzzlement. Wariness? Yeah, *Harley-guy* should have that, because clearly I didn't have enough.

"You need help?" he called out over the idling rumble, his voice deep.

I caught a distorted reflection of myself in the dirty window. Hair falling out of the expensive ornate up-do, poking out in unruly frizzy corkscrews above the short veil. Black spreading under my eyes from sweat and tears. Standing on a steamy sidewalk in a mountain of blinding white. It was probably a logical question, but damn the guy had to have balls to jump off into that crazy.

All I could hear was my racing heart and my breathing, even over the motor.

No. This is lunacy. All of it is lunacy, but what you're thinking of doing here is the cherry on top of the—

"Micah!"

I gasped so hard it made me cough, as I jerked in the direction I'd come from, toward the familiar voice I'd known since I was twenty-four. In eight years, I'd heard every possible inflection or emotion in Jeremy Blankenship's voice. I'd heard every range of happy, sad, and controlled anger, but I'd never heard this. Even from all the way down the road, I heard the timbre of mortification in his yell, maybe mixed with a little hurt and what-the-fuck. I'd give him that. He deserved the what-the-fuckedness of this situation.

He was standing in the church parking lot alone, until two other tuxedoed men appeared in the doorway behind him. Thatcher and Jackson. My eyes filled again as I turned away from them and stared back at Harley-guy. I couldn't face my brothers right now. I couldn't explain to them why—

"Micah!" Jeremy yelled again, this time in the tone I recognized. Not the one that told me he loved me last night. The one that said *How dare you embarrass me.* I glanced back to see him striding purposefully in my direction, and the panic seized my chest.

"Lady?" Harley-guy called out, yanking my attention back his way. "Light's green."

Fight or flight.

Fight or flight.

I looked into eyes I didn't know from Adam and felt the weirdest pull ever. My stilettoed feet made the decision for me, carrying me off the curb, into the street, hauling my weight in dress up to throw a leg over the seat and straddle his ass.

"You sure?" he said over his shoulder.

Fuck no.

"Are you?" I felt a laugh rumble through his body as he shook his head. "Yeah, touché. You aren't gonna kill me, are you?"

"Because if I was, I'd tell you?" he said, revving the engine. "Put on that helmet behind you and hold on."

Oh, sweet Jesus, what am I doing?

That was my last thought as I tugged the veil off, bobby pins flying in all directions, shoved the helmet on, shut my eyes tight, and wrapped my arms around his middle the best I could with all that dress. Shut them against the reality of the world I'd just created. Against the sight of my veil lying in the street. Of Jeremy running down the street after me. My brothers running for Thatcher's truck.

All there was, was the bike moving under me and the man between my legs as we sped away, out of Cherrydale. Toward the highway. To God knows where.

"Where are we going?" I yelled over the din as we hit the highway going south.

"I'm going to Charmed," he yelled back, turning his head slightly so I could hear him. The *I'm* in that sentence was stressed to let me know in no uncertain terms that anything after that was on me. "It's about an hour."

I nodded, trying to calm my heart rate and breathe like a normal person. I knew Charmed, or I knew *of* it. My family's flower farm rented beehives from Bash Anderson, the owner of an apiary there. That was fine. That'd be good. Not so far away that I'd totally lost my mind. Just maybe a little. Give me a minute to pull my shit together before the cavalry came. Also, it was good that the stranger I was straddling had a destination. Higher odds that he wasn't going to rape and kill me and leave me in a ditch.

My decision-making abilities needed an overhaul.

"Probably less than that, actually," he continued, making my heart skip in my chest as he upped the speed. "They are going to come after you and I don't feel like fighting today."

"You don't have to fight for me," I yelled.

"I'm not," he said. Well, so much for chivalry. "But that guy's gonna need to hit something, and it won't be you."

There was that.

"What are you going to Charmed for?" I asked.

He paused. I wasn't sure if he'd heard me.

"Work," he finally tossed back.

"You work there?"

"I will shortly."

We sped along the road in silence for the rest of about forty-five minutes, me attempting to look over my shoulder with a giant ball on my head while maintaining my death grip on some really good abs. A few cars tapped their horns at us, probably thinking we'd just gotten married, but no little old Mustang of mine whipped up next to us with an angry Jeremy inside. No big four-wheel-drive truck loomed, either. Which surprised me, because while Jeremy might give up, my older brother, Thatcher, wouldn't. They must have assumed I'd gone home first or was hiding in Cherrydale somewhere.

That would have been the logical thing to do. Well—if bolting for the door microseconds before walking down the aisle was the relative comparison. In that case, a logical person would have maybe just gone outside to calm her frayed nerves. Maybe walked around the block even. If *that* person had gone so off the rails as to climb onto a stranger's motorcycle and speed away, smart thinking would surely kick in after a block or two at which point she'd ask him to bring her back to the church. Or to Jeremy's house where we'd lived together for the past two years, after sharing apartments for five before that, to get some things. Somewhere that made sense.

They were looking for *that* person. The Micah Roman who had put away her spontaneous fly-by-the-seat-of-her-pants ways, along with her tendencies to ditch and run when things got too tough. The bar waitress-slash-sometimes artist-slash-whatever-made-money that had stepped out of those unstable shoes into business ownership with her brother, channeling her spirited creativity into the flower farming instead. The woman who packed up her beloved funky hats and shoes to finally adorn herself like a responsible businesswoman and worthy future wife to the heir of the Blankenship Resale empire.

Empire, my ass.

They ruled over Cherrydale Trade Days, mostly, which was several square miles of booth space for people to buy and sell their damn junk. That by itself was awesome. It's where I'd *met* Jeremy, while I was digging through a box of old retro hats and jewelry. The Trade Days was still relatively new at the time, since his family had relocated from farther south four years earlier. It was still growing, and the family roamed the grounds, interacting with customers. He'd stopped and teased me, and I'd found him deliciously adorable in that way a guy is when he's cutely making fun of your passion and you instantly think of fifteen ways you'll change him and you'll be picking out antique mosaic cabinet knobs together. Wearing matching plaid berets.

From that to now. In a ridiculous dress that was meant to say *I do* in, speeding down a highway with a nameless man to get as far away from Jeremy as I could—as quickly as possible.

So, it was just me and Harley-guy and speed. It was insane. *I* was insane! I could just hear my brothers now. Well, not Jackson. Jackson knew me. He knew my soul, my heart, my endless need for rebellion and nonconformity. He was my first shoplifting buddy when I went rebellious after our dad died, when I taught him how to pocket bubblegum from the corner store. He was the one who raised an eyebrow when I moved out of the house at eighteen into a friend's garage when I just couldn't live under my mother's roof anymore. And again when I put all my cherished old record albums and crazy prints into our mom's attic to move in with Jeremy and started wearing just one watch instead of four. Jackson got me. He probably saw this coming like a smoking volcano. He'd just give me a look and a hug and tell me he had my back. Thatcher—oh, man. He was going to get all puffed up, probably pace, and ask me, "What woman in her right mind did this?"

And he was right. I didn't know this dude I had my arms around. He could be twenty-one kinds of psycho, but oddly enough I felt nothing but safe with him. It vibrated off him, along with a primal intensity that was impossible not to feel. Okay, maybe that was the Harley's motor thrumming under my ass, but it felt like more than that.

Shit, yes, I was certifiable.

But the speed. It was awesome. It was like being out in the fields and the greenhouses with my hands in the dirt, textures and colors and aromas surrounding me, filling my senses. I loved being out there with the flowers, free, dirty, and reaching for the sun. This was close. When I closed my eyes, it was like flying, free and unchained. Unshackled from expectations and the limitations of boxes. Boring, cream-colored Blankenship boxes that had been trying to enclose me for almost a decade. I felt like something freeze-dried that had been dropped into water, or one of those vacuum-sealed packages that explode to three times their size when introduced to air. I wanted to cry from the joy of it, but I wasn't about to add *hysterical female* to what this guy probably already thought.

The exit for Charmed appeared, touting a big sign with bees and flowers on it saying WELCOME TO CHARMED. HOME OF THE WORLD FAMOUS HONEY FESTIVAL. We slowed into the curve of the exit, and I was surprised as disappointment washed over me, a new anxiety prickling my skin.

Exploding from my vacuum seal was great, but the adventure was ending. My fantasy was easy while adulting was put on hold and no words were exchanged, but shit was about to get real.

Another sign loomed before the turn, advertising a theme park called the Lucky Charm. I'd heard about it and the Honey Festival, but Jeremy never wanted to check them out, thinking it silly to drive an hour to buy bad food and ride a ride. Well, I'd done it now. Go me.

Rolling through Charmed, I was suddenly very aware of my attire. I felt every eye on us. Granted, I probably wouldn't have to be wearing a giant wedding dress for that. If Charmed was anything like Cherrydale, we'd get that same stare just for being out-of-towners.

Still, as we pulled to a stop in front of an old diner with a funky retro sign that said Blue Banana Grille, all I could think about was getting this thing off. This place looked like white bread, bologna, and apple pie, like crazy didn't land here much, and I had crazy radiating off me. I could feel it. I needed normal, and I had a feeling that anything resembling it was back there with my cell phone and keys. And—

"Oh, shit," I said, waiting while he grounded us.

"What?" he asked, his voice sounding preoccupied.

He pulled off his helmet, raking a hand back through short dark hair, while those dark eyes I'd seen earlier focused in hard on the diner door. I had the feeling the novelty of *me* had played out, and my new friend was ready to move on with his day.

"Nothing," I said, pulling my helmet off as well and hooking it back behind me, the reality of my situation rushing in on me from every direction.

I took a deep breath, smiling at a lady riding by on a giant tricycle, who waved and didn't miss a beat. Then again, maybe I could blend.

He held a hand out, supposedly for me, and when I paused, he blew out a breath.

"Well, I don't want to kick you in the face, so you need to get off first," he said, shoving the hand toward me again.

I gave the back of his head a look, resisting the urge to thump it. It was a good head, as heads go, but the part running his mouth was kind of a douche. Although what did I expect from my Harley-riding savior? For him to hold me while I had a good cry? Hell no. I'd pluck my head bald first.

"You should write Hallmark cards," I muttered.

Huffing a little, I tugged my dress up to almost my waist—at least high enough to catch sight of the blue glittery garter ribbon on my left thigh. So did he, I noticed, as the good head tilted downward. I grabbed his hand, expecting it to be for balance, but found myself nearly vaulted off the seat within a microsecond. I even forgot to let go of my dress, standing there with my girlie goods just about on display.

"You good?" he asked, letting go of me, swinging his leg over.

"S—sure," I managed, getting my balance and my first real look at him.

From the worn jeans to the black T-shirt to the really good arms rippling as he tucked his helmet under his arm. A little scruff peppered the hard lines of his face and balanced the sexiest full lips I'd ever seen on a man. Not to mention those soft, dark, haunted-looking eyes I'd already seen. Dear God, if I had to completely muck up my life today, at least it ended in this visual. This guy was jaw-dropping.

His gaze was dropping, too, sliding right down my bare legs.

"You might want to let go of that," he said, with a jut of his chin.

I dropped the fabric like it burned my fingers, cursing under my breath. *Shit, get it together, Micah.*

"Okay, so thank you," I said, pressing my hands to my hot cheeks. "I'd pay you, but—"

"*Pay* me?"

I pointed at the bike. "For the ride? For the gas?"

"I was coming here already," he said. "You looked like you needed help. At least in those shoes."

I nodded as I glanced down at the spikes attached to my feet. "Something like that. But I don't have my wallet anyway, so…"

"Didn't think that through very well, did you?" he said.

I narrowed my eyes at him. "Thanks for clarifying that."

"Do you have a plan?" he asked.

"Didn't you just establish that I didn't?" I said, rubbing my temples and wishing for an entire bottle of extra-strength something to dive into.

He blew out a breath and focused back on the door again, as if his attempt at polite small talk with the crazy lady had just run its course.

"I mean going forward," he said. "Obviously, you probably didn't start this day thinking this is where you'd end up, but I felt your mind spinning the whole way here. Do you know what you're going to do?"

I chuckled in spite of the barbs jabbing behind my skull. "That was survival prep you felt."

One eyebrow lifted in response. "Survival prep?"

"In case you were planning to chop me up and turn me into fertilizer, I had some defense going," I said.

Which wasn't total bullshit. I had thought of that for probably two minutes, before turning to the *What the hell do I do now?* channel.

The dark eyes narrowed with amusement, and it warmed his whole face. Like—serious *Push me backward and hold on to my ovaries* kind of warmth.

"Oh?" he said, taking a step closer.

No. I refused to take a step back. He was either being intimidating or flirty and I had no room in my brain for either. I couldn't help that I looked like an idiot doing what I'd done today. It happened. I didn't need this guy to scare me into some sort of lesson about stranger danger. No matter how hot he was. Because if he was just being flirty—well, my body might react to that because he was clearly carved from electricity and testosterone, but my heart said I'd just left one mostly-decent-basically-sort-of-nice guy at an altar, and my head said I didn't need any more alpha males. Period. I tugged at my dress to cover my boobs better, but it wasn't budging, so I crossed my arms. Which only drew his gaze to exactly there.

"And what was this defense plan of yours?"

His voice slid over my skin like butter. My body needed its ass kicked.

"I—I'd tell you but—"

He held up a hand. "Yeah, I know how that one goes, but just so you know—"

He glanced past me as the door opened and an elderly man walked out, carrying with him the sounds of clinking silverware and chatter before the door closed behind him. Harley-guy's expression disappeared on me again, all caught up in that building.

"Hey, don't let me keep you," I said. "If you have to get to work or something—"

His gaze snapped back to me. "What?"

I widened mine. "You said you were coming here for work? And you can't get enough of the view of this diner, so—if you need to go in there, go ahead. I'll—figure out what I'm doing in a minute."

"Don't you want to go clean up?" he said.

Awesome.

Just kick me in the face, already.

I smiled and averted my focus down the street. To—more of the same. Another little town pretty much like mine, where everyone knows everyone and nothing is private or personal. I swiped under my eyes, mentally groaning at the black on my fingers.

"Sure," I said.

"And call someone?" he added.

I slid my raccoon eyes up to meet his. "No phone."

He sighed, rubbing at his neck. "Of course not," he muttered.

"I'm not asking to use yours," I said.

"And I'm not offering it," he quipped. "Again—I have my own shit to deal with, lady. I don't need a pissed-off, jilted lover tracking me down making me have to hurt somebody."

I shook my head. Men.

"Let's just do this," I said, turning toward the door and then pivoting back. I held out a hand. "Thank you again if I don't see you when I come out of the bathroom."

Harley-guy looked down at my hand and took it in his. It was warm and protective and gave me all the good feelings I needed to run from.

"You gonna be okay?"

I took a deep breath and licked my dry lips. My ex-therapist would be proud. He'd always told me I played things too safe lately. I fired him last month, and now look at me. All fucking dangerous.

"I'll land on my feet."

"Do you have a name I can put with this story one day?" he asked, letting go of my hand to cross his arms over his chest. "Or do I just call you Miss Runaway?"

"Roman—" I began, automatically going into business mode, too late thinking I needed to not tell anyone I was Micah Roman. As in the Romans who owned and operated Cherrydale Flower Farm.

Then again, we weren't in Cherrydale anymore, Toto.

"—off," I added.

His eyes narrowed slightly. "Roman-off? As in *Romanov*?"

I opened my mouth, then closed it, going with a nod.

"First name Anastasia, I assume?" he asked.

Cute.

No, not cute. Nothing was cute.

"Sure," I said.

"Well, Anastasia," he said. "In case I don't see *you* again, the next time you're plotting a defense, here's a tip. Start with what's on you."

"On me," I echoed.

"You have heels on those shoes that can put an eye out, and five hundred pins holding up your hair. With enough force, any one of those pins can puncture an eardrum and bring a man to his knees."

"Wow," I said as my eyebrows probably moved up there with the bobby pins. The skin on the back of my neck prickled with recognition. Arrogance or confidence? My spidey sense twitched. "That's—a lot of observation."

He didn't blink. "That boulder on your finger?"

I glanced down at Jeremy's ring. Funny how I always thought of it that way. Jeremy's ring. Never mine.

"That thing could open a jugular," he said softly toward my ear, brushing against me as he headed toward the door.

"Okay," I said, turning with him, almost magnetically. As if being plastered to him for the last hour had bonded us and now there was this arc of electricity pulling at me. Ugh. Spray me down with something. "And you, Mr. Scowling-Harley-guy? Do you have a name?"

"Leo," he said as he kept walking. "Leo McKane."

CHAPTER TWO

The aromas wafted into my face like a blanket of happy as Leo opened the door for me. Meat, spicy, sweet, and salty all hit me at the same time, and the instant comfort of something frying in grease sent my mouth watering. Southern comfort food. I had never been one to claim the healing powers of it, but in that one moment I wanted it all.

It had to be noon or so, and my anxious stomach knew it. I would have been chowing on the grand spread my almost-mother-in-law arranged by now. Married. Micah Blankenship.

The relief that rushed over me was tangible, warming and chilling my skin at the same time. That had to say something, right? Surely that meant I'd made the right decision—even if my method was questionable.

"Micah Blankenship would be eating right now, though," I muttered as I eyed a plate of pepper-crusted pork loins and homemade mashed potatoes being devoured at a nearby table.

"What?" Leo said, startling me.

"Nothing," I said, moving to rake my hair back, then remembering it was manhandled into place by what were evidently lethal weapons.

A blonde waitress with an intimidatingly full tray of orders looked at us questioningly. Not the way the rest of the room was looking at us, like we might be aliens, but like we might just add to her workload.

"Table?" she asked in passing.

"Bar is fine," Leo said. "Is Nick McKane working today?"

"Bathroom?" I asked.

"Grab a stool," she tossed over her shoulder. "He's in charge today but we were slammed and he's helping Dave. And back corner to your right."

I laid a hand on Leo's arm as I moved around him, withdrawing it immediately as I felt his warmth and our eyes met. Why did I touch him like that? Familiar. Intimate. Like a lover. Or, at the very least, an extremely good friend. The question was all over his face as much as it bounced around my brain. *Why?* Hell, I was in no place to form logical thoughts. Maybe because it felt like we'd just gone through war together. But then no, that was really just me, because all he did was drive to where he was already headed anyway. I'm the one who jumped ship and turned my life upside down.

"Sorry," I whispered.

There was amusement in his eyes.

"Want something to eat?" he asked under his breath.

God, yes. Like a giant pig with a side of cow.

"I'm okay," I said, my stomach growling loudly right as I said it. I slapped a hand over my belly. "Go do what you have to do. I'll get a salad or something maybe after I—figure out what I'm doing."

Which I needed to do pretty damn quickly, I thought, as I weaved my way among the tables of smiling, curious diners. The longer I stayed there, dressed like a cake topper, the more that tongues would wag. The more that happened, the higher the likelihood that someone would find out who I was and rumors would get out. We did business here in Charmed, and Thatcher would have a shit fit if any of the local florists pulled their orders—especially *wedding* orders—just because one of the owners flaked out making a public scene on her own wedding day.

He would also not be happy if he heard it all secondhand. I needed to find a phone—

I pushed open the bathroom door sporting a sign with a stick figure in a skirt, and stopped short as the door shut behind me. The sight of myself in the mirror was too much.

Hair was all over the place. Not just sticking out from the pins, but falling down my neck, arcing straight up from my scalp, sticking to my forehead, and frizzing in very unflattering turd curls from each ear. That wasn't even the worst part.

"Sweet Jesus," I muttered.

My face looked like I had indeed been in the war I mentioned earlier. In it, lost it, came back for more punishment. The thick black eyeliner and mascara that the makeup artist had applied so perfectly for my portrait had bled way south. Heavy smoky eye shadow had gunked up to the north, and it appeared that my sexy, tiny, little drawn-in Marilyn mole I'd added to amuse myself had morphed into a fully grown beetle on my face.

No wonder Leo had suggested I clean up.

I began attacking my face with soap and water as the door opened. Great.

"Oooh, I love your dre—" the lady began, stopping as we met eyes in the mirror. "Oh, honey. You okay?"

Something resembling a choked laugh came out of my throat. I shook my head.

"I'm better than I look."

"Things not go as planned?" she asked, landing next to me at the counter to dive into her purse.

"Not even close," I said, scrubbing under my left eye, just smearing the greasy makeup further. "Kind of not at all."

"Oh, wow," she said. "I'm so sorry."

"No, it was me," I said, wondering who was remoting my mouth and why I was dumping my guts out to this woman. She did have an adorably kind face and her chunky-funky polka-dot heels endeared her to my heart. "I—well, let's just say my fiancé's mother probably wants my head on a platter right now."

"Here," she said, handing me a travel pack of wet wipes. "Works great on makeup."

I sighed as I pulled one out. "Bless you."

She leaned a hip against the counter. "So I'm guessing tall, dark, and moody who you walked in with isn't the groom?" I caught her eye and she shrugged. "Okay, so I didn't just stumble upon you in here. You looked like a hot mess who maybe needed a hand."

"No," I said, removing the beetle from my cheek. "I caught a ride here with him from Cherryd—"

What the hell, Micah? Shut up!

"Cherrydale?" the woman asked, her voice lilting up with her curiosity. She pulled in a little gasp. "Not the Blankenship wedding? You know, the Trade Days family?"

I closed my eyes and counted in my head. Of course it was just the Blankenship wedding. It wasn't the Blankenship-Roman wedding. Or Micah Roman's wedding. I got to eight and opened my eyes.

"I'm familiar with them," I said, the acid leaking into my tone.

"I didn't mean—" she began, touching my shoulder. "Oh, fuck balls. My mouth, I swear. I'm sorry. It's really none of my business."

I had to chuckle at her language, which didn't match the sundress and bouncy hair.

"It's okay," I said. "I get it. Probably not every day a runaway bride from a prominent family event shows up in your town with nothing but what's on her." I tossed the wet wipe and pulled out another one to take care of anything I missed, while blowing out a steadying breath. "So I assume you know them?"

She shook her head. "No, not personally, but my best friend, Carmen, is Mr. Blankenship's lawyer, and my friend Bash does business with the bri—" She stopped short. "With your family."

I rested my hands on the counter, letting my head hang.

"Bash Anderson?" I said, my eyes closing.

"The very same," she said. "And I just—know they were going to the—to your—" She sighed, sounding as frustrated as I felt. "Damn, I'm sorry."

Well, that settled the question of business contacts finding out. I felt the crush of a thousand soaking-wet blankets wrapping around me. That's what I got for letting Deidre Blankenship run the whole damn show and not at least finding out who was invited.

"Don't be," I said, handing back her travel pack with as much of a smile as I could muster. "You've been so nice." I put my hand over my eyes for a moment. "God, what was I thinking?" I said under my breath, thankful for her help but wishing she would leave me alone now to self implode all over the bathroom.

She laid a warm hand on my shoulder.

"Hey," she said. "Just breathe. Everything happens for a reason. I'm a firm believer in that, so take it one step at a time. I'm Lanie, by the way."

I nodded. "I'm Micah."

Lanie nodded with me. "Okay, Micah. Don't worry. People may buzz a little about a mysterious bride in here, but I'm not saying a word and it'll die down tomorrow."

As if on cue, a toilet flushed in one of the three stalls.

Fuck me. I never thought to look for feet.

We both looked toward the door, as a tall redhead with boobs the size of basketballs exited the stall.

"Don't mind me," she said, flashing a perfectly lined smile, flitting a hand carelessly as she all but shoved Lanie aside to step between us and wash her hands. "But I couldn't help but overhear. If you do decide to jump back on the wedding train, I can help you out." She reached into a wristlet wallet and pulled out a card. "Katrina Bowman, event management."

"Event *what*?" Lanie said. "Last month you were making jewelry out of your garage."

"I am a *certified* event planner," Katrina said, wheeling on Lanie like a ticked-off dog with a too-tight collar. "So don't stand there in that dimestore dress getting all high and mighty with me."

For about two seconds, I forgot about my plight. I froze in my reach toward my hair, zeroing in on Lanie's face in the mirror.

"Katrina—" she began slowly, drawing out the syllables calmly.

"What, you gonna pull out your boobs again?" Katrina said. "No thanks. I'm a business woman and I'm working here."

Lanie looked like she was counting in her head. Then she lifted two fingers in mock surrender. "I stand corrected. Plan away."

"Anyway," Katrina-the-event-planner said, turning back to me with an emphatic snub to Lanie. "Call me or visit my website. It's right there on the card in pink."

It sure was. Neon pink.

"I'm not getting married," I said.

Sweet Jesus, that was the most liberating sentence I'd uttered in months.

"Oh, I don't just do weddings," Katrina said, tossing that red hair of hers. "I'll do anything. If any of your friends have an event or a party to—"

"I don't know anyone here," I interjected. "And I don't have friends anymore."

That was both the saddest and most honest statement I'd ever allowed into my headspace. But it was true. The one quick scan I'd had of the wedding invitation list told me that. It was all Jeremy's friends. Even our common friends we'd hung out with for years originated with Jeremy. In an apocalypse or divorce, I always knew which side they'd land on. The only contacts on that list who weren't directly touching the Blankenship family in some way were the business clients Thatcher had provided.

All my old friends had fallen off the grid little by little. I met my own gaze in the mirror. I'd let that happen. I had let them disappear.

I let *me* disappear.

I sucked in a shaky breath as my eyes filled with unexpected tears, blinking them back quickly.

"Thank you, though," I called after Katrina-the-event-planner as she sashayed out of the bathroom. I pulled the last pins from my hair and shook the stiff, hair-sprayed locks free with my fingers. "God help me," I muttered under my breath.

"That 'keeping things on the down-low' plan?" Lanie said, making a chopping motion with her hand at neck level. "That's history, now."

"Yeah, I gathered that," I said. "There's a boob story?"

Lanie winked. "Another day. I've promised my husband to try to be less reactive and hotheaded over things I can't control, so I'm not going to let her stir me up."

I chuckled in spite of things. "I hear you. We have one of those in Cherrydale, too."

"Prepare yourself," Lanie said. "People you've never met will suddenly know all. Probably even know some things you don't."

"I need to do more than that," I said, speeding up the hasty finger-combing. I stopped, backed up, and took inventory. Good Lord, I looked like a themed Halloween costume. "I need to go find a phone and prepare my brother."

Lanie held hers out to me. "Knock yourself out."

This woman was too good. She was the kind of person I wanted to be when I grew up, and I couldn't let her put herself in the line of fire.

"I can't use your cell phone," I said, touching her arm. "Thank you. But my fiancé—or my ex-fiancé—is not one to take this without a showdown. I don't know where I'll be when he comes to find me, but I don't want him showing up at your door when he checks phone records." Those words bounced around on repeat in my head. I gripped the counter as a fresh wave of despair washed over me. I stared at myself in the mirror again, fresh-faced, no makeup, questionable hair tumbling down in dark waves around my shoulders. I looked more like me again, but what version? There used to only be one, and now there were all these fragments. "How did this get to be my life?"

Lanie sighed. "I was saying the very same thing last year, girl. It'll pass." She held out her phone again. "I'm not afraid of any man."

I shook my head, remembering what Leo said about having to fight a fight that wasn't his, just because Jeremy would be spoiling for one. "Your husband wouldn't like it. Can you maybe ask the owner here if I can use the landline?"

"Mmm, Allie—" Lanie pulled a cringing face.

"She's at my wedding, too, isn't she?" I said, the words barely a whisper.

"With Bash," she said. "They're engaged."

"Of course."

"But my husband is the chef and he's in charge while she's gone so I'm pulling spouse rank, bringing you back there myself," she said, grabbing my hand. "Let's go."

I let her pull me like a ragdoll, suddenly feeling just about as useless, dragging me into the chattering chaos of the diner, between the tables of curious onlookers, approaching the register touting a sign with a picture of a gorgeous blue-eyed man.

Sweeten the deal!

Vote our fabulous HONEY KING

Sebastian Anderson

for

Mayor of Charmed!

Of course.

Leo loomed at the end of the counter like a dark-haired Thor surveying his underlings. He didn't see me yet, and I had the wildest urge to keep it that way. To just stand there invisibly and rest my eyes on him all day. I'd spent worse days.

If only I *could* be invisible.

Our progress halted as a woman with light brown hair strode up to the register, a cell phone to her ear.

"Stop. Calling. Me," she said through gritted teeth as the girl behind the register looked on patiently. "Leave me alo—oh, believe me, I'd like nothing better than to never see you again, but now *you* get some of the misery."

She slammed the phone down on the counter with satisfaction, taking a deep breath with closed eyes before opening them and smiling tightly at the girl.

"Sorry," she said softly. "Call-in order for Graham's Florist. Apple pie and cake balls. Throw in a jar of that honey, too," she added, gesturing to the pyramid stack of honey jars sporting the Anderson's Apiary logo.

The girl nodded on her way to the back, and my new friend Lanie reached out to the cell phone woman.

"You all right, Gabi?" she asked, making the woman start.

"Peachy," she said, lifting the hem of an oversized T-shirt to shove the phone into the pocket of jean capris. She did a double-take on me. "Oh—wow, that's a beautiful dress." She glanced around as if trying to match me up with some equally decked-out man. "Congratulations."

It wasn't worth going through it all again.

"Thanks."

"So, cake balls from here?" Lanie asked, clearly changing tack. "Not the bakery?"

Gabi lifted her eyebrows. "I'm doing an edible bouquet, and Nick's balls are the best anywhere." Her jaw dropped as Lanie laughed. "I mean—"

"Oh, I agree," Lanie said, still laughing as Gabi's face went scarlet. "Cake balls included. And the pie?"

"Something to keep me sane," she said. "If lemon meringue was on the board today, I'd buy that, too."

Lanie and I both nodded. I didn't know about her, but it sounded like a fabulous plan to me. If I thought I had a place to eat a pie that wasn't on the curb, or didn't have to sell my body to pay for one, I'd totally copy this chick's plan.

"You've probably heard about me and Bart," Gabi said, blinking away.

Lanie gave a little shrug. "Just a little."

"Well, in addition to that, my parents have now added landlording to their endeavors," she said. "Being florists isn't enough for them. They turned the space above the shop into two rentable rooms, and I swear if I hear one more thing about communal bathrooms or feng shui I'm going to lose my shit."

The "florists" mention made my radar go up, and I searched my inner database for the local flower shops we worked with. Would she know me if I dropped my name? The last name, maybe. I wasn't the person on the phone or the e-mails or the invoices. I was the one outside with my hands in the dirt, talking to things that couldn't talk back. Or to Roarke, my helper, who didn't talk back much either.

"You might should have gone for two pies," Lanie said, squeezing her arm as she resumed our journey.

Gabi gave a small smile. "Nothing says I won't be back."

We continued on, pausing as we passed Leo, who Katrina-the-event-planner was touching repeatedly while laughing and tossing her red hair. He stood with his arms crossed over his chest like a club bouncer, an almost lazy amusement pulling at that amazing mouth, contrasting with the wary sharpness his eyes had taken on. The fact that he seemed more amused than turned on by her somehow made me happy. That thought did not.

Lanie turned as she passed him, nearly walking backward at one point as she peered at his profile. I'd never fault her for that. Married woman or not, Leo was hard to miss and impossible to ignore. But it was my turn to pause as his gaze locked in on me, completely tuning Katrina out.

His expression, his eyes, they were almost anxious as they took in everything. This place, the people, every conversation in hearing distance, body language.

Me.

God, the way he soaked me in made my skin go flush from my scalp to my toes. For one second, I missed the mask of the heavy makeup and fancy hair. I felt very naked as his gaze slid over my face.

"The real me," I said on a nervous chuckle.

"Better," he said just above a whisper.

Sweet Jesus.

"What the *hell*?"

A man's voice from behind the bar made me spin around, jerking free of Lanie's hand in automatic reaction as my heart slammed against my chest. My first thought had been Jeremy. I knew it wasn't; it wasn't his voice, but my reaction was the same.

"Babe?" Lanie said. My head swung back to see the befuddlement on her face that then morphed into something else. A knowing, a dawning of something crossed her features as she glanced back at Leo. "Oh, shit, I thought so," she said under her breath, adding something about "Barrett intuition" as she headed around the bar toward him. "Nick."

So that was the husband. As I looked back at him I noticed he wasn't actually talking to Lanie or even looking at her. He was staring hot fiery bullet holes at—Leo. With the same eyes.

Same everything, but more polished. Like a slightly younger, more *GQ* version of Leo. Something told me this wasn't about a job.

Leo, on the other hand, hadn't moved a muscle, a finger, or even an eyelash. He stood there like a mountain of bristling calm, his eyes gone softer as he looked at Nick.

"Hey, little brother."

CHAPTER THREE

Little brother?

Well, well. I had to admit, it was nice to get those hot spotlights off of me for half a minute. They were getting a bit warm.

"What are you doing here?" Nick said under his breath, pulling off a black leather apron in one tug as he glanced around at his patrons, moving to the end of the bar opposite Leo, his jaw tight with something fierce that wasn't just anger. No, that look ran deeper. Like the kind of deep wound only *family* can inflict.

Lanie had reached his side and had a hand on one arm like she was going to single-handedly hold him back.

Leo finally dropped his arms, resting his hands on the counter.

"Work," he said. "I got a job here."

"Here *where*?" Nick said.

"Bartending at a restaurant, for one," Leo said.

"In Charmed?" Nick asked, his eyes narrowing. "Why?"

Leo blew out a breath, holding on to the counter as if it might keep his answers levelheaded.

"Don't you dare say me," Nick continued, leaning in slightly. "After eighteen years—" He shook his head. "No. I didn't even know if you were alive, and now you want to drop out of the sky and be all *Hey, little brother* with me? Fuck, no. You walked away from being my brother. You don't get to come play this card with me now." He tied the apron back on with a yank. "I'm busy. I'm working. Go—be you somewhere else."

Somehow, he'd managed to miss me until that very moment, and now his gaze bounced from Leo to me.

"You got married."

It was more of an accusation than a question, and Leo's eyes dropped to me like he'd forgotten I was there. I wished everyone else could do that. There were two young guys eyeing me like fresh bacon, an old man shaking his head like I'd disappointed him, and Katrina-the-event-planner whispering to three other women while smiling at me.

I didn't care how much this thing cost Jeremy's mother; I was burning it. Okay, maybe I wasn't burning it; maybe I was just dumping it in a corner for a few days before having it cleaned and shipped to her, but in my head there was a bonfire from hell.

"No—this is—Anastasia," Leo said, as if that explained it.

I shook my head, eyes closed. "I'm not Anastasia."

"She needed a ride," Leo said, dismissively.

"From her own—" Nick began, glancing at his wife. "Same wedding Allie went to?"

Good God, didn't anyone else get married around here, ever?

"Yes," I said. "I bailed." I held my arms up and turned in a circle. "Everyone who is curious," I called out, "I bailed on my wedding. I was that girl. Judge at will. Now enjoy your lunch!" I turned back to Nick. "He saw I needed help and gave me a ride. That was nice. Can I use your phone?"

I'm pretty sure I'd hit the bottom that's under the bottom. Nick chuckled humorlessly, turning to go back to the kitchen.

"I'm sure he did," he said on his way. "He recognized a kindred spirit."

"Nick—" Leo began.

"Walk away, Leo," he said, his back to us as he turned the corner. "You're familiar with that. Whatever your name is, ma'am, I'd keep going if he's staying here."

* * * *

It was like a bomb had gone off, leaving us in the aftershocks.

Lanie said she'd be back and quick-stepped it to check on her husband. I stood awkwardly behind a sullen Leo, not knowing what to do. I needed to call my brother, like fifteen minutes ago, but I also felt a weird obligation to help this guy. At least be on his side. With the exception of Gabi, still waiting on her order and subtly giving us the side-eye, the other patrons had smartly either left or moved down to the other end of the bar during the drama, giving us a wide berth. Leo stared at the countertop as if he could climb into it. I could feel the heat coming off of him and I wasn't even touching him.

And why did I want to?

Because he'd helped me. And, arrogant or not, now this big rock of a man who'd just told me how to kill someone with my shoe looked like his insides had been rearranged.

"Are—are you okay?" I asked finally, crossing my arms before they did something ridiculous.

"I'm fine," he snapped, his voice growly as he pulled a phone from his pocket. "Go do—whatever it is you're doing."

My hackles went up.

"Excuse me?" I said. "Just because he dismissed *you* like a jerk doesn't make it okay to pay it forward." He turned a look on me that said *What the fuck* in about a hundred ways, so I just held up my hands. "You know what? You did something for me. I was just trying to be nice back, but I have no dog in this hunt and as you pointed out earlier, we have our own shit to deal with. Have a nice life."

I turned on my heel, nearly busting it, forgetting that said heel was nothing but an ice pick. One strong hand wrapped around my arm like a vise.

"Careful," he said in my ear, closer than I expected. "I told you those things were dangerous."

Shit. I yanked my arm free, glaring up at him. "You're just lucky I got rid of all the bobby pins."

There was almost the hint of a tug of a smirk there in that stupid sexy mouth of his. Just enough to piss me off. Then his eyes—they went softer. That kind of soft that dark eyes can do that makes people buy puppies.

No! No puppies!

Lanie poked her head around the corner and waved at me to come. I saluted him.

"Like I said," I threw over my shoulder as I hightailed it around the bar.

God, what was with me and irritatingly sexy asshole alpha males? What was the attraction? Knuckle dragging? It didn't matter. I didn't have time or enough energy left in my body to worry about Leo. Our weird little journey had ended. I had to figure out where the next one began.

"Here's Allie's desk," Lanie said, pointing when we turned through a short hall into an office. "Help yourself to the phone."

"Is—your husband okay?" I asked. "I mean, it's none of my business, but I feel like I'm somehow swirling in the middle of it. I swear I didn't know that my guy was anyone's brother—I thought he worked here or something."

My guy?

I'd just said that. What the living hell was wrong with me?

Lanie chuckled. "Yeah. He's—Nick will be fine. He just has to let it roll off him. This is a big sore spot with him." She widened her eyes. "He has a few of those."

I scoffed. "Don't we all."

She winked and disappeared. And just like that, I was alone.

Alone with my thoughts, my breathing, my heart still pounding in my ears, and the need for normal. Jeremy's ring caught the light as I reached for the phone.

My eyes filled with tears as I remembered the proposal. Not the typical grandiose Jeremy-style event I'd expected from him, asking me in front of a million people so I couldn't say no. He'd surprised me that night. Bringing me out to the patio behind the big greenhouse, a place in my comfort zone, going to one knee under the stars.

It was moments like that that had kept me with him. The moments that showed he knew me, the moments of pure raw joy that I'd think of every time I'd look at him—until he'd decide to be a dick again.

I sniffed and swiped under my eyes for the hundredth time, picking up the phone. I was done living my life on a yo-yo, putting up with the crap times in order to bask in the glorious ones.

Breathe in. One deep breath preceded another as I listened to a second ring and the beginning of a thi—

"Hello."

My stomach flipped at the stress and the worry and the ready-to-rip-someone-a-new-ass-for-bothering-him-right-now tone in my brother's voice.

Breathe out.

"Thatcher."

There was under-the-breath cursing, the sounds of shuffling, and a loud bang of a truck door shutting in my ear before I heard his voice again.

"Micah, where the fuck are you?"

Nothing like getting to the point.

"Thatcher, I'm sorry," I said softly, shutting my eyes tight.

Where my "little" brother, big six-foot-two bear Jackson, was my soul, my older brother, Thatcher, was my heart. He was the man of the house after our dad died, taking on all he could at the ripe old age of eleven. I was nine, Jackson was seven, and when our mom had to work all day on the farm and take side jobs at night to put food on the table, Thatcher took care of us. I was always better with that, anyway.

My mother and I—we had a strained relationship up till the day she died. Namely because she was a professional manipulator and I grew tired of watching her pull strings to get what she wanted. My dad, then my brothers, they all catered to her moods and desires. Even as a kid, I knew that I didn't want to be her, and I should have known that that meant I had the tough road ahead. I'd take Thatcher over her as a parent any day of the week. As a result, he was an old soul before he even hit puberty, too wise sometimes for his own good as a man. His ex-wife could attest to that. But he was the one I most wanted to be proud of me. And the one I kept disappointing.

I heard a sigh that was probably part relief, part wanting to throttle me. I was familiar with the tone. I could picture him closing his eyes and counting to ten.

"What happened?" he said finally.

"Are you alone?" I asked.

"For the moment," he said. "I'm in my truck. Jeremy and Jackson are talking on the porch."

"Whose porch?"

"*Your* porch!" he said, sounding exasperated. "We're here waiting for you."

I grabbed a pen to have something in my hand to squeeze. *Breathe in. Breathe out.*

It's not my porch.

"How is Jeremy?"

I heard a scoff. "Seriously?"

"Yes, seriously!" I said. "I didn't marry him—that doesn't mean I don't worry about him."

"Micah, what happened?"

I blew out a breath. How did I explain it? That I showed my true colors? Went back to my old ways? I knew that's what he was thinking, and to be completely honest I wondered, myself. The little niggling insecurity that had crept into my psyche over time was poking at me, dangling that question like a scribbled Post-it left on the fridge.

"I don't know, Thatcher," I said quietly, hearing the emotion wobble my words as it squeezed my throat. In my mind, I saw Jeremy's face last night, kissing my forehead, throwing back a foreign-sounding *Love you, Micah.* The same image I'd seen all night as I stared at the ceiling. "All I can say is that one minute I was standing there waiting to walk down the aisle, then suddenly it was all pretend. Like something plucked me out of my real life and deposited me there, fully furnished."

"Fully furnished?"

"Husband, house, June Cleaver heels, money," I said. "Like I'd scored the Barbie Dream House with Ken."

"And—that's a bad thing?" he asked.

I drew a shaky breath.

"Maybe I wanted to live in the Barbie van with the plastic fire pit," I said. "Maybe I wanted to be Rocker Barbie or Veterinarian Barbie or Bohemian Barbie."

"Micah, I was a boy, remember?"

"Maybe I wanted a choice," I said, my words choked by tears. "In my own life. Without Ken constantly telling me that my only option was the damn Dream House."

There was a pause, and I could only hope that my brother was using it to connect the crazy dots I'd just thrown out there.

"You've been with this guy for eight years," he said finally. "Lived with him for most of that. Were with him when he bought this house. You couldn't figure this out before today? Before leaving him standing up there by himself in front of everyone he knows?"

Bam. Gut kick.

"*His* house, Thatcher," I said, crying fully. "You just said it. He bought the house, not *we.* It's not mine. Not ours. I hated that house, but he wanted one just like the one they lost in the old fire, so my opinion didn't matter. And everyone there were people *he* knows, not me." Sobs pulled at my breath. "I had no one there but you and Jackson. You don't have to agree with me—and you don't have to like it, but I need you to be on my side." I pulled the phone away from my face for a moment as the burn enveloped me. I couldn't breathe as the reality that was my life vomited all over me. I heard Thatcher's voice saying my name from far away, and I lifted the phone back to my ear. "I'm here," I whispered.

"Baby girl, I'm always on your side," he said, the warmth of his words flowing over me like bath water. "I'm sorry. I just—" He breathed in deeply and let it go. "I've been a little stressed out since I watched you climb on a bike with a stranger and disappear. Dad would have died all over again, watching that."

A chuckle escaped my throat through the tears.

"Yeah, that probably wasn't my most shining adult moment," I said.

"Are you okay?" he said, his fatherly voice going into overdrive. "Where are you?"

"I'm fine," I said, deliberately avoiding the second question. "But I can't come back right now. I want to—Jeremy needs a minute to calm down."

"You need to talk to him, Micah," Thatcher said. "No matter what, he may be mad right now but he deserves that much."

I blew out a breath. "I know."

"So, where are you?" he repeated. "I'll come to you."

I shook my head, as if he could see that. He'd shit if he knew what town I was in. A noise behind me turned my head, and I smiled at Lanie leaning in the doorway with her back partially turned. She was either guarding the door so no one interrupted me or just eavesdropping. Really, I didn't care either way.

"Can you get my wallet and my car keys?" I asked, wiping at my face. "Maybe my phone? I'll meet you somewhere tomorrow if you can."

"I already have your bag that was in the dressing room," Thatcher said. "It has your wallet, makeup, a change of clothes, but Jeremy still has your car and he grabbed your phone the second we went in that room."

Of course he did. He was trying to find out if I'd planned some great getaway.

"That's okay," I said and sighed. "I can buy a new phone—once I get my credit cards back—"

"A new phone?" Thatcher said. "Micah, how long are you planning to be gone? Just come home and talk to the man and get your shit back. If you need a place to stay, you know you can stay with me."

In my childhood home that Thatcher now owned alone since his divorce, where the spirits of my parents still lived on in the walls, the curtains, the floors. Where the guilt and accusations still echoed from the ceiling, memories and judgment soaked into the very beams.

"I probably will," I began. "But—not yet. My head is all over the place right now, Thatch. I need a few days to figure things out."

Speaking of judgment, I could hear his whirling.

"I know you had mom issues here," he said after a pause.

"When can you meet me?" I asked, swiftly changing that topic.

"I have meetings with clients all day tomorrow that I can't cancel," he said. "But I can meet you somewhere tomorrow evening. I'd come tonight but he'll be all up my ass, expecting that." I heard a long sigh and I knew he was rubbing his face, wishing for a new sister. "I can't believe I'm having this conversation."

"Is my bag with you right now?"

"It's in the back seat."

"Quick, read out my Visa number." I grabbed a pad of paper. There was obligatory grumbling as he was probably extracting it from the back while trying to look like he wasn't. "Have I told you I love you today?"

"You suck, Micah," he grunted out over the sound of shuffling and a zipper and a grandiose release of breath. "Okay, here."

He read out the numbers while I scribbled madly.

"This will work for now. I'll call you when I get a phone," I said. "We'll make a plan. Please don't tell Jackson, because he has an awful poker face."

"What about clothes?" he said. "You planning to wear a wedding dress to go buy normal clothes? Isn't that a little backward?"

I'd rather go naked.

"I'll figure something out," I said. "Damn it, I'm a sitting duck without my car." I laid my forehead in my hands. "I can handle things for a couple of days. I just need to lie low."

He sighed. "I get it."

"Do you?"

"I get it better now that I know you aren't dead," he said.

"I know," I said softly. "Thatcher?"

"Yeah?"

I breathed out slowly, trying to quell the shake. "Thank you."

There was a pause, and I felt what was coming before he said it.

"I said I'm on your side, and I mean it," he said. "But damn it, Micah, I wish you made it a little easier."

My eyes filled with new hot tears. There were things he'd never know or understand, and that was okay. He didn't need to know everything.

"I love you, bro," I said.

"Always, baby girl."

CHAPTER FOUR

Leo was gone when I came out, which was both a relief and an odd disappointment that dug at my midsection like a dull butter knife. I stopped myself from peering out the window for his bike.

It was friggin' divine intervention, that's what it was. In my current weakened state, I had no business being around anyone whose cocky, irritating presence I missed after knowing him for all of an hour or two. God knew what He was doing, sending him on his way. In fact, God was kind of busy with me on all fronts today. That's probably all it was. In the crazy chaotic mess I'd kicked off today, Leo had been the only constant landmark I could keep looking back at to get my bearings.

Now, however, I was at a loss. I'd had one big mission—call my brother. Check. With that out of the way, I didn't quite know my next step. I'd never been without a car or money or even identification, with only the clothes on my back to my name. It was a weird, isolating, and very vulnerable feeling. Plus, my landmark had pulled up anchor and moved on.

That was okay. I breathed in, long and deep. It would be okay.

Lanie and Gabi were chatting, and I half smiled at a couple of newbies who'd come in, gazing at me curiously. They'd missed the floor show, and I didn't have the energy to catch them up, so I walked around to join the two women who were the closest thing to acquaintances I had at the moment.

"Hey," Gabi said as I approached, transferring her bags to one arm to hold out her hand. "I'm Gabi Lar—" She took a breath. "I should start saying Graham."

"So, you're giving him the divorce?" Lanie asked.

Gabi let loose of a slow breath with a mini head shake. "God, yes. Eventually. After he suffers for a bit. But I should get used to the name."

She inhaled deeply with eyes closed and opened them back with a smile. "I'm Gabi Graham," she said, shaking my hand with a grip that belied her softer appearance. "You're one of the Cherrydale Flower Farm Romans?" Yep. One of them. At my nod, she continued. "Lanie said you might need a place to land for a bit. Are you thinking for a night? Or to stay in town a while? Because we now have these rooms over the shop."

I laughed, a sound that felt as exhausted as I probably looked. Of course it would just be a night, maybe two, right? I mean, I had a job at home. Not that an hour commute was any big deal—and I did need to move out of Jeremy's house—but what was I thinking? I'd just move in with Thatcher for a bit, regardless of the shiver that gave me. *Don't make life decisions on traumatic days.* Move to Charmed? No!

"I'm not sure," I said. "But until I can get to a bank that will give me a cash advance on just a handwritten credit card number and no license," I said, waving the paper, "I have no money to make that decision with. No car. No—"

"No problem," Lanie said with a shrug.

I blinked. "What?"

"I happen to be heading back to work," she said, leaning over with a cocky expression. "At a bank."

"Oh, my God, seriously?" I breathed. "Do you think they would—"

"Yes," she said. "I can vouch for who you are and your family's business. Plus, my husband hooked me up with a to-go lunch and an extra slice of molten lava chocolate cake. My boss will *throw* money at me for that."

I closed my eyes, picturing freedom that included life's simple pleasures. Like cash at my fingertips, and clothes that didn't go on for miles or sparkle under fluorescent lighting.

And molten lava chocolate cake.

"Why don't you ride with me back to my house first and I'll lend you some clothes," Gabi said, looking me over. "You're a little taller, but I have some things that should work for you." She shrugged at what was probably my jaw hitting the ground. "Just to get you by."

"Oh, great idea!" Lanie said, shouldering her bag. "Then you'll feel much more at ease."

"The bank is walking distance from the shop," Gabi said. "So go get set up and then come down there if you want."

My eyes bounced between them. There are times when words just won't reach, and this was one of them. It was more than just small-town hospitality. I lived in a small town, too. These women were just rock stars.

"Why?" I said, surprised when the word came out all breathy and toneless. "Why are y'all doing all this for me?"

Lanie linked an arm in mine, steering us toward the door, probably needing to get back to work while all I was doing was rambling.

"Girl—"

"You're a hot mess," Gabi interjected, pushing open the door as we all filed out.

I blinked two hot tears free and chuckled. "No truer words."

"I've been there," Lanie said. "Maybe not exactly this same mess, but I've had my own version not too long ago."

"Paying it forward," Gabi said, nodding. "I'm a hot mess *now*," she said, making me laugh. "I'm just not *wearing* mine. So, let's go get that neon sign off your back, too, shall we?"

"Can I have some of your pie?"

* * * *

Two pairs of denim capris and a T-shirt and tank top later, I felt like a new woman. Or at least a normal one. Some cute flip-flops on my feet and I was good to go.

Gabi curled into an oversized chair with a small bowl of apple pie while I tried them on in the bathroom and came out to model for her like I was Julia Roberts in *Pretty Woman*. She'd smile and comment but I saw the sad that entered her eyes when she thought I wasn't looking.

"So," I began, watching her face as I folded my new temporary treasures into a plastic grocery bag, "can I ask what the story is with your husband?" Her eyes went wary and I held a hand up. "Or not. You don't know me, I get it."

Gabi shook her head. "No, it's okay. Not like it's some big secret. At least Bart's making sure it isn't." She took a deep breath but then caught my eye. "But you first. Did you really just hitch a ride with a hot stranger? You didn't know him?"

I chuckled, though the growing weight of the day made it sound heavy. Wearing another woman's clothes as one of many direct consequences brought a sadness to the reality.

"Never seen him in my life," I said, refolding a shirt for something to do with my hands.

My thoughts flashed back to that moment on the sidewalk, to running from the church, to feeling the front door pulling at me, to staring at myself in the mirror. Hair perfect. Makeup perfect. In a dress I would have never chosen, in the church I didn't want, with flowers I hated, and bridesmaids I barely knew. No one there for me but the two people I called family. To hearing what sounded like a recorded message from my fiancé's lips. *Love you, Micah.* We hadn't said those words in probably six months.

It was like being a porcelain doll on a shelf or an actress playing a role in a movie I could never change the channel on. It wasn't me. None of it was me.

"I wish I could say there'd been a plan," I said. "One minute I was looking in the mirror at someone I didn't know or like very much and the next thing I knew I was running down the street. I didn't know this guy's name till we got here. He said he was coming to Charmed for work so when he pulled up to the diner I thought he worked there."

"Yeah, that was quite the show," Gabi said. "I never knew Nick McKane had a brother—not that I would. He comes across as pretty private, but nothing really surprises me in this town."

"Why?" I asked. "Because it's small?"

She tucked a strand of light-brown hair behind her ear. "Because it's weird."

I chuckled, sinking onto her bed, pulling one ankle underneath me and reaching for my own little bowl of pie she'd dished up for me. "Okay."

"Don't get me wrong," she said. "I grew up here and I love Charmed. But there's some bizarre shit that goes on here."

"Like?" I asked.

"Bee stealing," she said. "Carnival people who appear from nowhere. Lanie's aunt was rumored to be psychic—I don't know if that was true but I did see her whispering to a pie once at the Blue Banana. The Lucky Charm only operates in cash, no matter how big the event is, and there's a really freaky old man who owns most of the town and lives in the woods like a hermit."

I laughed around a mouthful of pie that was so damned good, so full of all the feels that come only from food cooked with love and immense talent.

"Wow. All of that?"

"And that's just the highlights," she said. "Stick around, you'll see what I mean. Speaking of that," she continued, tilting her head, "you climbed on with a hunky McKane instead of walking down the aisle—what did the groom say?"

I shook my head. "I haven't talked to Jeremy."

Gabi's feet uncurled, hitting the floor. "Shut up."

I looked away, focusing on the perfect apples, glistening with glaze and cinnamon in the world's most perfect crust. I was almost unworthy of eating such a thing. I knew that what I was doing—how I was doing it—made me a horrible person. A heartless bitch. Evil troll. Unfeeling shrew. Or just a major cowardly puppet afraid of facing the puppeteer.

"Yep," I said softly, looping the plastic grocery bag of clothing on my wrist.

"I thought that's who you called," she said.

"I called my brother," I said. "We're pretty close, and I knew he'd be freaking out."

"Your *brother*? Holy shit, girl," Gabi said. "How long were you and Jeremy together?"

That wasn't going to make it better.

"Long enough to lose myself," I said. "To know I can't just call him and say I'm sorry. I need to do that in person." I remembered Thatcher's words. "The day I mortify him in front of a billion people isn't the day to do it."

Gabi's mouth opened to speak, then clamped closed as if she remembered we were still basically strangers and she couldn't tell me I was an idiot. Still, her eyes were kind.

"Did you love him?" she asked finally, in spite of the clamping, a hand coming up to cover her mouth that time. "I'm sorry."

I looked away, hearing his words again. Did I love Jeremy? Did he really believe what he said? I thought I did. I had to at some point. *You left him at the altar, then called Thatcher instead of him.*

"Your turn," I said, the smile I pasted on feeling like a picture I was holding up in front of my face.

Her gaze dropped to some spot on the floor.

"Have you ever been so blindly content that you just assumed everyone else felt that way?" she said finally, talking to the spot.

It struck me that most people would say yes. Most people would experience that at one time or another. I was with Jeremy for eight years; shouldn't I have felt that?

"No," I said.

Gabi's gaze lifted to mine. "That's good," she said. "Because it makes you complacent." She looked away, pulling her legs up in the chair with her again, linking her hands around her knees like a hug. "You might not notice while you bury yourself in fertility research and ways to get pregnant that your husband of ten years is way too fond of his new journalism intern at the paper. The one you recommended for the job." When Gabi looked at me again, there was a deep and festering wound in there. "Because you used to babysit her when she was a *toddler*."

I felt my jaw drop.

"Oh, fuck that," I breathed.

"Yeah."

"Gabi, I'm sorry," I said.

She shook her head. "No need to be," she said. "It is what it is. I learned a powerful lesson." A smile curved her mouth but didn't reach her eyes. "I always thought marriage was just automatically what my parents have. They are still stupid in love. Obnoxious, even. I was naïve to think that." She put her feet back down, rising. "That's a fluke that I'll never trust in again. In fact, I'll never even believe that *they're* really that happy. I think she just tells him they are, and then they smoke happy cigarettes and pretend."

I snorted. "Gabi."

"Seriously!" she said. "It's all bullshit. I don't buy it. The only thing I'm buying into for the foreseeable future is sex," she said holding up a hand. "Honestly, I can take care of that better myself, so to hell with men."

I laughed harder and it felt awesome. I couldn't remember the last time I'd had a good laugh. The kind where the tickle grows bigger and bigger, making your stomach hurt and your eyes water.

"I'm totally serious," she continued, looking befuddled by my giggling but chuckling anyway because it's contagious.

I held up a hand, as even that sent me off again.

"I know," I managed finally through deep inhales of air. "I'm sorry. I'm—probably delusional right now. But I get it, believe me."

She gave me a raised eyebrow. "I doubt it."

I set my empty bowl aside, stopping just short of licking it clean.

"Why?"

"You were engaged, still in that sexy stage where you have orgasms every day," she said.

"I wish," I said. "I mean, he could have done the wild thing every day, but the *he* in that sentence is key."

She frowned. "A self-server."

I smiled sarcastically. "Unless you call two seconds of foreplay *serving*," I said. "But that's my own fault for making that easy for him."

"*Your* fault?" she asked, getting to her feet, shaking her head. "Girl. You did the right thing today."

Goose bumps covered my body. Those were the first vilifying words said to me since I'd run out of the church. Every question, every doubt, every stab of guilt or selfishness hitting me all day had done a job on my head. Thatcher's words still rang in my head. Everyone's looks today. Even Leo's *You sure?* question made me wonder.

You did the right thing.

It didn't matter that she didn't really know me or Jeremy or anything about our situation other than the tidbits I was dropping. She hadn't heard the good stuff. And there *was* good stuff. Just the farther I was away from him, the harder it was to see.

"You think?" I asked, hearing the catch in my throat.

"I've got issues, Micah," she said. "I admit that. But I've never met a woman as twisted up in someone else's agenda as you."

I didn't know what to say to that. To feel insulted or relieved to finally have a diagnosis.

"You need untwisting," she said. "You need to unbraid all that crap you don't even know you're tied up with, pull it up by the roots, and burn it."

CHAPTER FIVE

I knew what I was afraid of.

We stopped at a little convenience store where she bought me deodorant and mascara, and I'd never felt more helpless and ridiculous in all my life. I was a grown woman. How had my life come to this?

It was like taking off the forty pounds of bling and lace opened my eyes. It put me in a different place—besides actually being in a different place. I was able to focus on what the hell my next step was. Or steps. Because this thing had a whole giant ladder to it.

Temporary clothing gave me the means to hit up those next rungs, like money, a cell phone, or possibly the ovaries to just go home and get the one I already own, along with my wallet and car. I didn't have to wait till tomorrow night to meet up with Thatcher. I could be a big *unbraided* girl, go get my wallet from my brother, and go straight to Jeremy to hash it out. Get it over with. I'd have my car and a plan and I could figure out where I was going.

But I wasn't going to, and I knew why. Because I *knew* what I was afraid of. Losing this clarity. Walking into familiarity. Hearing Jeremy's voice and falling into the fog—where what he told me was best for me, for us, for everything—made sense. Staying twisted, because twisted was normal. It was easier.

She was right. I was jacked up.

With Lanie's help, I was able to access my bank account and get a cash advance on a bank-to-bank transfer. So, with money in my pocket—or technically Gabi's pocket—I started down the sidewalk toward Graham's Florist.

It was heady, strolling past the shops of Charmed like a secret spy or a freed prisoner, the big Ferris wheel and roller-coaster of the Lucky Charm looming closer as I walked. No one knowing who I was, where I was, accountable to no one. I had no timetable to be anywhere, no one judging my purchases. No one to tell me I should get the frozen yogurt instead of the double dutch chocolate ice cream at the Charmed Creamery. In fact, marshmallow cream and chopped walnuts joined the party, with a drizzle of steaming caramel and honey.

Apple pie and an over-the-top sundae on what would have been my wedding day? It seemed appropriate.

I reached the flower shop, inhaling the scents already escaping through the mail slot. Gardenia was prevalent, filling my nose, making my fingers itch with the need for cool, fragrant dirt. There were customers inside, talking with a tall dark-haired woman, so I sat on a nearby wooden bench to finish my treat and listen to the sounds of the town. Cars driving slow. Two boys laughing on a nearby sidewalk. The thrum of a motorcycle nearby.

Small-town ambience wasn't new to me. Cherrydale had this same feel, this same look, the same smiling, friendly people strolling by, but this was different. It felt all kinds of different. Rebellious. Free.

I closed my eyes as I spooned the cold sweetness into my mouth. Gabi was right. I needed to unwind. I needed to feel this freedom and the sun on my face. To remember how to be me without anyone or anything else at the wheel. Where I could shovel pounds of caramel and honey-slathered ice cream if I felt like it, savoring all the flavor exploding on my tongue—

"Roman-off?"

The voice, the sound, the proximity, and the giant shadow suddenly blocking the sun made me suck in a breath as my eyes popped open and my heart rate doubled. Irritation flooded me as well when I realized I already recognized his voice. I knew it was Leo before I ever looked, and it had nothing to do with the cute name he used for me.

Jumping to my feet was a mistake, too, as he was too close and bumping chests was unavoidable before he stepped back.

"Sorry—" I blurted out, half choking on a mouthful of chocolate.

"Are you okay?"

"I'm—I'm good," I said, wiping at my mouth. "I was just—somewhere else. You startled me."

"You look different," he said, his eyes sliding over me. "Wasn't sure it was you."

I had to consciously tell my lungs to take the next breath, as the way he drank me in made me lose all normal function. *Shit, Micah, find your brain.*

I smiled sarcastically. "It's me."

"Did you mug someone for their clothes?" he asked, glancing down at my ice cream. "And steal their dessert?" At my look, he continued. "Since an hour ago you had no wallet or money."

I chuckled wryly. "Yep. You have me figured out. She's tied up behind that bush over there. I stole the rope, too."

Leo shrugged. "Logically."

He shoved the tips of his fingers into his front pockets, a move that made his arms do some delicious things.

"So, what are you really doing here in town, Mr. McKane?" I asked, pushing any thoughts about his delicious anythings from my head. He'd been the obnoxious asshole just an hour ago, so arms weren't on the menu. Nothing was on the menu. "If that's your real name."

I knew it was. At this point, I'd gleaned a few tidbits about the mysterious troublemaking-then-disappearing Leo McKane. "*You walked away from being my brother.*" All of which told me he was not to be trusted, but none of which told me why. Because nothing about his persona said he was undependable. He came across as quite the opposite, in fact, like he could take on the whole world. Even the few seconds where he stood off with his brother, I got the distinct impression that he was the Thatcher of his family.

Eyebrows went up. "*My* real name? You're one to talk."

"Nice dodge."

"Ditto."

I smiled at the face-off, realizing I might have met my match when it came to deception, feeling a small thrill at the game I'd let get dusty for years.

"I'm Micah," I said finally.

"Roman-off."

"Roman," I said, waiting for the recognition. When it didn't come, I continued. "My family has a business in—well, where you picked me up."

Leo nodded. "Did you talk to whoever you needed to talk to?"

"I did," I said.

"Headed back there soon?" he asked.

"Not—today," I said, my throat feeling weird as I said it. Like everything I said out loud from this point would seal my decisions in concrete. "I may stick around for a few days."

And there it was. A few days.

He appeared to study me for a beat or two. "I *am* here for a job," he said finally. "But there may be an ulterior motive or two."

I nodded, attempting casual as I spooned a too-big clump of ice cream into my mouth, a third of it slopping down my chin.

"Oops," I said around it, running the back of my hand over my chin. Boy, I had the sexy moves going, that was for sure.

His thumb sliding under my bottom lip stopped my goofiness cold. Every nerve ending in my body sat straight up and paid attention, sending all the blood in my head south. Just from that one touch. Jesus Christ.

"You missed some," he said, his eyes dropping to what he was doing, then raising back to meet mine.

It was everything I could do not to suck his thumb into my mouth when it hovered a second too long, then—*What the fuck, Micah?* There was no denying it. Leo was the devil, and I was losing my mind.

"Is there a full moon today?" I asked, my voice all weird and husky. I cleared my throat. "Or last night?"

He dropped his hand, looking confused. As you do when people babble nonsensical bullshit.

"No idea." There was noise behind us—thank God—as the customers I saw came out. "Hey, I was kind of a jerk earlier," he said.

"Kind of?"

It was the best I could do with no blood in my head.

"I should say I'm sorry for that," he continued, ignoring me. Or possibly not ignoring me, considering the passive apology.

"Well, when you decide, let me know," I said on a smirk, attempting casual and unaffected.

Thankfully, the door opened again, and the tall, slender woman from behind the counter strolled out with Gabi.

"Hey, you made it!" Gabi said to me, while the other woman smiled and shook hands with Leo.

"I made it," I echoed on a nervous laugh.

"Did Lanie hook you up?" Gabi asked.

"She did," I said. "She's awesome."

Gabi grinned. "Lanie definitely has the Barrett helping-people gene, just like her aunt did."

"Barrett?" Leo asked.

I looked up at him, my eyes seeing the narrowed gaze as he asked Gabi the question, but my brain still saw the heat and felt the tingle under my lip.

"Lanie Barrett," Gabi said, nodding, then rolling her eyes. "McKane, now. I still haven't sealed that in my brain. Wow, now that I look at you, the resemblance to your brother is amazing."

"Brother?" the other woman chimed in. "Wait—McKane—Nick has a brother?"

Leo didn't look super thrilled at the big reveal, or actually he just looked annoyed that it was getting off track, but he visibly dialed it back and gave a terse smile.

"Guilty," he said.

"Holy shit," the woman said. "If you're single, you'd better hide. The females of Charmed will sniff you out like bloodhounds."

Of Charmed, of Cherrydale, of planet Earth.

"So," I said, decidedly wanting to move past this party. I looked at Gabi. "You said there's a room?"

Gabi's eyebrows lifted. "You decided to stay after all?"

"For a few days," I said, feeling my scalp begin to sweat as I said those words again. "Nothing permanent. Just till I can get things figured out. Is that still okay?"

"Please," said the other woman. "They are so excited to rent these rooms out right now, they'd hand them to serial killers." She glanced between Leo and me. "You aren't serial killers, are you?"

"Killers?" I said. "Plural?" I looked questioningly at Leo, who was peering at me the same way. "You're staying here, too?"

"*That's* the part that bothered you in that sentence?" the woman asked.

"I'm sorry," Gabi said. "This is my sister, Drew, the rude one."

"Sorry," Drew said, cutting eyes at her sister as she held out a hand. "I manage Graham's Florist with Gabi and sometimes my parents when they aren't being hippies. So, you aren't serial killers, are you?"

I had to smirk at her no-nonsense directness. "Micah," I said, shaking her hand. "And no, not usually."

I wasn't usually a runaway from my life, either, so I figured the disclaimer was justified. But my question hadn't been answered. By anyone.

"Well, then, I guess we can do the paperwork," Drew said, looking at Gabi. "Is there paperwork?"

"I have no idea," she said under her breath. "You know how they are."

"So," I began again. "We—Leo and I—we're both staying here?"

"Evidently," Leo said.

"When did you even—"

"I'm guessing while you were getting naked," he said.

I refused to react to that. Gabi's gaze darted between us knowingly, a small smirk tugging at her mouth.

"Is that a problem?" she asked. "For either of you?"

"No," I said quickly. "I'll only be here to sleep, anyway. And not for long."

Why I felt the need to nail that down, I had no idea.

"I'm looking for a more permanent place," Leo said. "But this is fine till then."

"Well, then, let's go write it down at least," Gabi said. "Micah, we'll do a day-to-day thing or something. Mom and Dad are upstairs fiddling with everything and I know damn good and well they didn't make a form or a contract up so I'll type it up tonight more officially."

"Sounds good," Leo said, stepping around all of us toward the door, his tone inferring he no longer cared about any of it. "Let's do it."

Let's do it.

Why did I feel like those words would be my downfall?

* * * *

"Hey!" squealed an older woman with cheater glasses perched on top of faded blonde hair. She and an older man were arranging a rug that was already under a couch and two chairs in what was going to be my apartment. Both on the floor, tugging. She got from her knees to her feet in surprisingly good time, while her long, lanky husband took a little longer. "Welcome! Welcome! We're so glad you're going to stay with us!"

"This is Micah and Leo, Mom," Drew said. "Do you—"

"Oh, how lovely," she said, beaming, grasping both of our hands. "I'm Wanda. Martin, get over here! Are you just starting out, or—"

"No, no, no," I said quickly. "We aren't a couple."

"We're not together," Leo added at the same time, gesturing over his shoulder. "I'm across the hall."

"Oh, you're our other tenant!" Wanda exclaimed, grabbing Leo's arm, turning him around like she was leading a child. "Martin, come bring him over there."

Leo glanced back at me as the tired older man led him out the door, and for one second I felt a funny kinship with him. It was humorous and comforting and sexy—I dug my nails into my palm as I turned back to face the beaming Wanda.

"You okay, honey?" she asked.

"I'm great," I said, feeling like a mannequin. As I looked into her pale blue eyes, however, I suddenly felt like I'd grown up shelling peas on her porch and could tell her anything. "I'm just a little overwhelmed today."

"Big day?" she asked, pushing up her glasses as she pulled a tiny notebook from her back pocket.

"Well, I was supposed to get married today," I said. "But I ran away on some guy's motorcycle, and now I'm thirty-two years old with no house, very little of anything else, about to rent a room over a flower shop, wearing your daughter's clothes."

Wanda started to chuckle, but winked and squeezed my hand like I'd just said I had a hang nail.

"Remind me to tell you about my fortieth birthday," she said, to a chorus of low groans from Gabi and Drew. "The year my teenaged daughters blew up my house while their dad was out of town."

"Oh, my gosh," I said, glancing beyond her to Gabi, who was shaking her head with her eyes closed.

"Really, Mom?" Drew said.

"Let's just say that we had to start over a bit, too," she said. "So I know what you mean."

"Yes, my school project was *exactly* like Micah's situation," Gabi said, deadpan.

"So, Mom," Drew said, "did y'all do a boilerplate contract or anything?"

Wanda turned to her daughter with a befuddled expression. "A what?"

Drew nodded at Gabi. "Type something."

"Yeah."

Wanda waved a hand at her girls as if they were babbling gibberish, turning to me.

"Here's the living room, there's the kitchenette—it's small but very functional—"

Now, when Wanda said *kitchenette*, I paid attention. It never occurred to me that the apartment wasn't actually an apartment. Gabi had said *rooms*, and I heard *rooms*, but—my brain filled in the details like any other rental would have. A full kitchen you can cook in. What was before me was a stovetop over a cabinet, a small section of more cabinets, and a very small fridge. Like what a college dorm room mini fridge might look like one day if the kids didn't wear it out and it had a chance to grow up. No freezer.

Well, that was okay. All of this would help me not stay too long and work on getting my shit figured out really fast. There. That was a positive outlook.

"Over here is the bedroom," she was saying as we entered through another door. She slid a closet door aside. "Closet isn't big, but for a short time it should be enough, right?" She held her arms out wide. "What do you think?"

She was asking for my blessing. Pride emanated from her as she peered around at what they'd made, and she wanted to know if it was good enough. I wanted to hug her and tell her it was fine, and they'd done well, but there was still something missing.

"It's—it's great," I said. I could overlook the kitchen. It wasn't like I was going to cook gourmet meals or anything. "What about the bathroom?" I asked, turning in a circle, looking for another door I'd missed.

"That's right down the hall," Wanda said, the big smile back on her lips. I couldn't have heard right.

"I'm sorry, what?"

"Yes, ma'am, just a few extra steps down," she said, gesturing that way. "You walk right into it. A full bath with a toilet, vanity, walk-in shower, newly tiled and everything."

My tongue forgot how to work. Her overflowing glee was almost too much to bear in the wake of finding out I didn't just have a college dorm mini fridge. I had the actual dorm.

"Umm," I said, licking my lips. I looked at Gabi for help. Surely, she could have told me that part up front. That I'd be sharing a bathroom with my neighbor. With—"Oh, God."

"Sorry?" Wanda asked, adjusting her glasses.

"I wasn't aware of the bathroom situation," I said, feeling flushed at the thought of sharing a shower with Leo. Not sharing a shower, really. Not *like that*. Shit, the flush turned to a boil at the image of *like that*.

"Honey," Wanda said, laying a warm freckled hand on my arm, "I know it's not ideal. But for just a—"

"Few days," I finished with her, nodding. "I know. I just—"

"And let me tell you," she continued, leaning in like we were about to share a secret, "if you have to bump a little personal space with somebody, that guy is no hardship." She nudged me. "Know what I mean?"

"I—yeah," I said, nodding. Gabi was chewing her lip to keep from laughing. I sighed. "Okay, I'm—I'll deal with it."

When we walked back out into the hall, Leo was coming out of said bathroom, raking a hand through his hair. He locked eyes with me and not in a *Come get me* way. It was more like a *Did they tell you about this bullshit?* semiglare.

Why was he glaring at *me*? I didn't build the damn place, or rent it, or talk anyone into it. I didn't even know he would be there.

"Isn't the bathroom nice?" Wanda asked. "Martin tiled it himself. Didn't you, Martin?"

Martin nodded on cue, winking at his wife. I still hadn't heard him speak, but I assumed Leo got more than a mimed tour of his room.

"Yeah, great job, man," Leo said, gently slapping the older man's thin shoulder. "This will work short term."

"Wonderful!" Wanda gasped, clapping her hands together. "Wow, I never expected to rent them both out in one day. Isn't that exciting, Martin?" Martin nodded again, throwing a smile in the mix. "I suppose you both can start moving in your things any time."

I held up Gabi's wristlet and the plastic grocery bag of clothes.

"Done."

That night was surreal. Once it finally got there, that is. The longest day in the history of days finally gave in to the moon, and I didn't even have the energy to trudge down the hall to shower it off of me. I climbed in the mostly comfortable but foreign bed in my/Gabi's clothes, and stared at the ceiling for the second night in a row, the everythingness of it all landing on me with a vengeance.

Tears pricked at my eyes. I let them come, tracking hot trails back into my hair. How had my life come to this? I woke that morning to brunch and mimosas before getting ready to marry the man I'd spent nearly a decade of my life with. Now I was going to bed alone and still single, away from home and family and everything familiar.

And I was okay with it. That was the mind-blower. I wasn't crying because I felt sorry for myself, or over Jeremy. I was crying from the sheer overwhelming redistribution of crap as the weight lifted off me all at once. Like those people who have cars pulled off them, and they die from everything rushing in at one time—that's what I felt like. Relieved, free, and, oh, my God, the euphoria of having my life back as *my* life— followed on long loop by the crushing rush of *Holy fuck, what did I do and what do I do now and who do I have to face and is Jeremy hurt and oh shit oh shit oh shit...*

Rinse...repeat.

I held up my left hand, shining my phone on Jeremy's ring. I didn't get married, so was I still technically engaged?

Did I want to be?

The question made me start as if someone had yelled it in my ear. I instantly knew the answer without a second's hesitation.

No.

I did not.

Not anymore.

Screw a car. It was as if a dinosaur had been lifted off my chest, and I sucked in a huge breath like my lungs hadn't expanded fully in years. The epiphany felt amazing. Sad. Liberating. And a little scary. I slid the ring off my finger, setting it in a china dish on the nightstand, lifting my hand to shine my phone on my naked finger. It was done. In my head, at least, it was done.

It had been day one of a reboot I never saw coming, and my head spun with the dizziness of it. I shut my eyes tight against it and let the last of the tears go. On to day two.

CHAPTER SIX

The next morning was a blind fog. I'd totally expected to toss and turn and be unable to shut my brain down, but the opposite had happened. I'd fallen into a stress-induced coma and died. Like, I didn't even move. I was still in the exact same position, fisting the same handful of comforter close against my chest.

Instead of feeling refreshed, however, I had nap hangover. My head pounded, the room felt wobbly, my skin clammy. I needed about five showers, and I didn't care if I had to walk to China for it. It was time to start new.

I looked in the two closets for towels, but there weren't any, so either I was supposed to have my own—like normal people did—or they were already in the bathroom. Since normal people probably didn't rent apartments without bathrooms, I had to go on the hope and probability that the towels were in there. I dug in my plastic bag from Gabi and snatched the black stretchy workout capris and a flowy red tank top that wouldn't require a bra right away. At least until I could buy one later today. I couldn't stand another second of the strapless I'd worn all day yesterday, and the lacy white thong was about to join the burn pile. I could pull off commando in this getup; no one would know. So, off I stumbled down the hall, my hair still stiff from the hairspray and listing to one side, my contraband clothing under one arm.

This was going to be a better day. I would buy some new clothes, find a cell store and use my upgrade to get a new phone, meet up with Thatcher—

I turned the knob and pulled, but my foggy brain didn't have enough working cells to process the too-easy motion or the mountain of man-chest aimed at my face. My sleepy blink was a few seconds too long, and his momentum coming out of the bathroom was unnatural for seven thirty in the morning.

"Oh!" I exclaimed, just before the "oompf" and the soft-hardness of his sternum meeting my nose. "Shit."

Strong hands closed over my upper arms, as the scent of soap and man filled my senses, my heart hurtling over itself in a rush of panicked thumps. My hands went up on autopilot to stop myself from certain doom, landing against hard abs and chest hair. I had a tiny bit of experience with those abs on the ride here, but that was nothing on the full-frontal access.

Leo…communal bathroom…the logic was trickling back in as my heart—well, it sort of slowed down. The view just inches from my face did nothing to aid in that.

"Sorry," I mumbled, unable to step back or drop my hands because—I don't know. I guess nearly naked man before coffee rendered me stupid. Coffee. Where might I find that? "What—um."

"My fault," Leo said, bringing my eyes on the slow trip up to his face. "I didn't lock the door. Wasn't thinking."

Holy shit, the man was hot from head to toe, and as he rested his eyes on me I was suddenly awake enough to catch on that he hadn't let go of me or backed off in repulsion from my touch. Flashes of his thumb under my bottom lip yesterday joined the party, right about the time I became hyperaware of my own state and the very real possibility that I might have dried drool on my cheek. Not to mention breath that could stand on its own.

"Door," I blurted, licking my lips and backing out of his grip, letting my hands fall from his torso. I instantly missed the heat of him. "Yeah. We should—"

"Hang a tie?" he said.

I looked up at him again. He was joking. Amusement did an amazingly sexy thing with his eyes, causing a flutter in my belly, but I was too foggy to do witty banter.

"A something," I said, stooping to pick up the clothes and towel I'd evidently bailed on when groping Leo had presented a better option. The view on the way down was almost as good. Rough jeans carved around him, giving me further thoughts I shouldn't be having. Like what I might have seen had I made it down this hall ten minutes earlier and opened the unlocked door. "Or just lock it. That would work, too."

I heard a chuckle as he padded around me on bare feet.

"Enjoy your shower, Roman-off," he said. "The hot gets scorching pretty quick, so be careful."

I saluted his back as I then watched his back retreating. It was a really good back. All the way down.

"Jesus," I muttered, shaking my head. I was a piece of work.

I entered the bathroom, really and truly expecting it to be left like a man was just there. I mean, come on. I'd lived with one long enough to know the score. Stubble in the sink, piss on the toilet—or the floor—puddles of water on the countertop, globs of toothpaste left wherever they fell. It was a fruitless argument that I'd long since given up winning.

None of that was there. There was a little steam left on the bottom of the mirror from the heat of the shower, but everything else had been wiped clean. The sink, the countertop, the floor—even the toilet rim was clean. And the seat was down.

If I hadn't seen a big rough-and-rowdy guy just walk out of there, I'd swear there'd been a woman in there before me.

I met my eyes in the mirror then, and I wished it had been.

"Oh, my God, Micah."

My hair—let's just skip that one. We already conceded that it wasn't redeemable. But that didn't excuse the black around my eyes that morphed from somewhere in my sleep since I thought I'd washed all that off. The white of one eye had gone red in the process, I did have dried drool or snot or something very unappealing on my cheekbone, a rogue hair on my chin, and my lips were cracked and dry.

I not only needed a shower; I needed an exorcist.

First things first.

That's when it dawned on me. Soap, shampoo, lotion, toothpaste—

A knock at the door made me jump, and knowing who it had to be made me cringe. How many times did this man have to see me at my worst? I cracked the door and peered through.

"Yes?"

"You didn't lock it," he said.

"I will," I said. "I was getting to it."

"Lock it, please," he said. "Don't leave yourself vulnerable like that."

"Like you did?"

He smirked. "Do as I say, not as I do." He held up something in front of him. "And here. If you need it."

I cracked the door more. It was a Ziploc'd bag of motel shampoos and still-wrapped mini soaps, along with a travel-sized tube of toothpaste. He'd read my mind. It was possibly the sexiest thing anyone had ever offered me.

I opened the door and took the bag, apologizing in my head for subjecting him to the view of me again.

"Thank you," I said, nearly hugging the bag to my chest.

"Just set it outside my door when you're done," he said, turning to walk away again, this time with a gray-collared pullover covering the good back. "And lock that door."

I rolled my eyes and shut the door with my ass, leaning against it and waiting a full count of ten before turning the lock. Just because. Harley-guy did a lot of road trips to have such a collection of cheap motel toiletries. I opened it and the aroma wafted out. It smelled like him.

That was the catalyst that propelled me off the door, into the shower, clothes flying. I wasn't having any part of that train of thought. I'd unengaged myself the night before—disengaged—whatever the hell I did—and men needed to be off my radar for a while. Especially men who looked like Leo, making me think of things like *how he smelled.*

I stayed in that shower till the water ran cold, wanting nothing more than to be new. Ten minutes later, my hair up in a ponytail to dry of its own accord, my teeth finger-scrubbed with the toothpaste, and with not a stitch of makeup on my face, I headed downstairs.

If not for the boob bounce (that unfortunately wasn't as disguised as I'd hoped, but still wasn't worth the strapless from hell) under the tank top, I could have passed for a tall twelve-year-old. Or then again, maybe that was me feeling a little too new. Probably more like a frazzled soccer mom with no time for makeup or laundry.

I didn't care. I wanted coffee and maybe something to curb the growling in my belly, and then I could go buy a few basics to tide me over before meeting up with Thatcher tonight. Things like a toothbrush. A bra.

By the time I hit the bottom of the stairs, I was rethinking the strapless. It was evil and tight and belonged to yesterday's Micah, but I could hear people talking in the lobby and I wasn't a free-swinging kind of person.

"Micah!" Gabi exclaimed from somewhere I couldn't see, and then I did. In a mirror they had on the far wall, probably for this very reason. "Come here, we were just talking about you."

Crap. Fabulous.

I folded my arms across my chest, pasting on a smile as I rounded the entryway into the bright and sunny lobby. I hadn't paid that much attention to the aesthetics the day before, but I found it very pleasing to the eye. Being a corner building, the windows wrapped around, bathing the counter and the lighter, freshly cut delicate flowers in morning sun. In the afternoon, the roses and hardier blooms would get the light. It made for a beautiful palette against pale yellow walls and brick accents, surrounding the refrigerated case behind the counter. Very enticing. I wanted to pull up a chair and breathe in the gardenias. With a cup of coffee, of course. And no people talking about me.

"Oh?" I responded, as I approached Gabi with a tall hunky man with hair that swung sexily around his eyes. "Should my ears be burning?"

"This is Sully Hart," she said, as he held out a hand and I was forced to uncross my arms. "Owner of the Lucky Charm."

Well, well, high company. As I shook his hand, a blonde woman who was perusing a catalog at the counter turned and walked over, holding out hers.

"Hi, I'm Carmen Frost," she said, an air of professionalism about her. His hand landing on the small of her back said they were together, but something else said I'd heard that name before.

"Micah," I said, shaking her hand. I couldn't throw the last name in. Not this early, before my coffee. I wasn't up to the—

"Roman," she said, however, making that decision for me. "I know. You created quite the buzz in Cherrydale yesterday."

"Great," I whispered, withdrawing my hand to fold my arms back where they'd been, protecting my core. Holding me in. "You were there?"

"We were," Carmen said. "At least until it was pretty official that you weren't."

I closed my eyes. "I'm sorry."

"Carmen is—" Gabi began, making a tiny grimacing twist with her bottom lip.

Of course. The best friend. I remembered now. Shit.

"Jeremy's dad's lawyer," I said, nodding and taking a deep breath, staring at the floor as I released it. "Wow, they didn't waste any time."

"Wait—oh no, no, sorry," Carmen said, laughing as she put a hand on my arm. "I'm not here in that capacity. Sully and I are just ordering something special for tonight, and I told her about yesterday and she said you were here—blah blah blah."

I pushed down the panic that had risen to my throat. It never occurred to me that the Blankenships might go legal on me until that very second. Even though it evidently might not be the case right now, I felt like a *yet* was hanging over my head.

"And the house?" Sully prompted.

"Oh, shit, I'm so scattered today," Carmen said. "I have a rental house here in town that I'm not using," she said. "It's nothing special, two bedrooms, hardwood floors. My landlord won't let me out of the lease and I have another six months, so I'm essentially paying rent—"

"To shack up with me," Sully finished.

"Basically," Carmen said, laughing as she backslapped him in the belly. "I asked Gabi if she knew of anyone interested in taking over the lease or subletting. She said you might be?"

Oh, God. *Oh, God.* Committing to a few days was tripping me up already. Committing to rent? I felt the heat of a thousand volcanoes rise up my neck as my heart triple-timed it. I barely heard the jingle above the door over the rush of blood in my head.

"Oh, um, I—" *Full sentences, Micah. Use your words.* "I can't really commit to something that final right now," I said, chuckling. "And I realize that probably sounds weird to call subletting a rental house *final*, but—"

"No, truly I get it," Carmen said, holding out a hand. "Your life flipped all over the place less than twenty-four hours ago." Was that all? It felt like twenty-four weeks. "You need to figure things out. No problem, I'll keep asking."

"I'd be interested," said a deep male voice behind me that brought goose bumps to my skin.

I wheeled around, my arms dropping before I thought about why they shouldn't and I came face to face again with Leo. He sat on a stool against the wall, one leg cocked up at the knee, one arm thrown lazily over the counter. A pen casually rolled over the fingers of his left hand, knuckle by knuckle, almost as if he wasn't aware he was doing it.

"Shit, where'd you come from?" I said under my breath.

His eyes were soft as they met mine, lowering to see what was way too outlined and defined in that tank top. I folded my arms again, and to his credit, he blinked away.

That was it. I was going back to my dorm for the strapless from hell.

"Upstairs, same as you," he said, continuing the pen roll.

"Well, warn a person next time," I said, rubbing the goose bumps on my arms. Really? What the hell was that? "Don't just sit back there like Yoda and scare people."

An amused smirk pulled at his lips. "I'll be sure to announce the next time I'm sitting here minding my own business."

"You have to be Nick's brother," Carmen said, adding a self-deprecating little shrug. "Sorry, Lanie's my best friend and she kind of filled me in. Plus, you have the same—" She wiggled her fingers at him. "All of it."

"Just to be clear," Leo said, standing and letting the smirk turn into a grin that made my toes go numb. "*He* has the same as *me*." He held out a hand. "Leo McKane."

Carmen burst out laughing. "It's like that, is it?"

"Do I still get the house if it is?" he asked, moving from Carmen's hand to Sully's and locking eyes with him, doing that silent sizing-up thing that men do. Like there was some weird ancient caveman trading of respect arcing back and forth between them.

"Can you fix things that break?" Sully finally asked, not letting go. "Her landlord is worthless and I'm tired of playing Handyman Hank all the time."

"Not a problem," Leo said.

"It's yours."

Sully let go of his hand and slapped him on the shoulder. I felt like we needed to eat a side of beef or something. Smoke some jerky.

"Hey, *Handyman Hank*," Carmen said. "If you're through swinging your *hammer* here, maybe I can make my own deal."

I nearly choked on my own spit and had to turn around to pretend to cough. I liked this girl. She had spunk. She didn't take any shit. She was who I wanted to be when I grew up.

Sully lifted his hands, surrender style. "Deal away, baby."

Carmen lifted her chin toward Leo. "It's yours," she echoed, pulling a card from her back pocket. "You have a job? You sticking around for a while, or are you just looking for a month to month?"

Leo looked to be mulling that over, and I found myself leaning in to wait on his answer. Instantly, I backed up a step, mentally slapping my brain. Why the hell would I care?

"I have a job waiting for me," he said finally. "More than one, possibly. But I should probably do a month at a time right now. Till I get a feel for things." He crossed his arms over his chest. "This isn't going to be a problem, is it?" he asked. "You being Nick's wife's friend?"

She handed him the card. "Dude, I don't care what happened between you and Nick; that's your business. If you have a job and want a place to stay, I can have it ready for you by next weekend probably."

"Sounds good," he said. "Thank you."

Well, homeboy here just got his life issues worked out and solved in under thirty seconds. I needed something to work in my favor like that.

"Hart," Leo continued, lifting his chin toward Sully. "Like the carnival line?"

Sully chuckled, looking surprised. "There's a shot in the dark."

Leo shrugged, his body relaxed as he looped his thumbs in the tops of his pockets. "Heard someone talking about it."

Sully nodded, but something in his eyes went sad. "Once upon a time. My brother runs Lucky Hart now, God help them all." He took a deep breath and smiled as he let it go. "Now I have the Lucky Charm entertainment park keeping me busy."

"So, we're good for tonight?" Carmen asked Gabi, moving on.

"All set," Gabi said with a wink. "I'll have it ready by four."

Drew came in with a piece of paper and Leo took it, holding up his hand in a silent wave on his way to the door.

"Gone, I am," he said under his breath as he passed me.

How fucked up was I that that turned me on? I clapped a hand over the chuckle that bubbled up my throat.

"Nice to—okay then," Carmen said as the door shut behind him, widening her eyes at me. "Well, *he's* mysterious."

Why was that directed at me? Why would she say that, looking at me all cat-and-the-canary and wiggly-eyed, insinuating that I would have any idea about his mysteriousness? Just because I was acting like a silly *girl*?

"Is he?" I asked. "Huh."

Because that was better.

"What are you, his dealer?" Gabi asked Drew when she sauntered behind the counter.

Drew cut her eyes toward her sister. "What are you, thirteen?" She picked up two wholesale catalogs, setting them back on a shelf behind her. "He needed a bike repair shop, and I know a guy, nosy."

"What's tonight?" I asked, thankful for the distraction to move things off of Leo.

"Well, we're—" Carmen began, then looked at Sully. "We're just doing something fun for a friend, and tonight starts the whole honey clusterfuck extravaganza, so…what better time?"

"The Honey Festival is in a couple of weeks," Gabi said. "It's kind of a big deal around here."

"This year, Katrina Bowman is chairing it," Carmen said with an eye roll.

"I—think I met her yesterday," I said. "At the Blue Banana."

"Red hair, giant tits?" Carmen asked. At my chuckle, she nodded. "Yeah. She's hard to miss. Especially now that she's deemed herself *professional.*"

"She's doing a prefestival festivity week," Gabi said, gesturing with her hands. "All kinds of zany things. Some of it sounds fun, though."

"Then why don't you meet us tonight?" Carmen prodded.

Gabi laughed out loud. "Yeah, karaoke isn't one of those things."

"Oh, Lord," I said behind my hand.

"And you can be in charge of getting her there," Carmen said, wheeling on me with a wink. "Bring Gabi to Rojo's tonight," she said. "Y'all need to come have some fun. I know Gabi needs it, and I suspect you could maybe stand to relax for a minute, yourself."

Did I look that tightly wound? Maybe the death grip I had on myself gave that away.

"In my invisible car?" I said, chuckling. "Nah, I have to meet my brother to get some of my stuff. Is there Uber here?"

"Oh, that's right, you just climbed on big brother's bike and sped away," Carmen said to my dismay. "Did you know Nick had a brother?" she asked, turning to Sully.

"Yes," Gabi said, touching my arm to answer my question and bring us back to sanity. "But seriously, just take my car, and meet me back here. Rojo's is literally right around the corner, less than a block from here."

"But I don't know how long that will be," I whispered.

"Even better!" she whispered back.

"Hey, if I can get behind the celebration of bee vomit," Carmen said, "you can suck it up through a few drunk rounds of 'Feelings.'"

"I know," Gabi said. "Just—things get so insane this time of year with the festival, the Honeycomb Dance, the Wars. Everybody wants fresh flowers, everyone wants something different, and right now. I have no time for drunk karaoke."

"The Wars?" I asked.

"Honey wars," Gabi said. "All the local honey makers—from Anderson's Apiary down to the one-hivers making it in their garages—come out of the woodwork to shove honey in your face for two weeks for votes on the best honey."

"It's disgusting," Carmen said.

"She doesn't like honey," Sully said.

"It doesn't matter if it's on a card table on the side of the road," Gabi continued, "they want a wildflower arrangement or petals or a jar of daisies or *something* to bring the whole freshly pollenated visual home."

Carmen shook her head and did a little shiver. "Disgusting."

I knew this time of year was heavy for us as well, but I never knew why, in particular. I wasn't that involved in the customers and the ordering. I only knew I couldn't harvest fast enough.

"Is it wildflowers your customers want especially?" I asked.

"Mostly," she said. "I can have the most beautiful exotic flowers in here at the ready, but this time of year all they want are daisies and blue violets. I order from three different suppliers and still have trouble getting them in." She sighed. "One day, in a perfect world, I can have an entire field of it in my backyard. Problem solved."

Carmen glanced at her watch. "We need to get going, babe," she said softly. Then, turning to Gabi, "I'll see you at four, then again tonight, right?"

Gabi's expression faltered just the tiniest bit. "If Micah's able to get back in time, sure."

Carmen and Sully said their good-byes, and Gabi took a customer call. Drew was in and out again from a back hall. In the span of seconds, life was normal again in Graham's Florist.

Except I was still me. In my little aura, normal felt like a hundred years ago.

CHAPTER SEVEN

Bra…check. Two of them, in fact, just because they were better than anything I had. Some makeup I needed to replace anyway, and a brand-new shiny cell phone using my upgrade, making the one Jeremy had a useless rock.

I also bought a couple of shirts and some capris, a fedora hat in a boutique *because I could*, an ankle bracelet, a chunky-funky necklace, a retro jean vest, and some cute slip-on shoes. Just in case. I knew the one outfit that Thatcher had in my backpack, and it was a sundress. So if Jeremy didn't let me have my clothes…

I knew that was a crazy thought. And I knew that everyone I spoke to had to be thinking I was a loon for not just going to get my things. Or, hey, just going home. Like normal people would.

But they didn't know Jeremy. They didn't know that he was a master mind-game player and would easily hold my shit hostage just to jack with my head a little longer, punishing me for embarrassing him. Not in a mean way that would be obvious to anyone. But with a smile or a hurt look or guilt, or worse—being understanding, *giving me time*, with that underlying seething time bomb I could almost hear ticking.

I didn't trust myself not to fall for it. I'd allowed him to work me for so many damn years, it was like the air was just sweeter outside that bubble. I didn't want to chance losing it. If I had to face Jeremy, I needed a tether of some sort. Something to pull me out when the bullshit got too rainbowy.

I didn't know what that tether was. It couldn't be Thatcher. I mean, clearly he'd always come to my rescue, he was hard-wired for it, but only if I asked. He'd been friends with Jeremy now for too long to see the problems for himself. His wife, Misty, had even pointed it out once, to me, to both of us, but neither of us believed her at the time. That's how good Jeremy was.

Now Misty was gone, and there was no one with enough degree of separation to hold my ankles while I dove into the deep end. Maybe Gabi now. The woman I'd known for a little over a day, yet had lent me her car and told me she didn't trust men. She might definitely be a good candidate.

I passed a garage apartment for rent that had seen better days but was only a few blocks from Thatcher's house. No. I wasn't ready to go there, yet. I turned down the road I could find if I was struck blind tomorrow. The one I used to race my bike down and once rolled Jackson down when I convinced him to get inside an old tire.

I'd decided to just go to Thatcher's instead of meeting him somewhere. If Jeremy suddenly got a notion I was in town, well, good for him. I was visiting my brother, in the house where lies once shielded everyone from anything real. It had its own force field.

When I pulled into the driveway, Thatcher was outside pressure washing the garage door. He turned questioningly until he saw it was me, then went back to spraying off dirt and mold and God only knew what else.

"It's almost dark," I said as I got out. "You do notice that, right?"

"It's the only chance I have to get things done," he said. "It's not going to clean itself and it doesn't care if it's day or night."

"Of course not," I said.

"Whose car is this?" he asked.

"A friend's."

He turned again. "You already made a friend good enough to loan you a *car*?"

"I know; it's like voodoo," I said, wide eyed. "Except that, hey, people actually like me."

"Don't make me point this thing at you," he said.

"And what?" I said. "Scrub my sins away?" I attacked him from behind, wrapping my arms around his middle, burying my face between his shoulder blades. He smelled comforting, like home. "Too late, big brother. Nothing can do that."

"Hey, baby girl."

"Hey."

* * * *

An hour, two coffees, and a root beer float later—because that was always the universal comfort food in our house—I was eyeing the clock on my new phone, putting off leaving. It had been a long time since I felt comfortable there. In fact, every time Jeremy and I came over, I was the one looking for an out within an hour or two. This was different. There was no Mom, no Jeremy, no one pulling my strings. My neck muscles weren't knotted and painful. Huh. Who knew? I dug in the bottom of my glass for ice cream dredges for the fiftieth time, actually wishing I could stay sitting at that worn-out kitchen counter forever.

How many life issues/problems/dramas/dilemmas/celebrations/fights/confessions had occurred at that very counter over a root beer float? Too many to ever remember. Everything important in my life had been discussed right there, probably on the same stool, in view of my dad's mounted firefighter hat and our parents' wedding photo. It was one of the few things I felt my mother got right. Even the end of Thatcher's marriage had pretty much happened before my eyes, about a foot from where he sat now. I don't think there was ice cream involved in that one, though. Whiskey might have trumped it that time.

"You know your old room is still the guest room? I turned mine and Jackson's into the weight room, but you could come stay here," Thatcher said, getting up to rinse out his glass, grabbing mine before I started to lick it.

I knew he'd been holding that question back since I got there, saving it for my most vulnerable moment. I was savvy to his game.

"I know, Thatch," I said, watching him go through the motions of domesticity. Closing cabinet doors I'd left open. Wiping the countertop. There was something so lonely about it, knowing that all he had to clean up after normally was himself. He was good. He was content. But Thatcher Roman was born to take care of people. He'd wanted to be a firefighter, or a paramedic like our father, something to help people. Life kept dealing him other plans, however, and seeing him alone always broke my heart a little. I knew he wanted to take care of me right now, but I couldn't do that. "And I love you for offering. But—" I wasn't sure how to articulate it. It was better, but not *move back in* better. "This house makes me weak."

He turned around, one eyebrow cocked in question, shirt sleeves rolled up and the tails untucked from his jeans. Such a different image from the perfectly together guy he was at work. Maybe it made him weak, too.

"The house?"

I nodded. "It's like the floats, Thatch. It's my comfort zone and it's dangerous at the same time."

He gave me a look like I was about to make him tired.

"How is it dangerous?" he asked. "Are you on Mom again?"

And I was making *him* tired?

"It's home," I said, ignoring his question. "Yes, my memories here aren't as warm and fuzzy as yours, but also—it's like a time capsule."

"What the hell are you talking about?" he said.

I sighed. "You grew up here basically in charge your whole life." I watched him blink an uncomfortable moment away, and I paused a second, knowing that was a thing with him. "Nothing has changed there. You can be here and still be on top of your life. For me, though, I come here and fall into old habits. Old resentments. Bad choices. I left here to get away from something and ended up in another version of it. I can't get stronger, here," I let out a slow, calming breath as I felt the emotion thickening in my throat. "And I desperately need to."

Thatcher's eyes narrowed. "What did he do to you?"

I shook my head, my eyes burning with unexpected tears. Until a couple of days ago, I wouldn't have been able to point to anything. I wouldn't have thought anything was really wrong, other than I just wasn't happy. Funny how being outside the bubble for a minute gave a whole different meaning to clarity.

"Nothing tangible," I said softly.

The doorbell ringing made me jump, and I swiped under my eyes with a chuckle as he frowned in the direction of it.

"Booty call you forgot about?" I asked, palming my keys.

"I don't forget those," he said, following up with a look. "I don't have booty calls, Micah."

"Why not?" I asked.

"Because I'm not twenty-two," he said over his shoulder. "Or sixty-two."

"Excuses."

He started to make a smart-ass remark as he opened the door, but there wasn't time. Namely, because the presence in the doorway filled up all the space.

"Hey, almost-brother-in-law," the presence said loudly, in a voice that sent all my ice cream comfort to a bad, acidic, curdled place.

Shit.

"Not a good time," Thatcher said, his voice stern.

Fight or flight.

"Never a bad time for beer, man. Hope that car out front isn't a woman, because a bro in trouble trumps—"

He'd walked around Thatcher's attempts to thwart him and stopped short at the sight of me, now standing next to my stool. I didn't remember getting to my feet. I couldn't even feel them.

"Jeremy."

He blinked as if I might not be real, setting the twelve-pack of beer on the nearest surface.

"Well, well," he said after a long painful pause.

I swallowed, feeling the urge to run out the door, or up the stairs, or behind the fireplace to the little hidey-hole I'd found as a kid and didn't tell anyone about. The knotted-up feeling that had been blessedly missing before was back with a vengeance, requiring all the adulting properties I could muster. He'd already had some beer—his eyes told me that—but he wasn't so gone that the shock value didn't resonate.

"Well, at least you aren't dead," he said slowly. Too slowly. He'd had more than I thought. "That's good to know."

"Jeremy," I repeated, forcing myself to say it slowly, to not let him work me up.

"Although apparently your brother was already clued in on that," he said, dragging his eyes around to Thatcher.

Thatcher neither confirmed nor denied; he just walked up to Jeremy, putting a hand on his shoulder.

"Have a seat, Jeremy," he said. "I'll let y'all talk."

No!

"Thatch—"

"Talk," he said, raising an eyebrow. Not understanding. Walking away. He held up a finger in response to my silent plea and mouthed the word again. I closed my eyes and shook my head slightly.

Jeremy shrugged. "Not much to say, I venture to guess," he said as I opened my eyes. "Look at you, all hatted up again. That didn't take long. Getting a tattoo tomorrow?"

I felt my blood pressure rising as his backdoor insults swirled around me like a cage.

"Jer—"

"You didn't want to get married," he said, cutting me off as his eyes dropped to my left hand. "You ditched the ring, already?"

I automatically looked at my hand, even though I already knew the status of it.

"I didn't ditch anything," I said. "It's safe at—where I'm staying."

"And where is that, exactly?" Jeremy asked. "With the guy you're screwing?"

"What?" I yelled, expanding the word to at least three syllables and raising it more than one octave. I felt every nuance of boiling blood rise up my neck, threatening to explode out my eyeballs. "How could you say that?"

"Seriously?" he scoffed.

"I've never cheated on you, not once," I said through my teeth. "How dare you—"

"Yeah, well, you've never left me at the altar to run away with another man, either," he said. "So, my baseline is a little unreliable."

Begrudgingly, he had a point, no matter how slurred it was.

I took two slow breaths to cool the lava flow, dialing it back the way I'd been taught two therapists ago. *Imagine talking to a trickling stream and your words just need to land in the water and float with it.*

"Okay," I breathed. "Let's back up. Slow down."

"Screw this," he said under his breath, turning back toward the door.

"Jeremy, I'm sorry," I said. "Please don't leave. I know what I did was horrible. I know I'm a troll. I know you're mad—"

"You think?" he said, wheeling back around, nearly taking out an end table.

I swallowed. *Adulting.* "And you have every right to be."

"I know."

"Please sit down," I said, pointing to the couch next to him.

"I'm fine."

I sat purposefully in a love seat, facing him. Perched on the edge so that I could jump if I needed to, but still sitting.

"Please."

He rubbed at his eyes with a thumb and forefinger, sinking onto the couch with a disgruntled sigh, listing to the left. I waited for him to look at me again, and it took a while.

"I didn't run away with anyone," I said slowly, softly, concentrating on my own body language. No facial reactions that would trigger a bigger event. "I just ran." *Breathe in. Breathe out.* "I ran until there was another mode of transportation in front of me."

That probably wasn't a trickly, floating kind of statement, but to be fair, I hadn't been prepared for this. I should have been. I should have been thinking about what to say to him for the last two days, but I hadn't. I'd purposely steered my thoughts everywhere *but* there. Now he was looking at me like I was a strange food on a plate he didn't recognize and wasn't likely to try.

"Why?" he asked gruffly, the word drawing out. "Why run? Why didn't you just say something if you had doubts?"

"I didn't," I said. *Did I?* "Or I—wasn't aware of it, really." I covered my face with my hands, wanting so much to make sense, knowing I wasn't even in the ballpark. "There wasn't some thought-out plan," I said through my fingers. "There *was* no plan. I was just standing there, and—" *Love you, Micah.* "Then the music started and I was on the street."

His blinks slowed as I talked, to the point that I wasn't sure his eyelids were coming back up.

"Jeremy?"

"It was like that with the fire," he mumbled.

I frowned, confused. "What? What fire? Your old house?"

He never talked much about that, except that he'd been the one to come home to find it burning when he was twenty-one. His parents had been out of town, and Jeremy said he saw the guys leaving it. They'd left a cigarette lighter behind and robbery/arson had always been assumed but I guessed it was never proven. His family had money, so it was sadly logical, but I'd always felt like that was a hell of a thing to deal with alone at twenty-one years old. Not to mention, what if he *had* been home? That had to mess with a person's head. Much of the leeway I'd given him over the years was rooted in this.

"It just—was," he said, making a circling gesture with his hand. "It wasn't, then it was, and I had to deal with the consequences."

Sometimes it *still* messed with his head.

"I know," I said, placating.

Placating.

I glanced to where Thatcher had left the room. I needed someone to pull the tether.

"There has to be consequences," Jeremy said, his words almost lost in the mumble. "Can't take the girl with no consequences."

"What girl?" I asked.

His eyes sprung open then suddenly, as if someone pushed a button. "Whose car is that outside?" he asked.

"A friend's," I said.

"Same friend?"

I sighed. *Be patient.* "No. And on that subject, I need my car, Jeremy."

"It's at our house," he said, frowning. "My house. The house."

"Thatcher said you have the keys," I said.

"Well, of course I do," he said, the words slurring together more. "It's in my name."

It was my turn to pause. Possibly slur.

Wait, what?

"What are you talking about?"

"The car," he said, his eyes doing the slow dance again.

"*My* car," I reiterated.

"Meh," he said with a shrug. "You drive it."

"And pay the note," I said.

"But the title is in—"

"No," I said, shaking my head loose of the understanding I didn't want to see rise to the top. "No, you didn't," I said. "You told me you put it in my name."

My sexy little Mustang. That he had sitting in the driveway with a giant bow on my thirtieth birthday. Not as an actual birthday present, it turned out, since I paid the car note every month, but as more of an incentive to live a little fancier. Work a little fancier. Get my hands out of the dirt and into an office space. I'd been actively looking for a new car, so he just jumped ahead a little.

"Better rate under mine," he said, letting his head rest heavily back against the couch. "You never noticed you didn't sign anything?"

Was he fucking *kidding* me?

I couldn't breathe over the triple-time pounding my heart started doing. I pushed forward to the edge of my seat, barely able to keep my ass down. *Dial it back.*

"Jeremy," I said slowly. Deliberately. With as much willpower as I could muster. "I've paid every penny of that note. It's my car." I licked my lips. "I need my car."

"Well, you know where it lives," he said, sliding down onto a pillow.

I narrowed my eyes. "So, you'll let me have it? Sign it over to me?"

There was a weak chuckle as he descended into la-la-land. "Hell no," he mumbled. "Just saying you know—where it lives."

And he was out.

Consequences.

Motherfucker.

* * * *

"No, Micah," Thatcher was saying from somewhere behind the red haze.

I dug in Jeremy's pockets for his keys, tempted to sock him in his open, snoring mouth.

"He stole my car, Thatch," I said through my teeth. "From day one. Three years ago!"

Thatcher sighed behind me. "In all fairness, did you really not notice whose name was on the account?"

I spun around, nearly ripping Jeremy's pants as I yanked the keys out. Not that he noticed.

"Seriously?"

"I'm just saying," he said, holding his palms up.

I pointed a key at him. "Don't even. Don't you dare side with him on this."

"I'm not."

"He bought the car for me, set up the automatic draft—*for me*, all to be so fucking helpful," I spat. "Three. Years. Ago."

"Micah—"

"We weren't even living together yet," I said. "Not really. I was just blissfully sleeping over at his place because the plumbing at my apartment sucked. He was duping me way back then." I stared around the room I'd know blindfolded, seeing nothing. "What else did he fuck me over on?"

"You can't go over there right now," Thatcher said.

"The hell I can't," I said, grabbing my wallet off the counter. "He's out. I have his keys; he's not going anywhere. It's the perfect time to go get all the shit I can fit in my friend's car."

"And do what with yours?" he asked. "Strap it to the roof?"

Thoughts were pinging off the sides of my skull like a rogue pinball.

"I can at least find my keys, then come back for the car tomorrow."

"Micah," Thatcher said, stopping me with a firm grip on my shoulders. "You can't. He's a Blankenship."

I blinked, irritated. "And I'm a Roman."

"Well, unfortunately, that doesn't have the same knockdown power," he said. "They can have you arrested for trespassing. For theft."

"It's my stuff."

"You want to think about that in jail?" he said. "You have to be sure he's there, he sees everything, and bring witnesses. With the car being in his name...baby girl, you have no legal claim to it, no matter what you've paid."

I could hear my blood rushing through my head, my breathing in my ears. And his words—I knew they made sense. I knew he was right. But— *fuck.* Hot tears filled my eyes and I squeezed them shut.

"How did—how did I let myself get so screwed?" I said under my breath. "How did this happen?"

"You trusted," he said, pulling me into his big embrace. "You know, that thing we keep learning not to do?" He leaned back suddenly, looking down at me with alarm. "You didn't put your money together, did you?"

"No," I said. "It was my one holdout."

"See there, you had instincts," he said, kissing the top of my head. "You weren't completely duped. And you didn't walk down that aisle."

I looked up at him. "I thought you thought I was being flaky."

"I did," he said wearily, glancing over at the lump snoring on his couch. "But now there's this."

"*This* was your mother," I said, watching the understanding leave his eyes. "And almost your brother-in-law," I said.

Thatcher let go of me, plucked Jeremy's keys from my hand, and pocketed them.

Because little sister might look calmed down, but pissed-off female can skip the tracks at any time.

"Yeah, well, almost-brother-in-law can sleep this shit off here and I'll deal with him in the morning," he said. "Go—wherever it is you're going."

I nodded.

"When are you coming back to work, by the way?" he asked. "Regardless of where you lay your head, you have a job. Or is that too comfortable, too?"

I punched him in the arm. "Ha-ha. Yes, I'm coming back. Just—give me a few days. Hell, I was supposed to be on my honeymoon for two weeks anyway, so I'll be back in two weeks. Roarke can more than make up for me."

Roarke came to us four years ago to help me out in the houses with the physical labor. He was something of a side of beef mixed with a mountain, and he was a workhorse wonder who went about every single day moving, hauling, tilling, and harvesting with his earbuds in and his two turkey sandwiches on wheat bread for lunch. I think he once told me he was pushing sixty, but his body didn't know that.

"Of course he can, but he's mad at you right now," Thatcher said.

"Oh, no," I whispered. "Did he actually come?"

"In a suit, even."

I shut my eyes. How many people could I disappoint today?

"Shit."

"Just no going to that house alone in the meantime. Witnesses, Micah," he said, bringing us back on track. "More than me. Someone who isn't family."

Well, since my friends were long gone, that currently left about four people who even knew my name, much less could be called friend enough to step up for me. One was the best friend of Jeremy's dad's lawyer—probably not. One was Leo—*definitely* not. And one kept stepping up for me minute after minute.

CHAPTER EIGHT

"First round's on me," I said to Gabi as we walked into Rojo's and asked to sit in the bar area. I held up my strappy little travel purse that held $900 in cash in a secret pocket. The cash I'd taken out for our honeymoon trip to Turks and Caicos. That Jeremy had prepaid for. Karma's a bitch. "I have some pissed-off brain cells to kill."

I'd stopped by my room to update my ponytail from perky to side-shoulder sexy, put on a new black sleeveless minidress to go with my sassy new black strappy wedges, slapped on some face with my new makeup so I could feel like a woman again, plopped the hat back on top, and left to pick up Gabi. It almost felt normal. Like a person with a life. If having a life meant starting over with everything new and driving your friend's car because your ex-fiancé was holding yours hostage.

Katrina Bowman, the big-boobed redhead from the diner bathroom, was bent over a karaoke machine on a tiny stage in the back, in a low-cut tank top and shorts that didn't have much purpose. I could almost see her nipples. There was a nerdy little tech guy standing behind her who had probably been up there to wire it up but was now short-circuited by a giant boner straining against his zipper.

"Got it done, Gary?" said another guy off to the right, snapping him out of his porn fantasy.

"Huh? Yeah!" he mumbled, turning in a circle and adjusting himself. "Um, yeah. It's all hooked up."

"Thanks, you're a doll," Katrina said, standing upright and winking at him.

Poor Gary went red, then disappeared through a door to do things I didn't want to think about.

Sully Hart and Carmen-the-lawyer were at a big table with Lanie, Nick, and another couple, the guy I recognized from a poster.

"Shit," I said, slowing my roll.

"What?"

"It's Bash Anderson," I said, gesturing with my chin.

Gabi followed my gaze. "Yeah. So?"

"So, he's a customer," I said. "And he came to my wedding. The one I wasn't at."

Gabi flipped a hand casually. "Details. Come on. If I can do this, so can you."

"Really?" I said, looking around at faces. "Show up yesterday looking like a cake topper, did you?"

"Oh, my God," Carmen said as we wove our way to their table. "You actually came."

"Micah kind of needed to," Gabi said. "She's had a night." She winked at me as if to say, *Play along, let's make it about you.*

Why not? Everything was already about me, so ya know.

"Micah?" Bash said. "As in—"

Boom.

"As in I am so sorry you had to experience that drama yesterday, Mr. Almost-Mayor," I said, holding out a hand. "Please don't let that affect your opinion of Cherrydale Flower Farm or my brother will twist my head until it pops off."

Bash chuckled and took my hand. "It's all good. And I kept my gift, so I won't hold it against you."

I felt my face fall and my free hand went over my eyes. "Gifts. Oh, my God. I didn't even think about—"

"And we won't tonight, either," Gabi said, a hand on my arm.

I felt nauseous. "But people brought—"

"The gifts will go back, my friend," Lanie said, reaching across the table. "Or they won't. Don't stress about it. It's okay. Sit down. You look fabulous."

I could hear Deidre Blankenship waxing on in her uppity shrill way about that classless Roman whore who destroyed her baby and *Can you believe she didn't give a rat's ass about the gifts people gave her?*

Dee Dee Blankenship wouldn't say "ass," and probably wouldn't say "rat" either, but all the rest was pretty close to spot-on.

"Y'all missed Bash and Allie up there blessing the kickoff like a real king and queen," Carmen said with a grin.

"Oh, God," the woman next to Bash said.

"You just needed scepters and you'd be set," Lanie said.

"So that's what all the people outside giving away stuff was about?" I asked, thumbing over my shoulder.

"The endless honey prostitution?" Carmen asked. "Yeah, everyone thinks they have a new take on honey products around here," she said. "They can't hawk them inside the businesses, but the sidewalks get pretty full this week."

"I'm Allie," the woman with Bash said, grinning. "It's kind of dumb, but the town gets off to this stuff. I like your hat, by the way."

I reached for it automatically, the self-doubt waving its ugly head before I forced my hand back down. No. That wasn't self-doubt. That was Jeremy doubt. My skin flushed with anger at the thought of his name.

"Thanks," I said, clearing my throat, attempting to clear the toxicity from my head. "I used to have a thing for hats. I'm trying to remember that girl." I laughed. "Says the lunatic."

"Micah," Carmen said. "We've all had to find out who we were-slash-reinvent-ourselves at some point."

"I'm just sorry I missed the grand entrance," Allie said, kicking back in her chair with one hand lazily caressing Bash's.

Lanie started to laugh and I smiled distractedly as she and Gabi collectively told the story much funnier than I remembered it. Hell, it could have been made into a romantic comedy film the way they told it, but I didn't care. It was nice to be among people, laughing, not worrying about how I was dressed or if what I said was appropriate for the company, not having to put on a dog-and-pony show. Just me. Hanging out with some funny women and easily three of the hottest men I'd ever seen in one place. My God, these ladies had cornered the lottery. Even broody Nick was lighter and happier than I'd seen him the day before, but then his long-lost deserting brother wasn't standing in front of him.

A guy was mutilating "Wanted Dead or Alive" up there, but had a cheering section in the back nonetheless. Carmen was right. "Feelings" had to make an appearance at some point.

"So, who needs a drink?" I said, sliding my chair back. "I haven't seen a waitress."

"They're definitely short some help tonight," Gabi said, looking around. "Bad night for it."

"I'll go get," I said, mentally tallying the beer bottles on the table. Lanie had a glass in front of her with a lime in it. "Vodka seven?"

"Sprite," she said. "Just Sprite."

The designated driver, I got it. "Be right back." I glanced at Gabi. "What do you want?"

Katrina sashayed by, squeezing Gabi's arm in passing. "It's so good to see you out again with *people!*" she whispered loudly, a dramatic expression emphasizing the words.

Gabi cut her eyes toward me. "Something potent."

I made it five steps when the sight of the *fourth* hottest guy I'd ever seen in one place, standing behind the bar shaking a drink, stopped me silly. Leo was bartending. Leo was bartending *here*. Of course he was.

I glanced over my shoulder at the table where Nick sat, his back to the bar. Crap.

There I'd been thinking it was going to be a noneventful, nice evening to soothe my wounds.

I strolled up slowly, waiting my turn, as he and another girl cranked out orders. I noticed that Leo's crowd was mostly women, and I didn't blame them. Just watching him mix was like watching art in motion. He may be new to this bar, but he definitely wasn't new. He knew what he was doing, and how to work his assets. Eye contact with every patron, a panty-melting sizzling smile with every drink he handed over, and I would swear he could tell you the headcount of the room. He was a whole different Leo up there. In his element, alert, aware, those dark eyes missing nothing. Including me, just one head in a million. Goose bumps went down my spine when his five-thousand-degree gaze burned into me, while lighting some drink on fire.

I blinked away, pretending I didn't notice, but in truth, I'd have given anything for a freezer to stick my head in.

The girl kept eyeing him sideways like either she wanted to learn from him or she wanted to *learn from him*. The muscles in his arms rippled every time he shook a drink, did a high pour, or tossed a bottle from hand to hand, and I was pretty sure every other woman there held their breath through every one. Them. Not me. I was good. I was breathing. I wasn't light-headed at all by the time I reached the counter.

Nope.

Leo leaned his head back a little when I bellied up to the bar, regarding me with either wariness or weariness. I couldn't tell. Maybe I was cramping his style, spoiling his fun, reminding him of his not so exciting real life living above a florist shop, having to share a bathroom with his flighty neighbor.

"Roman-off," he said slowly, dragging out the word as he flipped a coin over his knuckles like he'd done with the pen earlier.

I raised an eyebrow. "McKane."

"You look nice. I like the hat." I smirked. That was a point in his favor. Not that there were points to be had. "What can I get you?"

"Um, I have a whole table, actually," I said, looking back to the left so he'd follow. "Including your brother."

Some of the cockiness drained from his expression, and I was struck with how sad that was. I wanted to take it back. Watch him light up again.

"Okay," he said, blinking quickly as if to regain his mojo. "Thanks for the heads up," he said more matter-of-factly. "What do you need?"

"Three Bud Lite Limes, one Dos Equis, one Corona Lite with a glass, a Heineken Dark, a Corpse Reviver Number Two, a whiskey sour, and a Sprite with a lime."

Let's see how good he really is.

The look of surprise on his face said the same.

"You've done that before," he said.

"In college," I said, wincing. "Instead of college, actually, most of the time." I looked around me. "Hopefully I won't have to do it again."

"Good to have a skill," he said, setting up the glasses, amusement playing at his lips. "You never know when you'll need a backup plan."

I rested my elbows on the bar, not caring about the hoard of women behind me waiting their turn.

"Like bartending when you just happen to land in the same town your little brother lives in?" I asked, adding a head tilt. I wasn't flirting. I was just soaking in some of his cockiness.

He gave me an almost-smile that nearly buckled my knees.

"No idea what you're talking about," he said, finishing off the drinks with a flourish, cutting me a knowing look before turning around to pull the beers from ice. "I'm also set to do some land clearing across the pond and some deliveries in Denning if you're nosy enough to need that information."

"Hmm."

"And you, Roman-off?" he asked as he returned, icy bottles between his fingers. "What's your story?"

I laughed. "I think you've seen my story pretty up close and personal."

He was already shaking his head as he opened the bottles deftly, grabbing a tray.

"I saw the end result," he said. "A desperate decision of a woman who felt like she had no other choice."

My eyes widened, my mouth opened, but the in-your-face shock sucked the words right out of my head.

"Desperate," I echoed.

"You don't think so?"

I looked away, *my* cockiness draining away. You can take the girl out from under the thumb, but you can't take—Or something to that effect. Leo saw me as desperate? Doesn't get sexier than that. Hat or no hat.

"Just give me the damn tray," I said, frowning down at it.

"Hey," he said. "Don't take it like that."

I barked a laugh. "Is there another way?"

I grabbed the tray but he held on, his eyes narrowed like he was studying a difficult problem.

"That guy must have really done a number on you," he said finally.

I felt the jolt in my gut as my whole body twitched.

"What?"

"To go to this much trouble to get away, to not even talk to him the next day," Leo said, his voice low. "Or have you now?"

His words hit every guilt trigger, bouncing off all the self-doubt and renewed anger on their way down. Especially on the heels of Thatcher asking me the same thing. Fight or flight hit me again, and I had to simmer it down. There was nothing to run away from now.

"You—it's not—" I let the indignation pull me together. "Thank you for being there for me, for giving me a ride out of my *desperation*. For giving me shampoo this morning." I shook my head. "You keep coming to my rescue, but my story isn't your business."

A spark of amusement flashed across his face, as he managed to scan the room again while never really leaving me.

"No, it's not," he said. "You're right. Just my curiosity taking over. People usually run for two reasons. Toward something or away from something."

"Yeah?" I snapped. "What was yours?"

The quickest of shadows passed over his face before he shut it down with a mini shrug of concession.

"Touché."

"Whatever," I said under my breath, pulling the tray from him, turning back to the table. "Move, people!" I yelled over the noise, making several girls jump away like the parting of the Red Sea.

Laughter was enveloping the table as I returned and passed out the drinks, and it was all I could do not to say my good-byes and leave. I wasn't feeling this anymore. All I wanted to do was go back to my sad, pathetic, *desperate* little room and figure out what to do with my life. Gabi was having a good time, though, so I bit my lip and took a healthy gulp of my whiskey sour, closing my eyes as it went down. Sully slapped Nick on the back, capturing my attention enough to open them again.

"Congratulations, man," he said. "No one deserves it more."

"Oh, what did I miss?" I asked, suddenly feeling very odd-man-out as they all looked my way. "Or—never mind. Maybe it's—"

"No, sorry," Allie said, laughing. "I just spilled the news that Nick will sort of inherit my greatest love and my biggest headache."

"That could also describe me," Bash said, giving her a side-eyed grin.

"I don't think Nick wants you," Allie said.

"You notice she didn't deny the headache part," he said to the table.

"Allie has invited me to be an equal partner in the Blue Banana," Nick said.

"Oh, wow," I said, taking another sip.

"For now," Allie said, smiling softly. "I feel other things coming on. My dad has dementia and will need full-time care soon. My daughter will be going off to college and while Angel loves the diner, she has zero interest in running it. So I need to start planning ahead. I learned not too long ago that I need to balance things and have more freedom." She smiled affectionately at Nick. "I need to know that one day maybe I can hand this off completely to someone who loves it like I do."

He lifted his glass to hers, emotion clear in his expression. Lanie dabbed at her eyes.

"I've never had anyone trust my work like you do, Allie," he said, clearing his throat. "You—" He shook his head and everyone chuckled. "You're the damn bomb, lady. Thank you."

Holy shit. Nick was having a monumental moment. Not the time to tell him that his very unwanted brother was back there tending bar.

"What is this you got me?" Gabi asked, sniffing it.

"It's called a Corpse Reviver Number Two," I said. "Taste it."

She took a tiny sip, her eyes lighting up. "Oh, my God, lemon!"

"Yes, ma'am."

"It's delicious," she said, sucking down some more.

"And ass-kicking," I said. "So be warned." I held up a finger to get Lanie's attention, thinking maybe that was the better course of action. "Um—"

"Unlike someone else's drink at this table," Carmen said, leaning over to bump Lanie's shoulder with her own.

"You're determined, aren't you?" Lanie said, chuckling.

"Actually," Carmen said, with a fake little grimace as she nodded to someone in the distance, "I have a little something for the table."

I turned to see a beautiful tall vase of cut lilies being brought to the table, followed by a second person with multiple bowls of something to place around it. It smelled amazing. Hot and steamy. Cinnamon. Apples. Lanie clapped a hand over her mouth, blinking back tears as Carmen hugged her, and everyone seemed to be in on whatever made this presentation special. Crap. Maybe I could just put up a curtain.

"Aunt Ruby would be so over the moon right now, my friend," Carmen said, swaying with her. "We need a little of her here, tonight."

"Excuse me," said a man's voice at the mike. I swiveled around to see Nick up there.

"Oh, shit," Lanie said, looking at the empty chair her husband had vacated. "How did he do that?" She looked at Carmen then with wet eyes and rolled them, laughing. "Aunt Ruby."

Shit. Nick would see Leo from there, easy. But then again, he appeared to only have eyes for his wife as he grinned at her. I was hit with an enormous wave of envy for a love like that, and it was the most foreign feeling. I'd never in my life felt like I was missing anything or that I needed that, but watching them was like some kind of gut check.

"Sing a song!" someone yelled from the back, but Nick just laughed.

"Believe me, you don't want that," he said, bringing a round of laughs. "I just need about fifteen seconds of your time, so I can announce that my wife Lanie is going to be really, really sober for the next several months."

My jaw dropped, squeals went to beyond ear-piercing, and Lanie went red-faced with laughter and love as Nick smiled at her like she was the only person in the room. She put her hands around one of the bowls of baked apples and closed her eyes. I had to think there was something interesting there. Something intrinsically private.

"Baby, since you picked me up in a diner parking lot and brought me here, it's been a hell of a roller-coaster ride," he said, an adorable grin on his face. The crowd went crazy with hoots and hollers. "I can't imagine my life going any other way. I love you, and I can't wait to meet our son or daughter. You've made me the happiest dad in the world."

Lanie blew him a tear-filled kiss. Instinctively, I turned in my seat to find Leo, and I did. Standing with a bottle in his hand, staring at his brother with a mixture of swelling pride and enormous regret.

"You walked away from being my brother."

I turned back around. It wasn't my business. But just as I did, it became Nick's. He had left the microphone and was walking straight to the bar with singular focus.

"Shit," I muttered.

"What?" Gabi asked.

"Leo is bartending," I said, pushing my chair back.

Bash and Sully were on their feet in seconds, ready to back their buddy I'm sure, or pull him off of someone.

I didn't really know these people. I couldn't very well tell them what to do, and a very irritated part of my brain was asking me why I cared, but I felt like someone needed to be Leo's buddy in this scenario.

Women parted for Nick like he was a hot knife through butter, moving aside and looking up at him adoringly as he approached the bar, probably wishing they were having his babies right then.

I pushed my way through, since no one was wanting to have mine.

"I'm working, Nick," Leo said before Nick even opened his mouth.

"Well, I was working yesterday and that didn't stop you," Nick said.

"My bad," Leo said, pouring a cocktail. "Won't happen again."

"None of this is going to happen again," Nick said, his hands going to fists. Noise and chaos erupted around us as someone started singing "I Will Always Love You." Thank God for that. "I don't know what your plan is, showing up here, disrupting my life, but—"

"Nick, grow up," Leo said, meeting his eyes.

"Excuse me?"

"It's not all about you, little brother," Leo said. "I have my own life and you have yours. I've made mistakes in mine, but I've learned how to make amends and move on. If you aren't mature enough for that, that's not my problem. But I can live wherever I damn well please, so like I said, I'm working. Congrats on the good news. Order a drink or move on."

His voice was soft and yet carried over the din, and I swear he never blinked. Which must have been a family trait, because from where I stood off to the side, Nick didn't either. Time seemed suspended as they stared each other down, until Nick turned, walking away, back to the table where Sully and Bash stood like bodyguards in waiting.

Leo visibly aged five years. His whole expression sagged as he watched his brother stride away in anger. He closed his eyes as if he were counting, then opened them, scanning the room for what had to be the eighty-fifth time.

"You know, you could show a little more of *that* reaction?" I said, stepping in front of what would have been the next customer.

"Hey!" whined a girl behind me with purple lipstick.

He did a double-take on me, ignoring her.

"Have you been there the whole time?" he asked.

"Wow, that's flattering," I said, laughing, resting an elbow on the bar. "So, like I said, you could try a little more emotional connection and a little less tough love."

"Seriously."

"I mean, he's already mad at you," I said. "If you're wanting to make good with him again, pissing him off more doesn't seem like a good plan."

Leo leaned over that bar so close to me I could smell the mint in his mouth.

"My story is not *your* business, either," he said. He stood up, effectively dismissing me. "Next."

CHAPTER NINE

Men.

They had the power to completely fuck up a fun night with nothing but words and some arrogance. Ugh.

What had started as a celebration of all the good news, petered out into a cooler mood at the table with major people-watching and Nick doing his damnedest not to sulk but failing every ten minutes. Bash and Allie called it an early night way too early, which made Gabi and me look like we were crashing a double date.

"You picked him up in a parking lot?" I asked Lanie, for the sheer sake of lightening the mood.

She laughed. "I did. There was this condition in my aunt's will that I had to be married in order to inherit her house—my house."

"Except that it was all a big lie," Carmen added.

"My Aunt Ruby was a character," Lanie said. "And she concocted a big mess, but I didn't know it was a mess—"

"You forgot to mention that you'd lied to her that you were already married," Nick said.

"And living in California," Carmen said. "Which was another lie since you were really in Louisiana."

"Yeah, that," Lanie said, her eyes sparkling with remembered mischief. "Okay, so maybe I inherited some of Aunt Ruby's stretching of the truth."

"She offered to pay me to come pretend to be her husband for a weekend," Nick said.

"Which turned into months," Carmen said.

"So, you aren't from here?" I asked Nick, noticing he glanced back at the bar.

"No, I was living about four hours from here at the time," he said. "But I'm originally from farther south, near Corpus."

"So was my ex," I said.

"Blankenship, right?" Nick asked, and I nodded. "I used to work construction for B&B, and I think one of the owners was a Blankenship."

"Oh, small world," I said.

The crowd got thicker and drunker. Louder. Especially in the middle. The far back edges held the people who didn't know if they really wanted to stay. We ordered food from the restaurant side, scarfed down chips and hot sauce to absorb the alcohol, but the room had a definite tilt going on. Almost enough to make that microphone action look like something I might want to do. Just as I formed that thought, Gabi was suddenly up there.

"Heyyyyyyy!" she squealed, doing a little shimmy.

"Oh…" I said, waving at her. "This can't be good."

"We need to go get her," Lanie said.

"Or go join her," I said, pushing my chair back. "Come on, let's do a ladies' version of 'Ride a Cowboy.'"

"I'm entirely too sober for this," Lanie said, getting to her feet.

"I'm entirely too everything," I said, glancing back at Leo for the hundredth time. He wasn't looking at me. He wasn't even looking our way anymore. It was as if he'd figured out how to block our table from his room-scanning spidey vision.

Carmen, Lanie, and I made our way up to the stage to wrap our arms around each other and a giggling, nearly-crying-with-alcohol-induced-emotion Gabi.

"Y'all," she kept repeating. "I love y'all so much. Y'all are my tribe, you know that?"

We just barely got the song going when I saw movement to my left. Which meant nothing, really. It was like a friggin' ant mound in there, people everywhere. Then something went lopsided as Gabi went up.

Up. In the air, as someone assigning himself the job picked her up to straddle him as we sang about saving a horse and riding a cowboy. Gabi, a few reactions too late, whooped a couple of times before realizing she was being dry-humped with strange hands on her ass.

"Hey," I said, frowning. I let go of Lanie and pawed at the man's hands groping Gabi. "Hey, that's not cool. She's drunk, man."

"So am I," he laughed, leering at her before burying his face between her breasts.

"Stop!" I yelled, pushing at his head.

"Put—me down," she said weakly as he jostled her again, her face going pale.

"Dude—"

Up she went again as Sully was there, lifting her effortlessly off cowboy-man and down from the stage just in time for her to grab someone's empty beer bucket off a table and hork for all she was worth.

"She should have puked on y—" I began, my words cut off by cowboy-man's putrid mouth on mine and the sound of Lanie yelping and struggling next to me. Boos from the crowd replaced the cheering. I shoved at him, screaming in his mouth, but his hand held my head by my hat.

"Get the fuck off—" Lanie yelled, right as he left my mouth and landed on hers.

Use what you have. Everything slowed down, and I took inventory. I didn't have much. I didn't have the weapon heels or the ring, but I stomped down on his foot as hard as I could with my wedges, and as soon as he lifted his face and let go of us I swung. My left fist landed square into his nose.

The cracking noise was nasty and the blood was even nastier, but the howling was worth it. Out of nowhere two Leos appeared. Or since it was in slow motion, I realized it was a Leo and a Nick, one yanking the guy into a full twist with his hands bent painfully behind him, and one grabbing Lanie protectively with one hand over her stomach.

"You're out of here," Leo growled, shoving the guy into the back wall.

"She hit me!" he cried.

"You're disgusting!" I yelled, wiping my mouth as I grabbed my hat from his still-fisted hand and looked it over. No blood. I shoved it back onto my head.

"Are you okay?" Leo asked Lanie, concern for her heavy on his face as he twisted the guy's arms tighter.

She was already wrapped up in Nick, but she nodded. "I'm fine," she said with a body shiver. "I need twenty showers, but yes, thank you." She gave her husband a pointed look until he nodded reluctantly at Leo.

Leo shook his head and turned to me as a security guy took the asshole off his hands.

"I'll sue you!" the guy yelled. "I'll sue this whole place."

"Please do," Carmen said. "I can't wait."

"Are *you* okay?" Leo asked me as if no one else had said anything. He grabbed my hand, which was swelling around the knuckles, leading me off the stage without another word.

"I'm—I'm fine," I said, following behind him like a puppy. I saw the scraped-up knuckles and the bruising, but it didn't really hurt much. Liquor and adrenaline.

I'd just punched a man in the nose.

Me.

I couldn't wait to tell Thatcher. He'd shake his head and roll his eyes but secretly be proud. Jackson would whistle into the phone.

Jeremy would be mortified.

"Oh, my God, I wish Jeremy could have seen that," I blurted as we went behind the bar. Leo grabbed a towel and filled it with ice.

He looked up from his task. "Because?"

"Shit, I said that out loud?" I said, wincing when he pressed his work against my knuckles. "Ow."

I felt it now.

"Keep that on there as long as you can tonight," he said. "It'll be better in the long run."

"Punched a lot of people?" I asked.

He narrowed his eyes, letting his focus move over my body. "One or two. Are you okay, otherwise? He didn't hurt you, did he?"

I grimaced. "He kissed me."

Leo curled his lip, and my toes tingled.

"I saw."

"With his *tongue.*"

"You should have bitten it off," said the girl with purple lipstick, back and waiting for a drink from the other bartender. The one who had had to take over when Leo went all superhero. "That's nasty." She then looked Leo up and down. "But him vaulting over this bar to take that guy down was the hottest thing I've seen in years."

I raised my eyebrows at him. "You vaulted?"

He smirked. "I don't really remember." Looking around in that way of his again, I felt cool, detached Leo coming back. His gaze landed on Nick and Lanie at our table, grabbing their stuff to leave, and a furrow deepened over his nose. "Shit."

"What?" I asked. "Lanie's okay."

"That just had to happen with me here," he said under his breath. "He'll find a way to make it my fault. Say trouble follows me or something."

"Does it?"

It was a simple question, but the myriad things that passed over his face were anything but simple.

"In Nick's mind it does," he said after a pause. Shaking his head as if his own mouth had betrayed him. "It doesn't matter—"

"Hey," I said, grabbing his arm. His skin was hot and I temporarily forgot what I was going to say. His dark eyes traveled from my hand up to my eyes. "You—you did good over there. You helped his wife. You helped me."

A hint of a smile touched his lips, and it had to be the whiskey but dear *God* I went weak in the knees.

"You handled things pretty well yourself, Roman-off," he said. "Used what you had." He lifted the towel and gingerly touched my finger. "Would have done a lot more damage with that rock you had." His eyes met mine with the silent question. An answer I wasn't ready to voice. "Wouldn't have figured you for a southpaw," he said instead.

"Like you."

He tilted his head slightly. "How'd you know that?"

"You're not the only observant one," I said. He gave a silent chuckle and nodded to the increasingly impatient cobartender who kept doing a neck jerk to indicate I needed to get on the other side of the bar. "Do I need to vault, too? Because I don't think I can do it as gracefully or *hot* as you evidently did."

He looked down at my bare legs in the mini dress. "Pretty sure it would be hot, but—"

"I'd land on my face," I said.

"And no one wants that," he said, not missing a beat. He pointed where to go. "Better to leave how you came. But you never answered me." He folded his arms over his chest. "Why do you wish Jeremy would have seen you do that?"

I needed to start carrying duct tape for my mouth.

"Shock value, I guess," I said. "Because he would have despised it." I saw Leo's look. "No, he didn't do *a number on me* or anything to me. I'm just—"

"Telling me it's none of my business?" Leo asked.

I pointed at him and stifled a grin. "That."

He reached out and adjusted my hat, and I was struck with the familiarity—the intimacy of the gesture. Which zinged me back in time to yesterday's ice-cream-thumb-to-lip escapade. Which made my tongue dart out to run along my lip before I could think better of it. Which made his gaze drop to watch. Which made me grip the counter closest to me before I swayed or swooned into him.

Holy fucking hell, I needed to get out of there.

"I'm gonna—" I said, pointing toward where my new friends for the day were leaving.

"You two aren't driving," he said. It wasn't a question.

"Around the corner?" I laughed. "No. We parked at her shop and walked in anticipation of this. She can crash in my bed tonight. I'll take the couch."

"Don't walk alone either," he said. "Nick," he called out with a wince, as if that was the last thing he wanted to do.

"Hey, don't," I said, grabbing his arm again. I didn't need a babysitter, or a rescuer. Again. "I can take care of—"

"Sully," he called out as well, making both of them turn. "Can one of you make sure these two get to the florist shop okay?"

Carmen was arm in arm with Gabi, who managed to grin while still looking a sickly shade of green.

"No problem, we got this," Sully said.

Nick stopped walking and looked at Leo. Looked hard. As if everything he wanted to say could just be shoved out there that way. I wasn't sure if it was *Thank you for rescuing my wife*, or *Fuck you for thinking I would let two inebriated women wander off in the dark alone*. Lanie moved in front of her silent husband, smiling up at Leo.

"Thank you," she said.

He moved his focus to her. "Anytime. Congrats, by the way," he said. "I'm happy for you. Does Addison know yet?"

"She does," Lanie said, chuckling but dialing it in as she glanced to her side for Nick. "She's over the moon to be a big sister."

That time, it was Nick's turn to show a flash of pain as he closed his eyes and turned his head, guiding his wife along. I'd bet that Leo didn't notice it, and I'd double that bet to say that Nick had no intention of showing it.

I looked back to Leo, but he was already moving down the bar.

Okay, then.

Not my business.

As I made my way around the bar to join Gabi and Carmen, I glanced back to see him talking to a bored-looking woman in a suit. Talking to her, but his eyes were on me, sending heat to every nerve ending.

Nope.

Keep walking, Micah. Keep walking.

* * * *

"I can't take your bed," Gabi slurred, attempting to get up for the seventh—maybe eighth—time. "I need to go home. I have fishhhhhhh. That's all I have. Just them."

I'd heard about these fish for the past hour. This tank I never saw one gill or scale in when I was over there the day before, but now was the reason for her entire existence.

"They will be fine till the morning, Gabi," I said. Again. "Or the afternoon, however this plays out. They won't be fine if you wreck your car on the way home, Miss Five Corpse Revivers and a shot."

"Mmm, all that lemonononony—"

"Yeah, you might not care for lemon much tomorrow," I said. "So enjoy the memory."

"I'm so glad you came to town, Micah," she said, hugging my pillow to her chest as she careened backward into the other one and rolled over onto her face. "You're my bestest friend, now," she mumbled.

I giggled and covered her up as she passed out instantly. I hadn't been anyone's "bestest friend" in a long time. It was kind of nice, even if a bit influenced.

My hand was killing me, now that my own *influence* was wearing off. I looked in the baby fridge for ice, but of course there was none. All I could do was run colder water on my towel and wrap it. First, though, the clothes had to go. Dress, underwear, hat were all tossed aside for the one thing I was glad I'd put in the getaway backpack. (The irony of "getaway" was not lost on me.) My favorite comfortably tattered sleep shorts and matching tank top. Not so much for honeymoon wear, but for after the action when Jeremy fell asleep and I would lay in bed reading whatever. They weren't meant for any other eyes but mine, but they possibly beat out root beer floats for comfort level.

I pulled them on, grabbed the afghan off the couch to wrap around me, and headed out the door to the bathroom to wash my face. Halfway down, a smallish door I hadn't seen off the hallway to the left caught my eye. My feet made the detour before I could think.

It opened to a small, almost hidden balcony. Not overlooking the street, but over the back alley, straight into another brick wall. The view made it pretty clear why this hadn't been presented as a selling point, but there were two lounge chairs with makeshift footstools out there. Probably Gabi's parents' little escape hatch.

It called to me. A little patchwork piece of privacy to think, absorb the night, and just—be. I commandeered one of the chairs and put my bare feet up on the stool, closing my eyes, hoping the quiet would soak in and dull the noise in my brain. I'd meant to ask Gabi tonight about going to Jeremy's with me tomorrow. To be my witness and ensure that anything that was said or done wasn't just for my eyes only. That would have to wait till in the morning, given the current state of her face-plant into my bed.

I sighed, opening my eyes to look at the shadows on the brick across from me. This was perfect. Some people might wish for a beautiful view, but to me it was like curling up in a cocoon with your own head where no one could see you. Right now nothing sounded better than that.

The door clicking behind me might as well have been a cannon going off, and I nearly took out the other chair in my flail to get to my feet. Without the afghan, which landed under the chair.

"Um," said Leo, taking in the view of not just bricks but way too much of me. "Am I interrupting?"

"Yes, actually," I said, wrapping my arms around myself unsuccessfully, then giving up and diving under the chair for the afghan.

"Sorry."

"No, it's—" I flailed again as I tried to gesture while wrapping a see-through blanket around me. "It's fine. I just found myself a little spot, and—"

"I found it last night," he said, sinking onto the other chair without further ado, closing his eyes before I even sat back down. "So technically it's my spot."

"Technically?"

"Squatters rights."

"Well, *technically*, you're supposed to still be at work," I said, sitting back down, wishing there was enough to cover my legs. It was either top or bottom, and I was going for most necessary. "So, how was the first day?"

Leo breathed in deep through his nose and let it go. "Well, the other bartender spilled sangria on me—"

"Explains the smell."

"And then this chick drinks too much and pukes everywhere, and I have to go save my sister-in-law and my—you—from a crazy madman," he continued, making me giggle. "Then of course there was my sulking brother wishing I'd stayed gone. Or dead. Whatever he thought I was."

"Sounds like a banner first day," I said. "Maybe even normal for this place."

"Why's that?" he asked.

"I don't know," I said. "Gabi said this town is weird. Things come out of nowhere, bees disappear, and something about an old man who lives in the woods."

"I think I might work for him," he said.

I looked his way. "The man in the woods?"

"If he's BBG," Leo said. "I'm doing some clean-up contract work across the pond for them and was told the owner was located remotely."

"Hmm," I said, closing my eyes. "Well, the two of you should hit it off like gangbusters."

"Whatever," he said on a tired exhale. "So, how's your friend?"

"She's snoring in my bed right now," I said.

"You left her alone?"

"She won't be moving again until tomorrow," I said. "She wore herself out arguing with me about fishhhhhhhh."

Leo laughed. An unexpected deep rumble of a thing that sent goose bumps rolling over my entire body, making me turn to stare at his grinning profile. Oh, my God. It was just unfair for any one man to be that hot.

"And you?" he asked, looking my way in the dark, nearly catching me gawking.

"She sobered me up," I said. "I wasn't that bad."

"How is your hand?" he asked, reaching for my hand with the towel wrapped around it and turning it over. "Hurt?"

"Throbbing a little, yeah," I said.

"Get you a freezer pack tomorrow," he said, setting my hand back down carefully.

I saluted with my other hand, and silence fell. Weirdly, it wasn't awkward. It was okay, like a blanket and dessert in front of a movie. Comfortable. Each in our own heads, except for the thoughts pinging around mine about how natural that felt with him. With a guy I barely knew, when eight years with Jeremy had never felt like that.

I closed my eyes and relished the fact that some of the internal noise had dissipated, and then he took a deep breath.

"I broke a promise," he said softly, the quiet of his words cutting through the night. "To Nick." There was a long pause, and I almost held my breath. "I broke his trust. I broke everything."

CHAPTER TEN

The goose bumps trickled over my skin again, slow, like they were picking their path. It felt like a moment, Leo confiding something personal to me, and I realized how foreign that was. Jeremy was either an open book or told me nothing, because I never got the sense that anything he said was a big deal. Was that kind of sad?

"We were on our own at a pretty young age," he said after another long pause. "Went to live with our uncle, but—" Leo scoffed. "He had no interest in parenting anyone. He was never there, so I kind of took that on. Made sure we were always at school and no flags were raised so that nobody would figure it out and report it or split us up. We swore to each other that nothing would make that happen."

"How old were you?" I asked.

"Thirteen," he said, offhandedly. "Nick was ten."

"Jesus."

"No, it was okay," he said. "We made it work. Most times our uncle at least made sure there was food in the house, but anything we really needed I learned to—be innovative."

He stole. Part of me wanted to raise my hand and say *Hey, me too*, and bond, but the grown-up inside me said to shut up. I stole things back then for the thrill of it. He did it out of need.

"I made a lot of bad decisions those years, though," he said. "Hooked up with the wrong people over and over, letting greed drive me instead of just getting us by the right way." He shook his head. "I was such a moron."

"How old were you then?" I asked.

"Twenty."

"Everyone's a moron at twenty."

He smirked. "I was a special kind of stupid," he said softly. Almost to himself.

"Oh, he told me tonight that he worked construction for a Blankenship, might have been Jeremy's family." Leo went silent. "They used to live in the same area y'all did before their house burned down."

The quiet was deafening.

"Small world," he finally said, echoing my earlier thought. "So, long story short, he came to me needing my help and I bailed on him. Then I had to leave, and—"

Leo stopped talking again, and I looked at him, waiting.

"Had to?" I asked.

He rubbed at his eyes and blew out a breath.

"Story for another time." His hand dropped to his chest. "Why am I telling you all this?"

"My magic power," I said on a yawn. "Makes men weak and talkative."

"Well, you need to dial that shit back," he said, making me laugh softly. "It's potent."

There was another stretch of silence, and I had the weirdest urge to touch him. To reach over and hold his hand. Speaking of being a moron. Thank God that hand was currently wrapped in a wet towel and not up for stupid activity.

"Jeremy swept me off my feet," I said instead. Because my powers clearly weren't done for the evening and didn't exclude me. "I'd had boyfriends, but nothing like that. No one could blow me away or pull me out of my comfort zone like he could. I was—kind of a free spirit up till then. I moved out at eighteen, went with the wind, did what I wanted, didn't answer to anyone, and then I met Jeremy Blankenship."

"And all that changed?" Leo asked.

"Times a million," I said. "But slowly. At first, I thought it was the way it should be, you know? I was twenty-four and all over the place, so I thought it was good for me. Growing up and being responsible and having someone help you, shape you, love you so much that you believe it's all for your own best interests." I tugged the afghan around me tighter. "Then all these years later, I wake up one day and realize that there isn't anything of me left. My *interests* are in a box in my brother's attic. My friends have disappeared. My way of thinking is pressed so far back in my mind that I can barely see it, because Jeremy's way—his words, his logic, his branding—has become the new me. 'That's not professional, Micah. Wear this instead. Hold your head up at parties, Micah. Look like you belong. Get out of the rain, Micah, you're not a child. Get your head in the game, Micah. Look like this. Act like this. Talk like this. Have a friggin' orgasm when I do, Micah, because I don't have time for the extra work.'"

My eyes filled with tears.

"I live in this pretty box. Like going to one of those all-inclusive resorts that have everything so you never want to leave?" I nodded at my own analogy. "That's my life. You said people run away from something or to something, and I honestly don't know which it was."

I was breathing fast and didn't realize it till I stopped talking. My heart was racing.

"Hey."

I head-jerked in his direction. "Yeah?"

"You aren't there anymore."

I drew in a shaky breath and let that simple sentence ground me. Darkness surrounded us, but I could see him looking at me, and it was intense. He reached over, resting his arm on my chair. Not on me, but it was the same as if he had. I felt the warmth behind the intention. I felt his touch in the same way I'd wanted to touch him, and it settled my rushing blood.

"Your choices are yours again," he said finally. "You took off the ring; you can put it back on again any time you want. You left, and you can go back; no one is pulling your strings now. Just breathe. Be you."

I inhaled deeply and let it go, staring forward again, listening to the ring of the quiet. *Be me.* I had to figure out who that was again.

"I was callous when I said that earlier tonight, Roman-off," he said. "I'm sorry for that." He faced forward, too. "I should know better than anyone that there's always a story behind the story."

I looked down at his arm, still resting on my chair. Not in a controlling way but—protective. Caring. Something I would have never gleaned from the big bear Harley-guy I first climbed onboard with. Then again, he did let me climb onboard.

"So there's a story behind coming to this odd little town to bartend at a restaurant and work for secret people that has seeing your brother as an ulterior motive?" I asked.

Leo chuckled and turned to face me, his feet landing on the ground.

"Remind me not to talk around you, Roman-off," he said, leaning close to my head as he stood. "You remember too much."

I grinned as he walked off. "Magic power."

"By the way," he said, stopping and turning back, "any man who isn't willing to *do the extra work* for you? That guy is an idiot and not worth your time." He held up a hand. "My opinion."

Oh, my God, that was out loud. I'd said that out loud. I'd said—

Kill me now.

"Good night," he said, opening the door with a click and closing it behind him.

I closed my eyes and pushed the mortification away, letting the silence sink in again, blanketing me. This time it came with the echo of words.

You aren't there anymore.

Be you.

Goose bumps.

"Good night," I whispered.

* * * *

"I've been mauled by wild animals," Gabi muttered, crawling onto my couch after a trip down the hall. The crappy couch I'd slept on because she'd commandeered the entire bed like a damn octopus. "I feel like I did the running of the bulls last night. And they won."

"They did," I agreed. "But you put up a good fight."

"Why is the bathroom so far away?" she mumbled into a pillow.

I laughed. "I feel your pain."

"Did I—was there a man who—did I hook up with someone?" she managed to get out.

"You don't remember?"

Gabi pulled her head out of the pillow and squinted up at me.

"So I did?" she said. "I was with some strange guy? Oh, my God. I haven't been with anyone besides Bart in—" She went even paler than before. "I'm gonna be sick."

I grabbed the wastebasket and set it close to her, shaking my head.

"Slow down," I said. "You didn't hook up with anyone. There was just this drunk guy that got handsy during karaoke and picked you up to—"

"Ride—oh, sweet Jesus, yeah I remember that now," she said, pulling another pillow over her head like a sandwich.

"I'd make you some toast, but I have no food," I said. "We could go get something."

"Don't say—food," she said, her voice muffled between the pillows.

"But I do have some headache medicine and a bottle of water in my mini fridge," I said.

Gabi grunted.

"I think I even have a *lemonade* in there," I said, testing my theory.

Pillows went two different directions, as she rolled to her side and dove her head into the wastebasket I'd be throwing away later.

"There you go," I said, getting up for the water. "Get that poison out of your system."

An hour and forty-five minutes later, I was dressed and Gabi was sitting upright and picking miniscule corners off crackers I'd raided from the shop's snack stash they use for gift baskets. And I was antsy.

"I know you feel like death right now," I said, sitting on the coffee table opposite her. "But would you mind riding with me somewhere? After we go feed your fish?"

She frowned. "How do you know about them?"

"They were vitally important last night," I said.

She chuckled as she broke another crumb off, staring at the cracker in her hand like it was a science experiment.

"What Nick did—his announcement—" Gabi said, a small smile warming her face. "That was cool. He and Lanie are so lucky."

I remembered her mention of fertility research.

"You and Bart were trying to have a baby?" I asked.

She scoffed. "I was." She blinked rapidly. "Everything turns out as it should, I guess. I can't have babies and he can't be faithful, so…"

"I'm sorry, Gabi."

She swiped under her eyes quickly. "Just take my car again," Gabi said with a wave of her hand. "I have *no* plans to do anything."

"Well, that's the thing," I said with a grimace. "I need to not be by myself."

She did her best to focus on me, blinking rapidly. "What is it you're doing?"

"Something I need witnesses for," I said. "In fact, I might ask Leo to come as well."

That was a thought I'd played with all night, and it had nothing to do with his words in my head or the weird chemistry between us. I just figured the more people, the better, and things were getting more and more comfortable.

Comfortable.

Yeah, there was a word for it.

"Leo."

"For backup," I said.

Gabi straightened a little more. "*What* are you doing?" she repeated.

"Going to my—to Jeremy's house," I said. "To get my stuff. My brother says I need witnesses."

"Holy Jesus, will Jeremy be there?" she asked.

"I—maybe," I said. "He was the first to pass out on me yesterday, so maybe he's up and sober and back home."

"Are you going to pitch for the car again?"

I sighed, rolling my stiff neck. "I don't know," I said. "I'll play it by ear when I see his mood."

"His mood," she muttered. "It's your car."

"Not legally," I said.

"What's he gonna do, have you arrested for grand theft auto?" she asked. "Come on."

"You haven't had the pleasure of the Blankenships yet," I said. "Nothing is ever off the table."

Twenty minutes later, we were standing outside Leo's door. Well, I was standing. Gabi was sort of holding up the door jamb.

"Are you gonna knock?" she asked. "Or are you two on a psychic level now?"

"I'm—I'm going to," I said, lifting my fist. It just seemed weird all of a sudden. I'd seen him a dozen times in the last few days, but it had all been accidental. This *on purpose* thing felt so—on purpose.

Suck it up.

I knocked, and clamped my lips together to stop the ridiculous little gasp that escaped my throat. Seriously.

The second one couldn't be helped.

Leo opened the door wearing only sweatpants. Granted, I'd seen him— smacked into him actually—in just jeans, fresh out of the shower and delicious, but this was fresh out of *bed*. Warm and tousled and sweatpants hanging a little low on his hips, rubbing his eyes and raking his fingers back through his short hair.

I glanced at Gabi and watched her hangover-riddled eyes light up in appreciation. Right before she slid her sunglasses back over them. In the hallway. Inside a building.

"What's up?" he said, his voice still husky with sleep.

Sweet Jesus, that didn't help things.

"I didn't know you'd still be asleep," I said. "Sorry."

"She used the same line on me," Gabi said.

Leo focused on her. "How are you feeling?"

"I've been better," she said with a pained smile. "But duty calls."

"Duty," he echoed.

"Micah duty," she responded.

He gave me a questioning look. "Am I missing something?"

"No," I said, shifting feet, suddenly uncomfortable with the comfortableness. "I was wondering if—um—you had some free time this morning."

"For?"

"Riding with me and Gabi to Cherrydale," I said, lifting my chin. "I need to go to Jeremy's to get some of my things, and my brother suggested I bring people so that everything stays neutral."

His eyes panned me in the briefest of a blink, but I felt it like it had been seared into me. I had on a low V-necked coral T-shirt with *Indie Woman* blinged across the boobs in rhinestones. My hair was down and silky, and I had on faded blue jean shorts and flip-flops. It basically screamed casual and *Look at my tits* sexy, while saying *I don't need you* at the same time. It was about as nonprofessional and un-Blankenship as I could get, and I knew that Leo knew that.

"Neutral?" Leo said. "He won't be thinking neutral if he sees me." His eyes fell to my chest again. "Especially with you looking like that."

"We'll be in Gabi's car," I said, resisting the urge to fan myself. "He won't know that you're you."

"He'll assume it," Leo said, turning around. "But Gabi and I can pretend we're together."

Gabi looked like she'd just swallowed the canary, looking at me with a shrug. Something in me twitched.

"Sure thing," she said.

"So—you'll come?" I asked.

Leo grabbed a gray T-shirt from a nearby chair and tugged it over his head, covering the good stuff. This was probably a good thing.

"I'm not letting you two go alone," he said. "Just give me a minute."

He grabbed his little bag of motel contraband and headed down the hall, and Gabi slid down the wall to a seated position, her legs flopped out in front of her.

"Not a bad plan," she said. "He's—"

"I know," I said. "Boy, do I know. Which is why I need to keep a distance. And not do things like this."

She blinked up at me. "I was going to say he's nice to drop out of a dead sleep and help, but sure, we can go with wherever you just went."

"You mean the same place you went, Miss Sunglasses Indoors?"

Gabi lifted a finger and slid her shades back with it. "No idea what you're talking about. I'm off men for the duration."

"Duration of what?"

"Of—whatever," she said. "See what you're about to do today? That's why men are the pits."

"A lot of men could say the same for women," Leo said, coming back our way.

Damn, he was fast.

"And they'd be right," Gabi said. "We all suck. That's why we should all stay single and just bang it out every now and then."

"I like the way you think," Leo said, laughing. "Let me change. I'll be right back." He disappeared behind his door and I was hit again with a twinge of something I couldn't define.

"You're still drunk, aren't you?" I said.

"I might be a little," she said, scrunching her nose.

Less than sixty seconds later, he was indeed back. Looking like a million bucks after being awake all of three minutes. It was so unfair.

"Holy cow," Gabi breathed.

"Come on," he said to her, holding out a hand and pulling her up. "You have to pull it together, girlfriend for the day."

Her grin wasn't even trying to hide.

"Lord," I muttered, rolling my eyes. "Give me your keys, Gabi. I'll chauffeur while you two kids make out on the way to prom."

"I think Mom is PMSing," Leo said in a loud whisper from behind me as we walked toward the stairs.

I turned with a look as he threw an arm around Gabi's shoulders and grinned just like she was. Oh—my—God. I knew what the twinge was. Jealousy. No, no, no, *hell* no. She could have him and his brick-shit-house body and perfect mouth and sexy rumbly laugh. All that stuff was good for nothing but a bang, just like Gabi said, and she needed it worse than I did. *Walk on, Micah.*

I mostly ignored their jokes on the way there, and briefly filled Leo in on the car thing, wishing I could read his expression in the rearview mirror through the sunglasses hiding his eyes. I wondered who he'd done *extra work* on and shook my head free of the visual that sent heat shooting to my neck.

"What?" Gabi said, looking up from her phone where she sat leaned against the passenger-side window scrolling Facebook.

"What what?" I responded.

"You just scoffed like you were disgusted," she said. "What happened?"

What the hell was with me and doing things out loud lately? Good grief.

"Just my brain," I said, shaking my head.

I watched a faraway farmhouse go by on my left that I'd seen go by the other direction on my right with Leo just a few days ago. I'd just done this last night, going to Thatcher's house, but there was something about Leo being in the car. Him being there, returning with me to the scene of the crime, as it were—it felt raw. And very real.

I had the dress in a garment bag in the trunk, and the ring in a cute little drawstring bag I'd had in my backpack for putting it in while on the beach on our honeymoon. Both were going to land at Jeremy's house and stay there. I didn't care what he did with them. I just needed for them to not be with me.

"Crap," Gabi said. "Do y'all know about the speed dating thing tonight?"

"I'm sorry?" I said, pulling out of my thoughts to—"Did you say speed dating?"

"I saw it on the sign last night," Gabi said, scrolling on her screen. "But I forgot about it. Kind of on purpose."

"What sign?"

"The—*Here's all the shit we're doing to kick off the Honey Festival* sign," she said. "Ugh, this is worse than karaoke."

"You don't have to go," I said, laughing.

"Yeah, I do, actually," she said. "The shop is sponsoring it. Different businesses sponsor a night. Drew signed us up for this one."

"Ohhhh," I said. "That sucks."

"You have to come," she said.

I nearly ran us off the road. "I can promise that I don't," I said.

"I'm coming with you for moral support today," she said, nudging me with her elbow. "You have to come tonight."

"You're only here right now out of guilt for making me carry you up the stairs last night," I said. "So we're even."

"Pay it forward, then," she said. "Micah, I will crawl into a hole and die if I have to sit through that shit alone."

"You said your sister will be there," I said. "And you actually have to participate when you sponsor?"

"A show of good faith," she said sarcastically. "To show everyone how *incredibly fun* it is. And Drew will likely disappear as soon as she can, leaving me holding the 'fun' cape by myself, and I'll need a straightjacket before the night is done."

"Gabi," I breathed, drawing out her name like I was in pain.

"Please, Micah," she whined back. "I need someone to make fun of people with me and make this light so I stay sane."

"Wait, you're still married," I said. "There's your out."

She shook her head. "Bart and Dixie-the-Barbie-Doll are all over the place being all over each other, so people think we're divorced already, anyway." She shrugged. "I could probably use the practice. Drew says I should take a step."

"Wouldn't that step be paperwork?" Leo piped in, then held up his hands when she turned around. "Just saying. Why aren't you divorcing the guy?"

I glanced at her frowning profile. "Principle of the thing," she said under her breath.

"Because it's what he wants," I said.

Her gaze dropped back down to her phone. "Like I said."

I blew out a breath. I was such a sucker for sadness.

"I'm sorry, did you say her name was *Dixie*?" I asked.

She held up her chin again. "I did. Dixie Dartwell of the wealthy snooty Dartwells."

Could it get worse than that?

"Fine," I muttered. "Where?"

Gabi did a little mini clap as her eyes lit up. "Rojo's again."

"Hold up," Leo said. "I have to be there for this fiasco?"

"Do you work tonight?" she asked.

He leaned his head back on the seat like he was searching the roof for a different answer.

"At seven."

"Aww," Gabi said. "Lucky you."

"So, does Jeremy know you're coming?" Leo asked, smartly changing the subject.

"Um, no," I said.

I saw the frown even through the dark glasses.

"Don't you think that might have been a good idea?" he asked, leaning forward. "What if he's not there?"

"No," I said matter-of-factly. "He would make sure he wasn't there, or have a block party going on or something. Anything to avoid being alone with me."

"Nothing like you, huh?" Gabi said. "Bringing your *witnesses*." I cut a sideways glance at her and saw her wink. She squeezed my hand. "Just kidding, girl. We got your back."

I listened to the road noise for the next half hour, knowing my exit was coming, and then there it was, the sign for Cherrydale and the pimping out of the Cherrydale Trade Days.

"I can't believe I've never been to that," Gabi said. "So close, and yet it never even floated across my radar."

"You aren't missing much," I said, turning onto the feeder road. "I mean it's cool, and you can find a lot of random stuff if you dig, but once you've been there, you've been there."

"Can we go by your flower farm?" she asked. "I've never seen that in person, either. Evidently, I lead a very girl-in-a-bubble kind of life, and actually that's work."

"We can drive by—in fact, let's do that first," I said, hitting the blinker. Yep, I was putting it off. The flower farm was on the opposite side of the highway from the town, kind of isolated from society. We drove past the open fields and the greenhouses, and I pointed out the main hothouse and office. "I'm technically on vacation for two weeks so I don't want to stop, but basically anywhere you see flowers or greenhouses, that's where you'll usually find me."

"Wow, that's a lot of flowers," Gabi said as we passed masses of color reaching for the sun. "And I just want one little field of wildflowers."

"It's impressive," Leo said. "Did you go to school for this?"

My hackles went up, draining my pride. It was a years-long argument I'd had with both Jeremy and Thatcher. I'd gone, but I never finished. Classrooms were never my strong suit, but I would have stomached it if I could have just taken what I wanted—the horticultural science of plants. Get my hands in the earth and teach me, but don't make me sit through years of unrelated basics and prerequisites. I just couldn't do it. So the library and I became fast friends to give me material to pour over, and the Internet after that. Thatcher didn't agree. He'd given up becoming a paramedic to be practical and snag a business major for the sake of the business. He was always pushing the selling point that having a horticulturalist onsite would up our worth. Jeremy just wanted me to up mine.

"I don't have a degree, if that's what you're asking," I said, trying to dial down the defense I heard in my voice. "But I know my stuff."

Leo chuckled. "I don't doubt that you do, Roman-off," he said slowly. "It was just a question."

"Sorry," I said, driving on. "I didn't mean to snap. It's just a really dead horse." I tapped the wheel with my fingertips. "Okay, time to do this."

I turned at a small road back toward the highway and headed around a curve and a slight incline, till we crossed over and drove through town.

"Déjà vu," Leo said as I landed at the red light. *The* red light.

I looked to my left at the sidewalk in front of the drugstore, and my heartbeat sped up as my mind's eye saw me standing there. *Micah!* I heard Jeremy yell my name. And Leo rev his motor, waiting, questioning me with those eyes I couldn't really see. Offering me an escape from that life. Or at least from a fate of baking on the sidewalk.

"Hey, you still with us?"

I jolted out of my vision with a start. "What?"

"It's green," he said. "We going?"

The ironic echo of those words pinged around my head while I met his eyes in the mirror. Eyes I could actually see since he'd taken the glasses off. I felt a smirk pull at my lips.

"Yeah," I said.

CHAPTER ELEVEN

I pointed down Thatcher's street—my street—to where I grew up. In the normal neighborhood made of trees and color and life, where kids sold lemonade and then broke down the signs to make ramps to jump their bikes over things. For some reason, it was important to me that they see that area before we arrived in the gated community of Cherrydale North, where various hues of beige, political correctness, and voting on important issues such as tulip placement prevailed.

I waved at the guard, who opened his little window.

"Miss Roman."

"Robert," I said, my little nerve endings standing up. He didn't normally open his window.

"Mr. Blankenship e-mailed that you don't live at the house anymore," he said, looking saddened.

That didn't take long.

"I'm still in the process of moving," I said. "Not quite out, yet."

The older man winked at me, and I hoped all my days of chatting with him and bringing him Christmas cookies while Jeremy treated him like gate hardware would pay off. He would let us in as visitors, of course, but that would entail taking down Gabi's license plate, and I didn't want that trail back to Charmed.

"He expecting you?" Robert asked.

Then he *was* there.

"No," I admitted, looking up at him as clear-eyed and innocent as I could. "But I just need to get a few more boxes we set aside. I'll be in and out."

Robert nodded slowly, and I gave him a rueful smile. I'd miss him. He was a little piece of nice and normal in a world of fake and phony.

"I'm gonna miss seeing your face around here, Miss Roman," he said, and my heart twisted.

"I might have to find my way out here around the holidays," I said. "I can't imagine not seeing you in your Santa hat."

He grinned huge and waved us in, and all my twisty sad feel-goods from Robert regrouped and braided themselves into tiny nooses.

"Wow, you're walking away from this?" Gabi said, her eyes taking in the big houses in various shades of cream, the immaculate angle-cut yards that no one did themselves, the smell of soft hands and pretentiousness in the air.

"And the first thing I'm doing when I get my own place is painting it red," I said. "I never want to see a beige wall again."

My own place.

There I went again, defining it a little more. I knew I wasn't moving in with Thatcher, and now Jeremy had told the guard that I didn't live here anymore. It was getting clearer all the time, in a smudged-and-dirty-window kind of way.

Jeremy's house loomed on the corner. Maybe it didn't really loom. Maybe that was just my projection. But it always felt to me like it was too much for the space, glaring at all its neighbors for being too close.

My stomach went sour before we ever made it to the curb, as the Cadillac in the driveway did all but shake its finger at me.

"Oh, crap," I said.

"What?" Gabi said.

"Monster-in-law is here," I said, rubbing a hand over my face. "We— nope, I can't do this today."

"Yes, you can," Leo said from the back seat. "She has no power over you, especially now."

"You haven't met her," I said. "She makes Cruella de Vil look like Glenda the Good Witch."

"So be Maleficent," Gabi said.

"Really?" Leo said.

She craned her neck around. "What? I can throw out movie references, too." She faced me. "Fight for what's yours, Micah. Be a badder bitch than she is. He's right; she has no power over you now. No leverage. So put that dress right in her hands and be done with her."

"There is no being done with her," I said under my breath.

We got out and I made it three steps before Deidre Blankenship and her son appeared through the doorway.

"And...showtime," Gabi said under her breath.

"Y'all hold back," I whispered.

"I'm sorry, what are you doing here?" Deidre was saying, her three-inch pumps eating up that sidewalk in record time. "You have some nerve—"

"Dee Dee," I began.

"Don't *even* dare to call me that now," she said as she crossed into my personal space, her well-lined lips curling into a sneer. "That is for my friends and my *family*. I took you in. I treated you like my own because my son loved you. And you spat in my face."

I backed up a step, every hair on my body standing up and gearing for bear, but the logical little voice of reason reminded me that I was on their turf. Deidre may be a lofty bitch, but she was a scrapper at her core. Twice, she'd helped her husband rebuild their life and fortune after misfortune hit them. She was no frail flower. She was a mama tiger.

"I understand that you despise me right now," I said, measuring my words and the speed in which they left my lips. "You have every right—"

"I'm so glad you approve," she said, speaking equally as slow.

Mama tiger was *mad*.

I got that. I hurt her baby, who was now standing behind her with his arms folded over his chest. I embarrassed him. I embarrassed her. Something in the squinty eyes told me it was more about the latter.

Fight for what's yours, Micah.

"Look," I said, putting my hands on my hips to portray that I was not going to be steamrolled. "I had the dress cleaned, and it's in the car. You can try to sell it."

I pulled the pouch from my pocket and moved around her to press it against Jeremy's arm. He grabbed it on reaction, but then looked like he regretted the move.

"What's this?" he said, his first words so far.

"The ring," I said softly, not wanting that part to be harsh. It had nothing to do with Queen Bitch. "It's yours."

The look on his face was stony. I knew that expression. It meant that nothing productive was happening today. We may as well leave. But Gabi and Leo were hovering somewhere behind me by the car in their pretend relationship, and I wasn't giving up in front of them without a fight.

"I'm only here to get what's mine," I said.

"Nothing here is yours," Deidre said, stepping between us again—making me back up yet *again*.

Shake it off, Micah.

"I'm sorry, this conversation doesn't involve you," I said. "This is between me and Jeremy. Can you please take a potty break or something?"

"I said," she repeated, ignoring me, "that nothing here belongs to you. You walked away from it all."

"Oh, I beg to differ," I said. "I didn't come here wearing a potato sack and a smile. I have things here that belong *solely* to me." My blood was rising to the surface and rushing through my head, and that little voice of reason wasn't talking loudly enough. "One of which was my car, but I found out yesterday that your son tricked me."

"Tricked *you*?" she sneered. "Who tricked *who* into an obnoxiously expensive wedding that she didn't even show up for?"

Breathe.

No.

Be the badder bitch.

"Please," I fired back. "That wasn't even my wedding, and you know it. That was a business party that *you* designed, orchestrated, and paid for, dressed up with some vows and a cake for entertainment. Nothing about that event was my idea. Or anything I desired. A one-armed monkey could have shown up in that dress to marry your son, and no one would have been the wiser."

"A monkey would have been more qualified than you," she said, inching closer, her eyes raking over my appearance. "Blinging you up didn't change the blood. Three days, and here you are, dressed like a classless street whore again. Didn't take you long to find your roots, did it?"

"Didn't take *you* long to put him back on your tit, did it?" I spat back.

Pow.

The slap across my left cheekbone was quick, stinging, and starburst inducing. And everything after that was a mix of slow-motion gasps and warp-speed action.

My left hand came up as if some internal launch button had been pressed, and it suddenly didn't matter who was on the other side of it. The pop across her cheek sounded just as powerful.

The shock in her eyes as she lunged at me was almost worth getting hit.

There was yelling and shuffling of feet around us, people grabbing at us, but Deidre Blankenship, high and mighty matriarch that she might be, had one singular primal focus. For once, we were on the same page.

"You little *bitch*!" she screeched, grabbing my T-shirt with both fists, taking my bra straps with them and snapping one of them as she ripped my shirt.

"Get off me!" I yelled, shoving her free, just as a flailing hand came across my mouth. I reeled, and that was it. I rushed her, just as strong arms wrapped around my middle like a vise, lifting me off my feet.

"You can't hit my mother!" Jeremy was yelling, his face red and angry as he wrapped his arms around hers to keep her still. She wasn't having that.

"Let go of me," she said through her teeth, spit flying.

"She hit Micah first," Gabi yelled. "She hit her twice!"

"I'll rip your slutty little ass to shreds!" Deidre screamed. "Nobody talks to me like that!"

"Shut up, Mother," Jeremy muttered, struggling to hold her.

"Would you be still?" Leo said against my ear, his squeeze tightening around me.

My heartbeat was so loud in my ears that I barely heard him. But I felt the words against my skin. I took a deep breath to calm my heaving ones, and swallowed hard. Jeremy and his mother were still bickering but I nodded.

"Please put me down," I said, my jaw tight.

"I'm holding your shirt on," he said against my ear again. "Care to take over?"

I looked down to see Leo's right hand propping up my left boob with a flap of T-shirt material and severed bra strap, an angry, almost bleeding line of a welt from her fingernails across the top of my breast.

I grabbed my shirt and held it to me, and Leo set me down and let go of my boob. Another save. Another thing I'd never live down.

"Oh, my God, your cheek is turning purple," Gabi said.

"Your mother ripped my clothes, Jeremy," I said, my voice shaking with rage. "She cut me. All I want is to pack up my stuff and get the hell out of here, and I get all this?" I let the flap of shirt go, and me and my scraped-up boob were out there for the world. "I could have her arrested for assault," I said.

"Our lawyer will sue you!" Deidre yelled.

"Your lawyer is my friend," I said, completely pulling something out of my ass. "I had drinks with her last night. Good luck with that."

Jeremy wasn't listening. He was staring past me at Leo.

Great.

Round two.

"You," he said, his jaws flexing madly. "I know you."

"I don't know what you're talking about, man," Leo said, brushing off his shirt like I'd been covered in sand or something.

"He's with me," Gabi said, sidling up to Leo and looping her arm through his. "What's your deal?"

"Jeremy!" I yelled, making him look at me. I pointed fingers back and forth between us. "Pay attention! This has gone very badly for you," I said.

Be the badder bitch. Even when you're spouting absolute bullshit. "You can thank your mother for that."

She yanked free of Jeremy and straightened her clothes, sticking that hoity-toity chin up in the air like that would pull her dignity back.

"You need to let me come in and pack up," I said. "I own two suitcases, and not that many clothes. What doesn't fit I can put in garbage bags. I brought my own. I have some knickknacks that should fit in a plastic tub I brought. I also got that tapestry when we went to Italy and I'd like to keep it. And the coffee table and curio—"

"You can't be serious," Deidre sputtered, stepping forward.

I stepped two to her one. "They. Are. Mine."

"They were her mother's," Jeremy spoke up. Well, finally.

"I'll have Thatcher come by for them with his trailer," I said. "Now—can we get this over with? You can follow me all over the house—I don't care—but I'd really like to change my shirt if you don't mind."

"Fine," he said, turning back to the house, but then looking at his mom. "Go home."

"What?" she said. "You aren't—"

"I will call you later," he said, his voice tight. "Please go home."

In a huff, Mama Blankenship got in her overpriced car and sped down the street, and Jeremy gave Leo another look over his shoulder.

I got the bucket and the dress and the bags from the car and walked into Jeremy's line of vision. I didn't want him studying him too closely.

"Let's go."

"Do you need help?" Gabi asked.

"She can come," Jeremy said, his back already to me. "The faster you're out of here."

"Hot diggety," Gabi said. "This place have a bidet? I always wanted to see one in person," she added on a whisper.

I glanced back at Leo, his sunglasses back in place, sitting against the hood of the car, arms folded over his chest. Good God, he looked like something out of a movie. He gave me a single thumbs-up, and I knew he was fine hanging back.

I felt it as soon as we walked inside. Not familiarity like you would expect after living in a place for two years. Not homesickness. Not sadness over knowing I was leaving it behind.

Cold.

I felt cold.

Emptiness and a sad waste of a beautiful house that never felt like a home. The belongings I laid eyes on looked out of place, as if they'd just been sitting there all this time miserable and waiting to be rescued.

How had I not noticed this before? Or maybe I did and just couldn't put a name to it. All I knew, as I wandered around looking for things, is that I couldn't wait to be out of that house. Even knowing I was going back to a room with no kitchen or bathroom—I couldn't pack fast enough.

Gabi hit my closet after I put on a new shirt, and filled the suitcases. I filled the plastic tub with my personal items and knickknacks, a few coffee mugs and plates and cutlery I'd come there with. A skillet I never used anymore because Jeremy's was better. And a garbage bag full of books I'd forgotten about but was in no way leaving them there for him to throw away.

In thirty minutes, we were done. The wedding dress garment bag was draped over Jeremy's recliner, and it gave me a sick satisfaction to know he'd have to physically move it to sit. I looked down at the two suitcases, the tub, and the trash bag, and was struck with how small my life had become. With how much my world had shrunk within his.

Nothing in the garage would be mine. But—

"I have stuff in *my car*," I said, my voice trembling. I gave Jeremy the most hate-filled look I could through the hot tears building there. "Can you unlock it so I can clean it out?"

He was looking at me differently. The stone face was gone, and it was like he was trying to work out a puzzle.

"Was your life here so bad?" he asked.

Oh, fuck to the fuck, we were going to do this now.

"Your mother just attacked me, Jeremy," I said. "What does that tell you about my life here?"

"You said I was on her tit, Micah," he said with a disgusted look. "What did you expect, a hug?"

I wiped at my face and under my eyes. "Okay. Fair enough."

"We had some good times," he said.

"Yes," I responded.

"So, what happened?" he asked. "Seriously, if it's not someone else, then what happened? And when?"

"We should have never gotten engaged," I said, hating how the words blurted out. I didn't want to hurt him. I was ungodly mad at him, but I didn't want to be mean. "I should have never moved in here."

"What?"

"It was better back then," I said. "You were still controlling, but I had my own place, my own things—"

"Oh, the control again," he said, clasping both hands on top of his head. "It's back to that."

"Yes, it's back to that," I said. "And since you remember the conversation—"

"Like there was just one?" he said.

I blinked and realized just how right Gabi had been that day telling me I'd made the right decision.

"And since you remember *those* conversations," I amended, "then you should realize that we would not be having *this* one, in this room, with my stuff in bags, if you would have paid any heed to what I said."

He shook his head, and I knew he hadn't heard any of it. As usual, he used my talking time to formulate his next sentence.

"I told you I loved you the night before," he said. "I did that to be romantic."

I frowned. "Do you hear yourself, Jeremy?" I scoffed. "You have to say I love you to be romantic? That should have been something we said every day. Every night." I stepped closer to him. "Do you know what it made me think? It made me try to remember the last time we'd said those words." I shook my head. "I couldn't."

"So you blew a whole lifetime together over words?" he said, arms flailing.

And there we were again, him driving, taking a detour, forcing me along with him. Not this time. Not anymore.

"Love isn't about words," I said. "And I'm done with this. Can I get in my car you screwed me out of?"

He turned and grabbed keys off the hook I never hung them on. I hated that hook. It looked stupid. My keys always went in my bag. Well, there was an argument he didn't have to have anymore. Score one for him.

"Where did you meet that guy outside?" Jeremy asked, striding to the garage door and hitting the button to unlock my car. "Did you know him before now?"

I passed by him, ignoring his question, and tried not to break down as I laid eyes on my beautiful little Mustang. Sitting there. Waiting for me. Looking out of place like everything else and waiting to be rescued, but I couldn't come through on that one. I laid my palm against the cool metal and silently apologized for having to leave it there. Which would normally be a crazy thing for me to do, but lately my crazy rankings were so high that it fell closer to average.

I didn't have much in there. Some personal things in the console, a cross hanging from the rearview mirror, an umbrella in the back seat, and a yoga mat I never used in the trunk. I grabbed it all through a haze of angry tears and marched past him.

Never again would I blindly trust anyone.

"You didn't answer me," Jeremy said, following.

"I don't care," I said, dropping it all into another garbage bag that Gabi held open.

"What's his name?" Jeremy said, his voice acidic. "He looks like someone from a long time ago."

A long time ago? Well, good, then he wasn't figuring out that Leo was the motorcycle dude sweeping me out of Cherrydale. Oh, except—

"He used to live down south near where you did. And his brother might have worked for your dad. Other than that, I don't know what to tell you," I said, grabbing everything I could hold while Gabi pulled both suitcases. I didn't want to make a second trip. I needed to get away from this soul-sucking place as fast as I could.

"Micah."

I glanced over my shoulder as I shuffled awkwardly through the door. "Bye, Jeremy."

When I got to the car, Leo was talking on his phone down the sidewalk. Animatedly. I'd know that angry-man body language anywhere. I couldn't really hear the conversation, but I caught a "What the fuck" that was pretty clear.

"Everything okay?" I asked, as he ended the call without a good-bye and shoved the phone in his pocket.

"Always," he said, but he stared unseeing at nothing down the street.

I remembered what he'd told me about his brother, and a messed-up conversation with him could certainly cause an expression like that.

And I could mind my own damn business.

CHAPTER TWELVE

It was a little better in the dorm room with all my own stuff there. Granted there was nowhere near enough space for all of it, and so I was kind of living out of one of the suitcases like I was in a hotel on vacation, but at least everything was mine.

Including the scratches on my face and neck and boob, and the purple shiner on my left cheekbone. I scoped it out in the bathroom, feeling really up to par for sitting across from strange men and having them judge me.

I must really like Gabi. This girl I'd just met days before and already felt like we'd been doing crazy shit together for years.

The bathroom door opened behind me and I jumped.

"Sorry," Leo said, starting to back out. "You didn't lock the door."

"Maybe we just leave it open when no one is in here," I said, peering at him through the mirror. "So, when it's closed, there's no question."

He stepped in behind me, and the generous bathroom got decidedly smaller. And warmer. He was so tall, the top of his head cut off in the mirror, and the rest of him filled the space around me.

"Or you could just lock the door," he said, his eyes narrowing as he studied my face. One finger came up to gingerly run down my bruised cheek. "Wow."

Fuck.

Wow didn't begin to cover it.

No, it didn't hurt that much, but Son. Of. A. Bitch. The electricity and chemistry that rocked and rolled through my body at that one simple touch nearly had me reacting in a very inappropriate way. Like backing up into him and—

"Yeah, I'm looking hot," I said, my voice all croaky and weird all of a sudden. "They'll *all* be wanting my number tonight. Aren't you supposed to be at work?"

"Leaving now," he said, eyebrows raised. "If I can have the bathroom for a second."

"All yours," I said, moving too quickly and *actually* backing into him. Then jolting forward and waiting for him to step back out so that I could slide past him.

Jesus.

"Are you okay?" he asked.

Don't look up.

I looked up. At genuine concern mixed with a little *Did your brain get rattled today?* questioning. I huffed out a breath and nodded.

"It's just been a day," I said. Which seemed to pretty much describe the last three. I needed to get my shit together or come up with a new tagline.

"Does that hurt?" he asked.

"Only when I smile," I said, smiling.

* * * *

I was accosted by something called Cajun honey-drizzled bacon outside of Rojo's, and if one has to be force-fed something, it wasn't a bad way to go. I thanked some gray-haired lady who smiled at another gray-haired lady, the second of whom was sitting on the giant tricycle I'd seen before.

"Just remember that one, sweetheart," the first lady said, handing me another one on a napkin. "When it comes time to vote, remember the Feed Store."

"She can make anything," the second lady said as she started to pedal away. "Trust me, I get around."

Wasn't even odd. I don't know what that said about me.

It was kind of like returning to the scene of the crime, going into Rojo's again. Except without Lanie and Carmen and even Allie, who'd been much quieter but I loved watching how she looked at Bash. How they looked at each other. Like all this was just icing and fireworks and ponies that they were just there to tolerate. Because all that mattered was the one they were looking at.

I wanted that. Theoretically. Not right now, and not with anyone in particular, but I'd just had the anti-that for nearly a decade. I knew what I didn't want, and they gave me the visual for what I did. One day.

One day not to be decided upon tonight in a room full of tequila-driven sex drives and a phone app. That's right. A phone app. Because speed dating wasn't contrived and robotic and cold and slightly pathetic enough without giving everyone a *reason* to stay in their phones.

I glanced toward the bar for Leo but I didn't see him. Which meant nothing. I was just looking for my friend.

Gabi waved at me from a little powwow with Katrina Bowman, which led Katrina to do the same and get this little look on her face that scared the living shit out of me. She excused herself with Gabi and strode purposefully my way, big breasts contained—barely—in a pleather zip-up vest.

I panicked. I looked in all directions for somewhere to go, to be, to see, but she was on me like white on rice in seconds. I shoved my leftover honey-slathered bacon into my mouth and smiled around my chewing.

"Micah!" she crooned. "I'm so glad you came! Oh, my God, what happened to your face?"

Because every woman likes to start a conversation like that.

"Mm-hmm!" I mumbled around my food, covering my mouth. "I had a little incident with my non-mother-in-law, and you know how that goes." That was the dumbest ball drop ever, but I figured it would at least keep her guessing for a bit. I swallowed and widened my eyes. "So how does this work? What do I do?"

"Well, I wanted to talk to you about that," she said, handing me a little white button to put on that said *I'm #2!* "Put this on, it's your Charm Factor number."

"My—"

"I'll explain later," she said, waving off my confusion. "So since you're new in town, do you mind if I use you in my intro as a little promotional bait and catch?"

I must have looked more horrified than I already was, because she continued.

"I just mean using you as an example, and playing you up," she said, smoothing hair back that honestly wasn't budging. "And then everyone will be intrigued to talk to you and it builds the excitement for the rest."

"I—don't think so," I said. "I'd like to just blend if that's okay. I've had enough spotlight this week."

"Oh, girl, that's what makes you the perfect one for the job!" she gushed, squeezing my hand like we were besties. "Everyone has already heard about you!"

"No thanks," I said.

"It'll be great," she said, beaming. And walking away.

Wait.

Why was she beaming? I said no.

I felt my scalp start to sweat, and my palms joined in.

"You look about to bolt," said Gabi, suddenly at my side.

Fight or flight.

I was back in the church and staring at the door, except that the door had sombreros on it and the smell of salsa and fajitas was everywhere. And Leo had just appeared behind the bar and gave me a double-take around Katrina, who was doing her best to invite him into her chest. He wasn't paying attention, and there was a split-second before someone called for her that I thought she might climb a nearby stool to get on top of the bar.

"Katrina wants to use me as bait and—fuck." I took a deep breath and patted my face. "I said no and it was like she never heard me!"

"She's good at that," Gabi said.

"I might go," I said, feeling fidgety and wishing I had keys or something in my hands to mangle.

"Just—start with getting a drink," Gabi said. "Relax for a second while I go make sure all my signs are out. I'll come check on you in a minute."

She steered me toward Leo, which made sense considering the three of us had somehow become a weird little band of misfits, but he might also be the last person I needed to hang out with. He looked preoccupied tonight, a line pressing downward over his nose.

"Make her something delicious and strong," Gabi said.

"And for you?" Leo said, humor pulling at his lips.

She widened her eyes. "I'm drinking water tonight. Dr Pepper if I get really ambitious."

She strolled off, looking adorable in black jeans, hurt-me heels, and an off-the-shoulder black-and-white top. Her hair silky with flirty curls at the ends. She was making a statement tonight, whether Bart was there or not. She was probably terrified, so if she could do this, I could too.

"A beer is fine," I said. "Actually, no, I'm not drinking tonight either. I'm—" I blew out a breath.

"What?" he said.

"Okayyyyyy!" came Katrina's voice, loud and shrill over the microphone. "Let's get started! Tonight's festivities are sponsored by Graham's Florist, if you haven't noticed that already, so a big hand for Drew and Gabi." Gabi waved as she made a pass around sprinkling rose petals on each table, and Drew just grinned from her stance next to what looked like a giant stoplight. "I have a surprise special *dater* guest here for you tonight, and I'm going to introduce you!"

"Oh, God," I said, gripping the counter. "That."

A surprised chuckle came out of his mouth. "You?"

"Do you see what I look like?" I asked, pointing at my face.

Leo leaned over the bar a little and took his gaze all the way down my body. I know, because I felt the trail. I'd tried to step it up a little without really stepping it up. I wore black leggings with little red flames on them, with a black fitted tank top that hugged my boobs really well without saying *Hey, I'm Katrina!*, and a long sleeveless dark red cardigan. And kicky little sandals because the tight clothing was enough sexy for a speed dating night. I had to balance it out and yet take the focus off my face.

"I do," he said, meeting my eyes again slowly.

I glanced around, surprised I hadn't spontaneously ignited.

"Well," I said, clearing my throat, "I'm going to be sitting at tables staring at people, so pretty much this is what they're going to get." I said, gesturing circles around my face.

"Hopefully she got as good as she gave," he said, holding up a finger to a customer trying to get his attention.

"Go do what you have to do," I said, resting one hand on the bar. "I'm—"

"So, without further ado," Katrina crooned, wiggling a finger at me, "come up here!" she whispered loudly, which sounded horrifyingly creepy through that microphone.

"Kill me now," I said under my breath, as some bizarre spotlight found me.

Maybe it wasn't a spotlight. Maybe it was just someone's phone flashlight, but it felt like the heat of a thousand suns had landed on me with a *phoomp*.

A warm hand covered mine and slipped something under it. I blinked away from the light and looked to find a bar toothpick—the kind with the little flags—in my hand.

Use what you have.

I laughed out loud and looked up but Leo had already moved on to a paying customer. That was okay. I laughed again as Katrina cleared her throat and smiled at me. I clenched the toothpick in my fist like a talisman and took deep breaths as I made my way up to the little stage I'd almost made a singing debut on the night before.

Claps were all around me, and when I stepped up and looked out, I wanted to throw up. Where did all these people come from? I'd been there all of five minutes. Maybe. Were they hiding under the tables? There were this many single people in Charmed who didn't already know every single detail about each other?

"Now everyone here in Charmed knows about this lady," Katrina said on a sexy little chuckle. I gave her a side-eyed *What-the-fuck?* that she didn't see. "She made quite the splash the other day, but all you Denning and Lakeforest and other lovely townsfolk that came out tonight to have some fun and meet great people—you might not know about her yet."

Katrina nudged me like we were conspiring about something and all I could do was stare.

"What are you doing?" I said under my breath.

She covered her microphone. "Building up some mystery," she whispered. "Adding an edge. All the best event sites do it."

"Well, stop," I said through my teeth.

"I'm not even gonna tell you her name, because that's part of the fun," she said, all flirty and winky and—oh, my God, it was like being in a cattle auction.

Look here, everyone, look at those gams...

"So, without further ado, you'll notice all the two-seater tables are kind of in a circle, with numbers taped on top. Guys, take a seat on the inside. Ladies, you get the outside." Katrina stopped to smirk. "In case you need to bolt."

The best thing I'd heard, yet. I started slinking out of the limelight while she was so shiny with it, and had plotted a path for the door when Gabi grabbed my hand.

"You're next to me," she said. "Drew managed to get out of it, the wench."

I looked back at the stage where Drew wiggled her eyebrows at us. She'd been put to work on stage.

"I'm out of here," I said. "Did you see that dog and pony show she put me through?"

"Have fun with it," Gabi said, nudging me. "She didn't give a name, be somebody else for the night."

"Who are you going to be?" I asked as she pulled me to a table and sat me down, then sat at the next one catty-corner over.

"Well, if I can find enough people who don't know me," she said in an undertone as she skimmed the choices, "I'm feeling like a Natasha, tonight."

"Natasha," I said, giving her a discreet high-five down low. "Nice."

"Everyone have a seat?" Katrina yelled into the microphone. The girl really didn't need one. "Everyone's phones charged?" She giggled as if that were utterly brilliant. "You'll see the app address on your table as well, so download the Wham-Bam-Charm-Me-Ma'am app now!"

"She did not," I said, feeling my jaw drop.

Gabi started laughing so hard that she snorted, and the guy that was thinking of sitting across from her turned and made another choice.

I turned to see if Leo was catching all this fiasco and was surprised to see him leaning on his hands as if all the weight of the world was pulling at him. A woman with really ugly pants walked up and he stood back upright, but something—something—in his eyes wasn't quite right. And tension was obvious in the set of his jaw. I hadn't really seen Leo angry yet, except for maybe that phone call earlier, but if I had to guess, he'd look kinda like that.

"Heyyyy."

The attempt at cool coupled by a teenager-worthy flop into the chair across from me, didn't bode well for—#7.

"You all have your Charm Factor numbers," Katrina was saying. "Make sure they're visible, and if you're interested in someone, add their number to your Charmed By list and feel free to add anything else in the comments. Name, interesting facts, anything that will help you remember them. Please do not give out actual phone numbers or addresses," she added. "Unless you want to give it to me," she whisper-squealed-squeaked into the microphone and then laughed at her own joke and wiggled her ring finger. "Just kidding! I'm married, of course."

"Of course," Gabi said, deadpan.

"Once you register in the app, you can contact your interests by their Charm Factor number," Katrina said. "You can actually talk and text without ever giving away a stitch of your private information."

"That's actually kind of brilliant," I said.

"Unlike the name," Gabi said. "That's kind of dumb."

"So, like, what happened to you?" number Seven said, pointing toward his own face as he winced a little.

I blinked back to him and chuckled. "Wow, I've evidently been in a long-term relationship for way too long, because—wow."

He frowned. "You're in a relationship?"

"Ding ding!" I called out, tapping the toothpick on the table. "Time to move on yet?"

"We haven't started yet," Katrina said from the stage with a polite smile. "But on that subject, you'll have one minute with each person, starting with this green light and chime." She pointed to Drew, who demonstrated said light and chime, and tinted the whole room green. "And ending with this red light and buzzer."

"Feels like traffic court," Gabi muttered, rolling a cardboard coaster on its side.

"So, are we ready?" Katrina asked, holding up an arm like she was the girl to hold up a scarf at a road race.

She swung her arm down, Drew hit the switch, and the room went green, bathing everyone in a sickly hue as the chiming noise tinkled away and my stupid friend nodded at me.

"Well, I'm Gary," he said.

"Are we supposed to say names?" I asked.

"Yeah," he said, looking confused, like I'd thrown him off. "Just not numbers. So what's yours?"

"My what?" I asked, looking past him to Leo, who'd moved on from pants lady to shiny-buffed-bald dude and then another woman with sparkly fringe swinging from her tits. He smiled at this one, and she did the head tilt and made her fringe move a little more. He looked, but then blinked away and grinned his thank-you as she tipped him. Sorry, fringe-girl, his mind's not in the game tonight.

"Hello?" Seven said, tapping on the table. *What was his name again?*

"What?"

"I asked what your name is," he said. "Where'd you go?"

I glanced over at Leo again.

"My name?" I said. "Anastasia."

CHAPTER THIRTEEN

I didn't stay Anastasia. I might have used it two or three more times before I decided to go rogue and become Callie, Isabelle, Lauren, and even Mary Beth. Because, you know, I'm such a Mary Beth.

I was about to give Brooke a try, when Katrina announced we were taking a fifteen-minute break.

"Thank God," I mumbled, or I thought I mumbled. The questioning look someone named Macon-not-Mason gave me as he left my table told me I might have been a little louder.

"Men are—just—I can't comprehend this," Gabi said as we stood and stretched. "What the hell happened to people while I was married?"

"No shit," I said. "If this is the best that the world has to offer me, I'm good with my vibrator for the duration."

Gabi gave me a fist bump. "No truer words, my friend."

There had been a waitress coming around with drinks so we didn't have to get up, but my cranberry and Sprite had run dry a while back. I was down to chewing the ice.

It was slow around the bar, as Leo's groupies had temporarily dispersed.

"Your fans left?" I asked. "Did you break their hearts?"

"Of course," he said. "It's what I do." He nodded toward my empty table. "Your suitors taking a break?"

I slid my ass along a stool as he wiped up some spilled liquid.

"Well, two of them I think I scared when I told them I got this shiner playing roller derby with my bitches," I said.

Leo laughed out loud, and my ovaries clenched.

Stop.

"One was kind of normal but he had this nervous twitch thing going on with his hand," I said. "I thought he was going to bang a hole in the table." I glanced at Leo's left hand as he rolled a quarter over his knuckles without even looking at it. Hell, possibly without even knowing it. "Kind of like that, but not as cool."

He palmed the coin without looking down. "My uncle taught me that," he said. "One of the few things he was around long enough to do. Another cranberry and Sprite?"

"Sure," I said, suddenly remembering something I'd forgotten to ask him. "Hey, this is a weird question, but you don't know Jeremy, do you?"

Leo turned to fill my glass, a pause in his reach. "How would I know him?"

"From the same area?" I said.

"Do you know everyone in your town? In your county?"

"Okay, smartass, I'm just asking," I said. "Or if your brother worked for his dad."

"You'd have to ask my brother."

"Oh, my God, whatever," I said. "But he acted like he knew you. Something about a long time ago," I said. "Or something like that."

Leo grabbed a slice of lime and slid it onto my glass. "I must just have one of those faces."

I doubted that. The only person who could come close to Leo McKane was Nick, and neither of them had *one of those faces*.

Katrina flashed the green light, making circle motions with her finger.

"Looks like she's summoning the troops," Leo said.

"Seriously," I said, frowning her way.

"Rachel," a guy with too much cologne said, touching my arm as he passed. "Time to get back at it."

"Rachel?" Leo asked after he was gone.

Oh yeah. *Rachel*. Forgot about that one. I opened my mouth and closed it, giving him a shrug.

"What can I say?" I said, grabbing my glass.

"I don't know," he said. "I'm not sure I've met you yet."

The next round was almost numbing. There're only so many times you can tell your story. Even the made-up ones. After a while, I couldn't remember which was what and a little bit of reality got mixed in, and before I knew it, I was staring into the eyes of the sweetest but clingiest man named Jeffrie-with-an-ie, who held my hand and didn't care that my ex-husband sold crack or that my ex-mother-in-law had punched me because I'd left him for my Roller Derby team but then decided I didn't like women after all. This guy was enamored. And I really needed that red light to come the hell on.

"Anastasia," he said, because I'd decided to loop back. "You deserve so much better. No one should ever treat you like that. You should never settle for anything but pure, one hundred percent *all of me* kind of love."

Ooookay.

The red light came on and I bolted from my seat, raising my hand.

"Can we have a bathroom break?" I asked.

Katrina smiled like I'd just said something brilliant. "Awesome idea," she said. "From our special attendee tonight!"

Oh, fuck.

I headed for the bathroom as Gabi ducked off to take a phone call. Even just five seconds alone would be priceless right now, but an exit sign just past the girls' room door called to me. Glancing over my shoulder and hoping for no alarms, I gingerly pushed. No beeping. No yelling. Just quiet.

"Oh, thank God," I said, pushing into the low hue of a nearby security light. Not so bright to really be able to see, but not so dark that a stranger could sneak up and—

"Can I help you?"

"Shitfuckhell!" I yelped, flattening myself against the now closed door and trying desperately to remember what shoes I had on and if they were weapons. Where was my fucking toothpick?

"It's me," Leo's voice said to my left, a chuckle following it. "Take a breath."

"Jesus Christ, Leo," I breathed, willing my heart to back off its superspeed mission. "Don't ever do that to a woman alone."

"Sorry," he said. "You're right, I wasn't thinking."

I took a deep breath and blew it out, wiggling my fingers to return the blood.

"What are you doing out here? Hiding?" I asked, now that I could see him. He was sitting in a plastic chair, legs kind of sprawled, his arms folded over his chest with a cigarette between his fingers. "Smoking?"

He unfolded his arms and looked down at the cigarette. "Nah, this thing is ancient," he said. "I quit, but I still like the getaway and holding it somehow gives me peace."

I nodded as I strolled slowly over and leaned against the wall next to him. "I get it. Thatcher—my brother—he does the same thing."

He nodded, and we existed in silence for a few beats. Again, I had a moment of amazement that we could do that. Just—be. No words, no expectations, no needing to fill the space. It was nice. I felt the troubled vibes coming off him, however.

"What's wrong?" I asked, keeping my voice soft in the spirit of the silence. He just shook his head, but I nudged his arm with my knee. "Something's eating you. You aren't your normal chirpy self."

He chuckled at my wit and pulled out a worn wallet, putting the even more worn out cigarette into it and pocketing it again.

"Ever feel like you've been trying to put something behind you forever?" he said, almost to himself. "Logging millions of miles, just to find out that you've been on a treadmill the whole time."

"He asks the runaway bride?" I said, making him chuckle again. "Lord, I hope not. I hope getting away from Jeremy is real."

Leo nodded. "I hope so, too."

Curiosity pulled at my brows. There was something in his tone that was about more than just wanting that for me. "Why?"

He paused. "Because he's—what do you know about him?"

Warning bells started to tinkle in the far recesses of my brain.

"Well, pretty much everything, considering I was with him for eight years," I said. "Then again lately I'm not sure. But I thought you didn't know him."

Leo shook his head. "I don't," he said, still staring forward. "But he reminds me of someone I used to know. Another time and place."

Funny that Jeremy had said nearly the same thing.

"And who was that?" I asked.

"Someone who was bad news," Leo said. "Who was cold and freakish and would stop at nothing to get what he wanted. Including terrorizing his ex-girlfriend, selling out his own parents, and buying into his own lies."

"And you think that was Jeremy?" I asked after a pause.

"I didn't say that," he said. "I just think you need to be careful with people like him."

My control trigger yanked, and I pushed it back. He was trying to be helpful, but it felt an awful lot like—no, I didn't need to get defensive. I blew out a breath. I'd already had enough of that today.

"Well, I don't have to be anything with people like him now," I said. "It's over." A long stretch of silence waned before I spoke again. "So, you gonna expand on what you've spent all these treadmill miles getting away from or do I just get the metaphor?"

"Let's just say karma's a sadistic bitch," he said.

"Well, that's helpful."

"So, Thatcher, the nonsmoking brother," he said, changing the subject with the subtlety of a neck snap. "Is that your only sibling? I feel like I should know this after the big escape and all, but all that conversation seems like a blur."

"Yeah, it does," I said, laughing. "God, that seems like a hundred years ago." I shook my head free and leaned against the wall next to him. "And no to your question. I'm the middle. I have a little brother who lives down on the coast. Jolly Beach."

Leo nodded and gazed off into the night. "Family is important."

I looked his way. "Yes, it is." I took a shot. "Have you talked anymore to Nick?"

He shook his head. "I haven't tried, but I don't think it would matter if I did."

"You don't know that."

That head kept shaking. "I'm just glad he's getting the chance at another family."

"Another one?"

There was a pause. "Nick was a father at seventeen. Addison's her name." Even in the almost dark, I could see the look of pride on his face. "She's in college now. Art school." His expression changed. "I missed all that, and now I'm going to miss this one, too."

I recalled him telling me that Nick had needed him and he'd bailed. Teenage fatherhood could fit that bill. It could also explain Nick's bitterness.

"If you know she's in art school, then you haven't missed *everything*," I said.

He gave me a look that probably said I was too nosy for my own good. "I've kept tabs."

"Leo, you don't have to miss this," I said. "You're here. You can be there, be a brother again. Be an uncle. Mend things."

"That's easier said than done," he said. "And it's not enough that I want it. He has to want it, too, and that's—" He took a deep breath and let it out slowly, leaning his head back against the brick. "That's not happening." He frowned and gave me a sideways look. "Why are you out here?"

I rolled my eyes, not that he could see it.

"I was excused to go to the bathroom," I said, making him chuckle. "And this looked like a few blessed moments of quiet."

"Sorry," he said.

"No," I said, nudging his shoulder with my wrist. "This is good, too. A little piece of normal."

His chuckle burst into something heartier. "If I'm a piece of normal for you, you're in deep shit."

A laugh bubbled up my throat. "No kidding."

The door squeaked open to my right, just a smidgeon.

"Anastasia?"

I gripped Leo's shoulder like a vise. "Shit," I whispered.

"Anastasia?" Leo whispered on a chuckle.

"Shh."

"You out here?" came Jeffrie's voice. The door pushed open farther and he was about to appear around it. "I saw you come out here. I don't think we're supposed—"

I couldn't do it. I couldn't have another lame, meaningless conversation with someone I had to lie to just to get through sixty seconds. What could I do? *Fight or flight, Micah?* What I did next wasn't planned or even thought out in the next second. Call it a reaction, call it running again, call it panic, but my leg swinging over Leo's lap was as much of a surprise to me as it was to him.

Especially considering I couldn't have nailed that landing any more *precisely.*

My gasp as the sensation shot through me was cut short as his hands automatically spanned my thighs, fingers spread wide, as he inhaled deeply and I wound my fingers into his hair.

"Follow my lead," I managed to whisper, trying not to think about what I was doing or the overwhelming sensation overload that flooded my body. About how close his mouth was, how he felt against me, about the heat of his hands on my thin little leggings and exactly where his thumbs started making tiny circles. I saw his eyes, and yet I didn't. I couldn't see the words behind them, and I didn't want to. My head was spinning with too many *what the fucks* to go adding knowledge to the mix.

"Anastasia?" Jeffrie called out again, rounding the door.

"Follow mine," Leo whispered against my lips. Heat claimed my skin in waves of goose bumps as his mouth took the lead.

One of his hands slid up my back under the cardigan, all the way to the nape of my neck, while the other one moved to my ass and gripped me so tightly against him I saw stars. I sucked in a gasp as our mouths met and wasted no time with the small stuff. His lips were wet. Soft. Demanding. My toes curled under as his kiss instantly deepened, our mouths searching each other hungrily. My hands went from his hair to the hard lines of his shoulders and back again, all in the span of—

"Anastasia!"

—of *that.*

I jumped, and stared straight into Leo's eyes that time, our breaths mingling as we struggled to catch them. How was that—it had to only be seconds, but—

Fuck.

Both his hands were firmly on my ass now, mine were fisted in his hair, some poor scarred sap was standing somewhere in the vicinity wishing he'd never held my hand, and my stupid plan to quickly get rid of him now had me fighting the urge to wrap my legs around Leo and ride him till the cows came home.

"What are you doing?" the guy sputtered. "Oh, my God, he isn't even—is that the *bartender?*"

"Not at the moment. I'm on a break," Leo supplied helpfully, not breaking eye contact. I could still feel his breath on my skin and my hands were still in his hair.

"I thought we had a connection," Jeffrie said, his voice full of disdain and disappointment. That was me. Double Ds. "I came to check on you."

"I'm sorry," I said, my voice wobbly and gravelly and not sounding at all like me. I cleared my throat. "I'm—I just—"

"Do you even know what she's been through?" Jeffrie asked Leo, accusingly. "Do you *know* what her ex-husband did?"

"Actually, Leo's the one who turned me back on to guys," I said, backing up an inch and holding out a hand. "But you can join us. The more, the merrier."

Jeffrie's mouth formed a perfect O as he made some snort of irritation and stormed back inside.

"Oh, my God," I said under my breath, closing my eyes as I rested my hands back on his shoulders and Leo laughed.

"I didn't realize I'd turned you," he said.

"I'm sorry," I said. "You keep having to save me."

His hands hadn't left my ass, either. In fact, I was fairly certain that his fingertips were growing roots. Every nerve ending in my body was zinging at top speed, however, including the ones in my lips. They were reaching for more of his mouth like food to the starved.

"I'll send you my bill," he said, closing his eyes as I opened mine. I watched something change on his face as he shook his head as if to himself and then open his eyes again. "We had to make it look good, after all. Give them something to talk about. People don't sneak out of places to hold hands and keep it PG."

I raised my eyebrows. "Right," I said. "Making it look good. Something to talk about." I took a steadying breath, trying to catch up to the coolness chilling the heat between us. "All pretend."

His eyes dropped to my mouth again, however, fire sparking in them again as he slid his hands slowly off my ass and along my thighs. His fingers spread wide. "I assume that's where you went."

CHAPTER FOURTEEN

"Of course," I said in response, my words echoing in my ears. *Of course.* Pretend. All a big show. Yep.

So why was I still in his lap with no one out there, my lips still tingling from his kisses. Kisses that in just mere seconds had rocketed me further than years of being kissed by Jeremy.

"You okay?" he asked softly, blinking logic back into his expression again.

I blinked, too. Maybe that was the trick. "Why?"

His hands traveled down to my calves. I felt the trail of every finger. It was a bold move for something supposedly pretend, and it drove me to slide my own hands slowly up his neck. I felt a rush go through me as my fingers found his hair and his breathing quickened, but I couldn't look away from the—something. The need, the want, the raw desire mixed with *this is a bad idea*—that, I understood. That was probably all over me, as well. This was something else.

"You're trembling," he said.

Shit. He was lucky I wasn't pole-vaulting. It was like a supermagnet was pulling me to his mouth, and I couldn't breathe until I tasted him again.

The door squeaked open again, and I inhaled sharply through my nose. *God, get it together.*

"See?" came Jeffrie's voice from somewhere over the rainbow. "I told you."

"Micah!" Katrina Bowman exclaimed.

"Who's Micah?" Jeffrie asked.

A nervous laugh escaped my throat, and Leo chuckled too, as his hands spanned my hips and helped me off him. The weirdest disappointment washed over me as we separated, like the missing contact was needed. Too needed.

"You know, if you're just going to make a mockery of everything here," she said, all the nicety of earlier, gone, "why don't you just go back where you came from?"

"Relax," Leo said, standing with me. "We were just blowing off a little steam. Not that it's your business."

"Not my business?" Katrina asked, her voice moving up an octave as she put her fists on her hips. In that pose, in that leather outfit, she looked like a cross between a pissed-off Viking and a dominatrix. "I'm running a dating event tonight if you haven't noticed. And when the featured contestant skips off to get nasty with the bartender—"

"Hold on, there was no nasty," I said. Not yet. But, oh man, my body was still thrumming with the trip that direction. "It was a show so that John-boy there would stop stalking me."

Yep. Pretend. Blowing off steam. *All pretend.*

"What?" Jeffrie said, his voice rising, too.

"And two," I said, holding up fingers. "This isn't a reality show, Katrina. This is a one-night event in Charmed. Calm down."

"I gotta get back," Leo said, one hand on the small of my back as he moved past us. Goose bumps trickled across the area after he left it. "Break's over."

"Yeah, why don't you do that?" she said.

"And three," I continued, watching Leo shake his head as he disappeared through the door. *Breathe.* "I never asked to be a featured anything. In fact, I asked you *not* to do that. So leave me out of it."

I went back in, leaving Katrina and Jeffrie there to do whatever they needed to do. I didn't care. In fact, that *going back where I came from* wasn't sounding all that bad at the moment. That garage apartment I saw in Thatcher's neighborhood couldn't be that bad, and I could kiss and fondle whoever I wanted.

Holy fuck, I kissed Leo.

Big time.

He kissed me back. Just as big time.

And God help me, I wanted more of it.

* * * *

I couldn't stomach any more date night. After what just happened, I was useless. I was—I don't know what I was. I could still taste him. I could still feel his hands on my body, his hair under my fingers, his—yep, all that. All up in my grille.

I hadn't touched or kissed anyone except Jeremy in years, and the fact that I'd not only done that but climbed on him without a plan or a forethought—it just blew me away. Kind of like running from a church and saddling up on a stranger's motorcycle.

Who the hell *was* I?

I texted Gabi, but she was all into playing the game, so I ordered myself some queso and chips, found myself a dark corner, and hid. I watched Leo work the bar, smiling politely, laughing sometimes, but mostly there was a quiet trouble about him. Was that because of me? Was it about his brother? And why did it matter? I couldn't stop staring at his mouth and I was about to start pulling off my own fingernails to distract myself when Katrina made it back up to the microphone.

"Okay, y'all, that was the last round!" she said, giggling. "We lost a couple of people," she added sourly. "But that's okay, feel free now to mingle and meet back up with ones who tweaked you!"

"Really?" I muttered.

"Oh!" she continued, stepping back like she forgot something. "And don't forget tomorrow night!" She circled an imaginary lasso over her head. Calf roping? "The bachelor auction!"

"Oh, wow," I said.

"I hope everyone got their votes in for the esteemed victims—I mean bachelors!" she said, laughing at her lame joke. I'd never heard about any voting, but it all could have happened before I landed in Charmed. "I'll read out all the names now, and, guys, if you're here, be sure to show up at the Lucky Charmed pavilion tomorrow at six to practice your strut!" She giggled again, doing a little shimmy thing that made me want to hurl.

One by one, names were read and catcalls were done. I didn't know any of them except Sully, who wasn't there, and probably was exempt from the shenanigans. If he wasn't, I was pretty sure that Carmen would change that.

"And one more who was written in recently," Katrina said, her voice teasing. "Give a hand to the new boy in town, Leo McKane!"

My jaw dropped. My gaze shot to the bar, where Leo turned from a bent stance at the sound of his name and frowned. Women whistled, and I could almost hear the plans and strategies being devised in the seconds that followed. In fact, I *could* hear them. The table next to me started arguing over whether his bidding should start at $100 or $200.

Gabi was laughing as she approached my clandestine little table.

"Could you be more hidden?" she asked. "I was beginning to think you left."

I barely heard her. All my senses were spinning out of whack as I watched the vultures descend upon the bar. "Nope. Just—um—how'd you do?"

"Idiots," she said, dropping into a chair. "All of them. Hear about your boy?"

"My boy?" I said, probably way too fast. "What—he's not—why are you calling him that?"

Her eyebrows shot up. "Breathe."

I rubbed my temples. Breathing had gone by the wayside long ago. "This day is just eating me alive."

"So, are you going to bid on him?" Gabi asked, gesturing with a tilt of her head and a glance backward.

I followed her line of focus, not that I'd been looking at much else.

"I don't think—" I began. "I mean, I probably should take a night off. Stay in."

"It's not here," she said, leaning back in her chair. "Out at the pavilion. Fresh air."

"Still," I said, giving her a smile that she probably wouldn't understand meant *Let it go*, seeing that we'd known each other for about a minute.

"Speaking of fresh air," she said, "want to have a picnic tomorrow?"

I blinked, aiming all my focus back on her. "I'm sorry, what?"

"There's something I want to show you," she said. "Some land out across the pond. I have an idea and I want to see what you think." She shrugged. "We can grab some burgers to go and eat lunch on the boat."

"Boat?"

"A rowboat."

I nodded. "Of course it is."

"So, you up for it?" she asked.

"Why not?" I said. "Sounds awesome."

Gabi narrowed her eyes. "Are you sure you're okay?"

I smiled stiffly. "I'm awesome," I echoed.

She gave me a sideways look. "Uh-huh. Be at the shop at eleven?"

I would likely already be there, since I planned to go home tonight and stay there till it was time to meet her tomorrow. That or stick a glass to the door and listen for Leo to leave so there was no chance of running into him in the hallway or the bathroom. This is what my life had come to—running away from men, hiding in new towns, making out with them, and then hiding again.

My brother might have a point. I should be past this shit.

"See you then."

* * * *

I didn't actually have to listen with a glass, but I did hear Leo come home. This, because I was lying on my couch wide awake and staring at the popcorn texture on the ceiling when I heard his footsteps down the hall. Did I imagine the pause by my door? Probably. Did I know what I would do if he would have knocked? I would love to say no, or even an emphatic yes that I would ignore it. But every nerve ending in my body tuned in to those footsteps, especially when I heard the door squeak open to that secret back patio. I was pretty sure what those same nerves would do if given the opportunity.

My nerves were absolute sluts.

But he didn't knock. And I didn't leave.

And the next morning, I didn't either. I slept till past when I knew he'd probably be gone, and I snuck out like the big kissing chicken coward that I am.

The Grahams were downstairs when I went down, Gabi's dad lugging in some flowering plants while her mom directed.

"Perfect, Martin," Wanda was saying. "Those begonias are the perfect swatch of color for that corner. They catch the afternoon sun."

"Agreed," I said, crossing my arms over my chest and smiling as she looked my way. "Something else that would really draw the customers' attention would be tiger lilies."

"Tiger lilies," Wanda said, looking surprised. "You sound like Gabi. She likes the wild blooms, too."

I shrugged. "There's something magical about natural beauty. Independent of us. In spite of us, even."

Drew wandered in with a big white binder that said "Weddings," followed by Gabi and a young woman with a pink streak in her hair. Wanda pushed her glasses up on top of her head and gave the young woman a double-take before looking back at me like I was something to study.

"That's quite a perspective," Wanda said, the studied look turning to a frown as she peered closer. "Honey, what happened to you?"

It wasn't as bad as the previous day. Less purplish and more just a weird red with a little bit of brownish green. Makeup helped, but it was still there.

"It's a long story," I said. "Everything's okay, though."

She blinked a couple of times as if trying to decide if she believed me.

"Gabi tells me you're one of the Romans from the Cherrydale Flower Farm."

"I am," I said on a sigh. "My brother really runs it. I work in the nursery. I'm more of a hands-in-the-dirt person than sitting at a desk."

"You and me both," Wanda said, to which both daughters guffawed.

"Since when?" Gabi said. "That's Dad."

Their dad lifted his eyebrows in a little chuckle and left the room, and that's the most noise I'd heard from him yet.

"Well, whatever," she said. "I couldn't sit at a desk for a living, either." She laughed. "I couldn't sit anywhere. My dream is to take off one day. Sell the house, leave the business to the girls, and see the world."

Gabi smirked, but Drew looked like her mother had just sent down a life sentence.

"The business is with the girls, anyway," Gabi said under her breath.

"I heard that," Wanda said.

"It's not a secret," Gabi retorted. "So, Drew will finish up your paperwork, Macy," she said, turning back to the nodding girl who'd been standing there taking it all in. "Micah, you ready to go?"

"You're coming back, right?" Drew asked. "We have to finish designing the Honey Games set."

"I'm aware," Gabi said. "Relax. Just taking an early lunch."

We left, and instead of heading for Gabi's car, we walked toward the Lucky Charm. Rides loomed ahead, and I wondered what her plan was.

"You mentioned a boat?" I asked. "Are we talking a real boat or the theme park version?"

"Oh, real," she said. "But there's a pizza kiosk out here that is to die for. You up for that?"

"I'm always up for that."

We grabbed a small pizza from a little artisan pizza place called Jimmy's, eyed an old-fashioned ice cream parlor along the boardwalk, made plans to come back for the two-scoop special, and then loaded ourselves into an old dilapidated rowboat that might have seen better days. Like maybe before we were born.

"How far are we going?" I asked. "Because this thing looks to have about a ten-minute shelf life."

"It's fine," Gabi said, taking up the oars. "Better than it looks. And it's just right around this corner." She gestured with a tilt of her head.

I looked where she was pointing.

"Like this bend?" I asked, squinting to take in a pile of flora and fauna that gave way to a kind of sandbar and then a wild-growing field.

"Yep," she said, pulling the first stroke and sending us on the move.

There were people over there, standing by a truck.

"It looks accessible by road."

"It is," she said, pulling again.

I blinked at her. "Then why are we going this way?"

"Because it's more fun," she said.

Couldn't argue with that. Until we got closer and I saw the truck and people more closely. It was two men. Sully and—

"Damn it."

"What?" Gabi said, stopping her action.

They looked our direction as we approached by water, and I saw the double-take on Leo's face. I was pretty sure his expletive was the same.

"Did you know they would be here?" I asked, making her twist around.

"No." She turned fully around. "What are they doing here in my field?"

"Your field?"

"Hey," Sully said, making his way down the sandbar to pull us in before we'd even touched. "Throw me your line."

Gabi did, and he hauled us up on the sand and tied the boat to a stump.

"What are y'all doing here?" she asked.

"Working out the clearing plans for Bailey," Sully said.

"Clearing?" Gabi said.

"He wants this cleared out for development next year," Sully said, thumbing over his shoulder toward Leo, who was strolling up behind him.

Or as much as you can tell when you're trying not to look at someone.

"No, no, no," Gabi said, clamoring out of the boat. "I thought you owned this."

"Not this parcel," Sully said. "He hung on to this little piece for some reason, and he's wanting to develop it. Put houses here or something—"

Sully stopped talking when Gabi started pacing.

"Crap, that's not good," she said.

"Gabi, what's up?" I asked.

"It's what I wanted to show you," she said. "Look at what's growing already. The soil. The proximity to the water. The proximity to the shop. Wouldn't this be an awesome place to do a controlled wildflower field?"

I looked around with a different eye. With Gabi's perspective. With mine, if I was truly a Roman and meant to do what I do. I walked past the guys and shut down the magnetic pull coming from one of them. This wasn't about that.

The field was thick with weeds and needed an overhaul, but it also grew Indian Paint Brush wild, along with buttercups and a very wild daisy strain.

I stooped to dig my fingers into the earth. It wasn't sandy like the bar; it was rich and pungent. It was good soil and looked to go back for several acres. With a careful clean-out and flower mapping to get just the right types together, with cross-pollination and natural nutrients feeding back into the soil—Gabi was right. She could have a gold mine here.

"What do you think?" she persisted. "Am I crazy?"

"Oh, you're crazy," I said, chuckling as I rose to my feet. "But that's separate from this."

"So?"

"I think it would be perfect."

She made a squeal of joy and hugged me, and then just as abruptly left me and wheeled around.

"It would be perfect, except that Mr. Bailey owns it," she said.

"BBG owns it," Sully said. "The corporation he set up recently to protect his assets."

BBG. Where had I heard that before?

"Was he being threatened?" Gabi asked.

Sully gave a side shrug. "He hasn't been as private lately as in past years, so he's more exposed. I think he's just being careful."

"Do you work for him?" I asked, realizing then where I'd heard it.

The big guy standing behind him with his arms crossed like a bouncer had once told me he came here to work for BBG, along with other things. Like bartending and taking nonsmoking breaks with old unlit cigarettes so that you end up with your tongue down the throat of the town's latest gossip sizzle.

To his credit, he wasn't looking at me, either. He looked very casual, and even lowered his hands to rest in his pockets, as though he didn't have a care in the world. Least of all about me. Well, that was fine. That was good. He shouldn't have a care in the world about me. I'd be willing to bet that he didn't sit in his living room listening for *me* in the hallway. Or spend half the night thinking about every nuance of those five seconds kissing me.

"No," Sully said, as if answering that question. I had to blink a couple of times to remember that I'd asked him a whole other one. "Not in any official capacity. But he's sort of a family friend."

"Like the kind of friend you could ask not to develop this and instead rent it to me?" Gabi asked, looking a little off guard that the words came out of her mouth.

Sully regarded her. "If you're serious about it," he said. "Bailey's a— different kind of person. To the point. He doesn't have the best people skills," he added with a chuckle. "But he's fierce when it comes to helping the tiny circle of people he considers family."

"How did you make that circle?" Leo asked, speaking up for the first time. His voice sent a sensuous trickle down my spine.

Sully licked his lips and raked back his hair. "I'm where I am now because of him," he said. "Bailey had an odd kind of kinship with my father, the details of which are too bizarre to explain now, but in turn he took me under his wing when I left the carnival circuit and came back here. He offered me the land for the Lucky Charm at an insanely cut price. And he's helped me out a couple of times personally as well."

Gabi was nodding. "So, in return…"

"In return, I'm there for him." Sully shrugged. "Some might say he engineered it that way so that I'm always indebted to him, but that's okay. End result—his business sense is sharp as ever, but his health isn't, so I'm sometimes the front man." He smiled softly at Gabi. "So if you're really serious about this, I'll approach it, but get something together to back it up. He likes numbers."

She nodded and suddenly looked a mix of euphoric and nauseated.

"Want me to hold off on this then?" Leo asked. "Just in case?"

Sully gave a small nod. "Yeah, I'll tell him you'll start in a week or so, pending what Gabi comes up with."

"This guy has millions, I gather," I said.

"Probably," Sully said, chuckling.

"So why would he hire a one-man contractor to clean this up and level it for development?" I asked, ignoring Leo's indignant look. "I mean, he can afford a professional team to come in and do it in a week."

Sully grinned. "My guess? Family."

Leo frowned. "What?"

Sully slapped him on the shoulder. "I think you might be in the circle, my friend, because of Lanie."

"Lanie?" Gabi asked.

"Lanie Barrett," Sully said. "Married Nick, who is Allie's right-hand man at the diner." At what was probably a group look of confusion, he continued. "BBG is Bailey, Barrett, and Greene. Ruby Barrett and Oliver Greene—Lanie's aunt and Allie's dad—were Bailey's best childhood friends. His only family."

"Ohhhh," Gabi said under her breath.

Sully turned back to Leo. "You're attached to Nick."

Leo looked at him warily. "How would he know that? I literally just answered an ad."

Sully laughed and walked back up to the truck. "We should probably have the Albert Bailey conversation soon. It's kind of like questioning the universe." He nodded our way. "I've got to get back to work, but keep in touch on this, Gabi."

"Will do," she said. "And thank you."

Leo gave a half-hearted wave and followed Sully, so I turned and climbed back into the boat. I wasn't going to give him any more than he was giving me. And I had pizza to eat.

Gabi watched me sit and unwrap the food, and then nodded.

"Okay," she said, climbing back in and sinking onto her seat. "This works."

CHAPTER FIFTEEN

"Gabi, I meant what I said," I mumbled around my last bite of pizza. "This is seriously a good idea."

She met my eyes with a glimmer of hope. "I thought so," she said. "I've wanted to do this for so long, and when I saw this spot, it just—" She sighed. "Of course, I also thought it belonged to Sully and would be an easy in. And now I have to do a business plan? Gah."

"Well, it sounds like if you're a friend of his or anyone in the Barrett-Greene world, you might have that in," I said, shaking my head. "How weird is that?"

She pointed at me around a massive bite of pizza. "Did I not tell you? This town is so odd." She put her pizza down and turned to relocate the oar out of her way. "Speaking of which, what's up with you and big brother hottie?"

"Ugh."

"Yeah, it's not reading *ugh*," she said, trying to balance the oar on the side.

"I kind of kissed Leo," I blurted.

Gabi's head snapped around.

"You—what?" she said, drawing out the word as she scooted back around to face me. "When?"

"Last night," I said, covering my face with my hands.

"When?" she repeated. "Where was I?"

"You weren't outside behind the bathrooms," I said, peeking between my fingers.

Her eyebrows shot up. "Tell me!"

"Well, I was escaping the weird guy I told you about," I said.

"Right."

"And—Leo was out there. And I might have left out the part about straddling his lap and face-planting him when the guy came looking for me."

Gabi grabbed for the oar as it slipped from her hand and set it in the bottom of the boat. Laughing. Hard.

"Holy shitwaffles, girl!" she sputtered.

"I know."

"Seriously!"

"I know," I repeated.

She dropped her hands and looked at me expectantly.

"Well? Was it hot?"

I chuckled. "What do you think?"

"I think he's sex on a stick, and you need to tell me every detail," she said, holding up her hands when I widened my eyes in amusement. "Hey, I'm not off men. I'm just off dating them. Throw a girl a bone." She laughed. "No pun intended."

"I was in a wedding dress less than a week ago," I said.

"So?"

I chuckled. "So, what does that say about me?"

"It says that the asshole holding your car hostage never deserved you and the hot guy who whisked you away does," she said matter-of-factly. "Seriously, Micah, he made you pull your shit out of your own car while he watched."

The memory of that indignity heated my blood a little.

"True."

"I wouldn't be worried about him," she continued. "Mr. McKane, now, what did he say? Or do? Or either?"

That memory warmed me in a whole different way. The feel, the taste, the smell of him—they were still all over me. I still felt the trail of his hands, felt his body as he pressed me to him. Those full, delicious lips of his taking my mouth like a man starved.

"He participated," I said.

"I'll bet he did," she said, laughing again.

"No, I mean he—" I stopped. "It was—"

My mouth worked, but I couldn't find the description.

"Oh," Gabi said, her tone changing as she drew the word out.

I met her eyes. "Yeah. Like as if we'd thought about nothing else for days, and now—"

She narrowed her eyes. "Christmas?"

I loved that she got me.

"So much Christmas," I said. "Because—I might have maybe not been thinking about much else for days." I covered my face. "I suck so bad."

"So—then you—" she inferred, her tone lilting up.

"No," I clarified. "And he made sure to tell me it was all for show."

"Did it *feel* like it was all for show?"

I thought of his reaction when I'd touched him. The way he'd inhaled sharply and curled his fingers into me. When we'd almost kissed again. Hadn't we? Had I imagined that?

"I'm not the greatest judge of anything, anymore," I said. "What do I know?"

"Are you coming out here tonight?" she asked. "Because you know these women here are going to kill each other bidding on him." She took another large bite and gave me a knowing smile. "If it really was just all for show, then you're okay with that?"

The thought of his hands sliding along another woman's body like that, of him kissing someone *like that*, sent spikes of not-so-pretty jealousy zinging through my veins. Not that bidding on him automatically meant a romantic date or a sexual encounter, but what if it did? What if someone straddled him like I had and he thought, *Hey, here's another woman sitting on my dick. Let's do this.*

"Here's the flip side then," she said, continuing while I was silently ranting.

"What?" I asked.

"If it *wasn't* for show," she said. "If it was real. Are you okay with *that*?"

Why was that scarier?

I swallowed hard. "I don't know."

"Do you want to find out?" she asked.

I looked her in the eye. "I don't know."

* * * *

It was like being in high school. Or hell, not even that mature. Let's go with junior high. When you kind of avoid the guy you're obsessed with, so he won't see that you like him—not that you like him. More likely, you don't like him because he can be an arrogant ass who drives you bat-shit crazy, but yet then he does these things and says stuff and looks at you all... like that, and you can't think and you can't make any sense and you can't adult. But wait—we were talking about junior high school—sigh—okay, so then you make sure you aren't where he expects you to be, and then you accidentally-on-purpose place yourself where he doesn't expect you to be, and he can't help but see you so he'll have to talk and you can then analyze his reaction for the next three hours.

Yep. That's where I was. Envious, anyone?

Gabi had something come up with her family that she had to run off and deal with, so I was left to my own devices. My own devices were proving to not be very trustworthy of late, and without a wingwoman to keep me on the tracks, I just held back. Watching.

Tables and chairs had been set up on the grounds around the pavilion, oddly transforming the very casual park into something formal. I had to give Katrina this one. Black tablecloths and candles under the stars was a weird mix that worked.

Leo and the other guys were gathered around the pavilion stage across the park, talking to people and generally schmoozing and working the crowd. Well, the other guys were doing that, at least. Leo was sitting on the edge of the stage, dressed in all black, scrolling on his phone, looking up occasionally to smile and talk to the women who came up to him, but mostly looking pretty annoyed.

It was the time for my junior high school moment, to go up to the guy. Except that I had no business liking this one. It was stupid and crazy and really probably just sexual chemistry and bodies wanting each other, but—but that would make more sense if we'd had blindfolds on and those eyes hadn't—

"Micah!" Katrina Bowman's shrill voice intoned behind me. "Of course you'd be here." She was smiling, but her expression and body language hinted that she'd rather I be anywhere else. "Need to 'blow off steam' again tonight? Looking through your choices?"

My *choices* looked up from his phone, and the look on his face before he shut it down nearly took out my knees.

Fuck.

He wanted it as much as I did.

But what? We wanted *what*? Sex? Gabi made the separation sound so easy, but that had never been my strong suit. Sex was emotional for me.

Which greatly explained my choice of a red strapless dress that I rarely ever got to wear in public because Jeremy found it too revealing and sexy. He didn't like other men looking at me that way. So here I was, very much in public in the dress that hugged every curve and flared out flirtatiously above my knees. With cork wedges to dress it down and my hair swept up in a messy updo to dress it back up. Because I wanted nothing to be sexy or emotional tonight.

Yeah, I couldn't even sell it to myself.

"Are you bidding tonight, or are you just stalking?" Katrina asked.

"I don't know yet," I said, grounding myself by latching on to a nearby chair. "I'll see how I feel when it begins."

"Well, just so you know, Leo will likely be the big ticket, so don't expect to win him," she said, throwing me a look over her freckled shoulder as she walked away.

"Oh, what a bitch," I said softly, not even realizing that the subject matter had walked up slowly to me and was only feet away.

"Problem?" he asked.

The lack of blood to my head, maybe. Leo wasn't just in all black. He was in black dress pants and a silk button-down.

"Sweet Jesus."

His eyebrows raised, and I realized my mouth had once again overridden my brain. "I mean, you look nice."

"You look—stunning," he said, his eyes taking me in.

That was it. We were toast.

"How was your picnic today?" he asked.

"Can't go wrong with pizza," I said. "And if Gabi gets her deal, then…" I poked at his arm. "Didn't realize you were part of the cool crowd."

He huffed out a breath. "Neither did I," he said. "Inclusive only by means of a brother who doesn't speak to me."

"You can work on that, Leo," I said. "It just takes time."

"We'll see," he said, shoving his hands into his pockets. Dear God, he looked good like that. "I didn't know if you'd be here tonight."

I swallowed. "I didn't either."

"We're okay, right?" he asked. "I mean, nothing's weird after that—"

"No!" I exclaimed, way too animatedly. *Calm down.* "Of course not. That was just—" *The hottest kiss I've ever had. The thing that I've obsessed about all day.* "That was just craziness."

He nodded. "Right."

"Right," I echoed.

His eyes on mine were intense, and I had to do something in that heated *What the fuck are we doing?* pause. Something to keep me from crossing that small space between us and climbing him like a monkey.

"Katrina just told me you're going to be the big ticket," I said, for lack of better words. "You up for having a hundred women salivating over you?"

He grinned lazily before shaking his head and rubbing at his eyes wearily. "I've had worse evenings."

I rolled my eyes. "Of course."

"But this is about as stupid as the speed dating," he said. "I'm doing it only because Rojo's is sponsoring it, and it's for a good cause."

It had been rumored that the week's proceeds from all the activities might be going to build an epic playground in the park very close to where we now stood. Something magical for the children of Charmed, and call it the Tiny Charm. As if growing up with a theme park down the street from you wasn't magical enough.

"So, just being a dedicated employee?" I asked.

"Why else?"

He almost looked dead serious.

"Maybe you'll get your own stalker," I said. "Your own version of Jeffrie with an *ie*."

"If I get a Jeffrie, I'm out of here," he said. "You could rescue *me*."

"I could," I said slowly, watching his eyes process that. "But then again, I don't think I can afford you," I said. "Have you seen the money walking around here? These women are hard core."

"They scare me," he said.

I laughed, and he did a double-take on me, his eyes going soft.

"You really do look beautiful tonight," he said, his eyes staying on mine instead of my body.

It stole my breath, that simple choice. It was so—intimate. Real. Foreign. That wasn't pretend.

"Thank you," I managed, the words coming out breathy. My hands flitted to my cheek. "I—managed to cover up the bruise pretty well."

"Can't even see it."

My gaze dropped to his lips, and every sensation from the previous evening washed over me. My head was dizzy with the need to be all up in that again.

"Okay, guys, let's rally up," Katrina yelled into a microphone, startling us both back into reality.

"Well, go do your thing," I said, clearing my throat. "Work up that money for the greater good."

"Good grief," he muttered.

"Let's see you strut," I said as he turned around to walk off, ignoring me. I watched the really good back and ass saunter away all swathed in black perfection. "Yep, you've got it."

I breathed in deeply as he left, sinking into the nearest chair. Humor was easier with us. We could go there. It was safe there. This other—whatever we were doing—it was dangerous and exhausting. Had it really been less than a week? It felt like we'd been doing this dance for an eternity.

Men pranced throughout the evening, and women acted like they'd never seen one before. Seriously, it was as if some invisible switch was flipped and normally intelligent people turned into the worst version of any stereotypical horndog you'd ever seen. Catcalls, whistles, body shimmies, anything to draw attention to themselves—it was entertaining in a somewhat horrifying way.

Even men who wouldn't normally be viewed as studly—put them in a suit and march them around a stage, and the female feeding frenzy below did not falter.

I nursed my one glass of wine, laughed with the other people at my table, and did my best to blend. For once, I wasn't the focus of anyone's attention. No one at my table knew me or remembered me. I was just one of the masses. It was heavenly.

And then it was Leo's turn.

"Okay, ladies, we saved the best for last," Katrina said with an eyebrow wiggle. "No offense, all you other hotties!" She giggled. "But you've all met our newest resident, Charmed's very own drink slinger, Mr. Leo McKane!"

She drew out his name in a ridiculously long manner, and I covered half my face with my hands in anticipation. Part of me was sympathetic and embarrassed for him, knowing how uncomfortable he was about this. And part of me was hideously turned on.

Leo came out on stage from behind a red partition and stopped short when a spotlight landed on him with the brightness of the sun. He held up a hand, and they backed it off. Yeah, this isn't *Project Runway*, people. Let's keep it real.

Cheesy music played, and he walked the stage from one end to the other, one hand in a pocket like he'd come out of the womb meant for this. The females lost their minds, a couple of them climbing over each other, not caring about decorum or proper behavior. They had been primed and readied with the other bachelors and now were pulling out all the stops. Bidding cards were popping up everywhere, and Katrina had her work cut out for her, keeping up with them.

A woman with long immaculately curled blonde hair raised her card repeatedly, getting up from her table, even, as the bidding went higher. Katrina zoned in on her, working her bids against the others as people methodically bowed out of the rising price. It was down to her and one other older woman in a red netted hat that looked to be pushing sixty.

"One night with the handsome Mr. McKane," Katrina said. "We're at four hundred ninety dollars. Do I hear five hundred?"

Five hundred dollars.

For a date with Leo.

It was insane.

But the blonde sleeper cell hell-bent on going home with him didn't think so. She was walking steadily closer to the stage, looking up at him like she wanted to do five hundred dollars' worth of nasty. Leo smiled down at her, and my nerve endings twitched.

She held up her card. "Five hundred twenty," she called out.

"Who is that?" I asked the woman next to me.

She shrugged. "Never seen her before. Must be from Denning or somewhere."

"We have five hundred and twenty," Katrina said, as blonde-woman strolled ever closer to the stage.

Leo walked to the other side of the stage again, and the woman slowly mimicked his direction. He glanced down at her again, and in that second it became a sexual dance. A game. And my blood went sharply south of warm. My image of another woman on him now had a face and a body and a little black dress that would too easily be shoved out of the way.

No one else was bidding. Red-hat lady shook her head. That was out of her budget for a dinner with a handsome hunk, but blondie was willing to shell out her life savings. I was pretty sure dinner wasn't anywhere in her plan.

"Going once," Katrina said, holding up a hand. "Going twice—"

Leo's gaze landed on me, and in that microsecond we were back in the chair.

"Six hundred dollars," I blurted out, grabbing my unused card and holding it over my head.

Katrina widened her eyes in a mixture of euphoria and irritation, as all eyes swerved to me. Including Leo's, still hardwired into mine, now with a spark of amusement added.

"Six hundred," she echoed, not bothering to hide her annoyance. "To the lady in red at the back table." She glanced around the room. "Anyone for six fifty?"

There were mumblings and murmurings, but no other cards went up. *Please, someone, bid me out.*

"Six hundred, going once," Katrina said. "Going twice."

What did I do?

CHAPTER SIXTEEN

I didn't leave my table until the night started shutting down and I was physically required to go settle up my purchase.

My *purchase*.

I'd bought a man. A date. I was a john.

"Oh, God," I whispered, palming my phone and my wallet and starting the walk of shame.

Leo was talking to two other men when I approached the cash-out line, and he excused himself and joined me. I couldn't look at him. I just couldn't. He'd be all smirky, and make some comment, and—no. I temporarily lost my mind. Let's get it over with.

"I assume you take credit cards?" I asked the woman softly as I held out my Visa.

The woman gave me a look of disdain. "This was a cash event."

"Well, I wasn't prepared," I said. "And most of them went for fifty bucks and under. I don't have six hundred on me."

"Then why did you bid it?" she asked.

Question of the night!

"Can we just focus on how to finish this?" I asked. "I have PayPal."

"That's fine," Katrina said, strolling up like a queen bee. "Send it to mine and I'll transfer it over." She gave Leo a seductive look from under her lashes. "Goods like this just take away a girl's better sense. Two nights in a row, even."

Oh, my God. I couldn't tap on my phone fast enough. *Goods?* It was mortifying. I was weak and frivolous and pathetic and just spent six hundred dollars over spontaneous jealousy.

"Done. Let's go," I said, turning on my heel.

"Thanks for your support!" Katrina called after us.

"You okay?" Leo asked, picking up his stride to keep up. "Damn, Roman-off, slow down."

"I can't," I muttered.

"Why?"

"Because moving right now is keeping me sane," I said, stopping abruptly. "What the hell are we playing with, Leo?"

He stopped too, and his expression turned more serious. "I know."

"Do you?" I said. "Because I'm clueless. I just shelled out six hundred of my hard-earned dollars over—what?"

"Why did you?" he asked, folding his arms over his chest.

"I have no idea," I said, flailing mine. "Except—"

"Except what?"

"That blonde lady," I said.

Damn it, why did I say that?

His eyebrows lifted. "The blonde lady."

"Don't play stupid," I said. "It's beneath you."

He huffed out a breath. "Okay, what about her? She was bidding."

"She was not bidding on a dinner with you, Leo," I said.

"I'm fully aware of that," he said, chuckling. "I have been around the block a time or two."

Oh—the arrogance.

"You are such a pig," I muttered, resuming my walking.

"What?" he said, following me. "I'm a guy, Roman-off. A hot woman hitting on me is not repulsive."

"Oh, I got that," I said. *Stop talking, Micah.* I reached the end of the grass and my wedges hit the parking lot pavement. *Listen to your footsteps. Stop talking.* "You certainly didn't throw me on the ground last night when I climbed aboard, so why would this chick be any different?"

Shit. All of that fell out of my mouth. Where was a roll of duct tape when you needed it? Earplugs?

"What? Rom—"

Keep walking.

It was all I could do. Keep walking and pray he would turn around. Realize what a freaky moron I was, and just turn the hell around and go home.

The problem was *home* was currently the same place I was headed, and I had nowhere to detour with. I kept walking in silence, my ears keened for his footsteps behind me. I felt him more than heard him, his strong presence far outweighing his physical one. He wasn't done, and he wasn't going to be put off until he said his piece.

What were the odds I could just disappear into my apartment, put on my pajamas, and crawl under my covers in shame without another word spoken?

"Roman-off," he said as we entered the florist shop and the stairway to our floor.

Fuck. Pretty much what I expected. I closed my eyes and kept walking upward. Screw my apartment; it suddenly sounded too confined. I strode past it and headed down the hall toward the bathroom, except for a sharp turn to my left. I twisted the handle and pushed back out into the night air, inhaling deep gulps of it.

"Micah."

"What?" I muttered, not that I was surprised.

It halted my feet, though, and turned me around. He was standing in the open doorway, his silhouette outlined in glowing warm light, looking like something out of a movie. The kind that was likely to get me into trouble.

"Thank you," he said. "I at least deserve your face."

"Let's not do this," I said. "I'm not up for a conversation right now. I'm probably a little too keyed up for this to go anything other than bad, so—"

"I don't care," he said. "You don't like being controlled...Well, neither do I."

All my little hairs stood on end, and yet it was different. His tone wasn't authoritative or domineering. It was standing up for himself and making us even without taking over.

That was new to me.

That was probably worth exploring and thinking about.

But I was a hot mess of emotion and irritation and I was just out a shit-ton of money over something ridiculous. It wasn't the time.

"Okay, I hear you, and I'm sorry," I said quietly. "And maybe that's not a lot of money to you, but it's a car note to me." I closed my eyes. "Not that I have a car anymore, so I guess buying a man is totally affordable—"

"I'll cover the money," he said.

"It's not about the money."

"No, it's about feeling manipulated," he said.

"I—what?"

"That asshole has you so wired to do what you're supposed to do that you're jumping off cliffs just to resist," he said.

Goose bumps trickled down from my neck as his words touched all the right nerves.

"Don't act like you know me just because—"

"You didn't like the thought of me touching her like I touched you," he said, cutting off my words. My thoughts. My brain. Fuck, he may as well have short-circuited me completely with that sentence. He let the door shut behind him. "Or was it the kiss itself?" he added, tucking his hands in his pockets. "I'm guessing it's been a long time since another man kissed you like that," he said.

Like that?

Try never.

But the arrogance of him saying that to me. How dare he assume that—

"I know it has been for me."

I blinked and backed up a step, the fire draining from my fury.

"What?"

Leo shook his head as he closed the space between us. His moves were slow, yet the energy coming off him was palpable. He pulled one hand from a pocket and tucked a rogue lock of my hair behind my ear, letting his finger trail down the side of my neck.

I inhaled sharply, every nerve ending in my body reaching in his direction like flowers to the sunlight when I should be shutting this shit down. I opened my mouth to do just that, but then that finger traced up along my jawline, and all my breath left me.

"What the fuck am I doing?" he asked under his breath as if it wasn't meant to be out loud. "What the hell is it with you?" he said, his voice gravelly. "You make me crazy."

"I know the feeling," I breathed.

I wasn't sure the words even made it out of my mouth or if they stayed lodged in my head. It didn't matter. All that mattered was the entrancing heat of his fingers on my skin and the nagging memory that this was not the right direction. I was supposed to be shutting it down. Saying good night. Telling him to take his know-it-all crap and kiss my ass.

"I can't get you out of my damn head," he said. "You make me—need to be near you," he said, his brows furrowing into a frown as his gaze followed his finger along the underside of my bottom lip. "Damn it, I don't do that. I *can't* do that."

I was dizzy with his touch and fighting the urge to let my fingers do some walking of their own.

"Do what?" I asked.

"Need," he said, his eyes finally landing on mine.

I felt that look in my bones and everything inside me turned liquid.

"Then why are you out here?" I asked.

He shook his head slightly, both hands moving up to my face. Fuck, that was more than I could bear. My fingers found his shirt and tugged him closer.

"Because I never do what's good for me," he said, his mouth achingly close. "I make horrible choices."

"So do I," I said, drunk on his nearness, on the feel of his hands moving on my skin. "I spent six hundred dollars—"

"So that I wouldn't touch another woman," he finished, his head detouring to brush his lips against my ear. *Oh, God.* Instinctively, I leaned my head to give him more access and he dragged light kisses down my neck while one hand dropped to pull me snugly against him. All my breath left me in a whoosh as his scruff scratched across my skin. I had no words, no utterances, no—coherent thoughts. "That was the hottest thing I've ever seen," he breathed against my skin.

"You might want to get out more," I whispered, pulling that sinful silk shirt free of his pants.

A laugh rumbled through him, but it turned to a growl when I slid my hands up under his shirt to feel the really good back for myself. It didn't disappoint. Muscles rippled under my touch and his hands came up into my hair, pulling it down in a tumbled mess.

"God help me, I should stop right now but I can't help myself," he said. "And I damn sure shouldn't kiss you, but fuck if I'm not about to do it again."

The pull was too much. His lips were right there, his hands were hot and sliding maddeningly along my throat, and I was humming like a friggin' power plant. I shouldn't do this. I shouldn't want to. I was too green. Too newly damaged.

That ship had sailed. My body didn't care.

I pulled him to me as his mouth came down on mine and I kissed him like there was no tomorrow. Like I wasn't tainted goods. Like I had every right to be making out with the most gorgeous man in town, just days after leaving someone else at the altar.

I needed, too. I needed so badly.

Leo lifted me effortlessly and I wrapped my legs around him, lost in the sensations and no longer caring about choices or rights or the way things should be. All that mattered was this man's hands on my body and the delicious way they roamed my skin. With reverence and awe and barely restrained hunger. The low moan that escaped his throat when his hands slid up under my dress to grip my bare ass sent shivers of desire through my core.

He sank onto one of the loungers, pulling my legs around him so tightly I could feel every straining stitch over his zipper. His mouth was hot and hungry against my skin, searching out my cleavage. His fingertips dug into the soft flesh of my ass as I moved against him, the tiny swatch of fabric from my thong no match for it, serving only as friction against an already maddening build.

"Leo," I breathed, unable to stop the rhythmic motion.

"Slow down, baby," he said, his mouth soft and wet against the inside of my right breast. "Fuck, you taste so sweet." Unzipping my dress just enough to pull down the front and expose my tits, he palmed a breast and took my nipple into his mouth with a groan.

Lightning shot through my body as his tongue sucked me and flicked in fast little shots, sending white-hot heat to that place rubbing against his giant hard-on. My back arched as I grabbed his head and rode him harder.

"Fuck, Leo, that's not slowing down," I breathed. "Please—" I gasped as the pressure mounted almost unbearably. "Please!"

His fingers slid from my thighs to under my soaked panties, making me cry out as his fingers mimicked what his tongue was doing on my nipple. Circling, tugging, teasing, making love to my clit with his touch.

"Fuck, you're so wet," he growled against my breast, his voice sounding like he was in pain.

My fingers fisted in his hair, pulling his mouth away from me as I arched without trying to. Nothing I was doing was a choice anymore as I gyrated against his fingers shamelessly. Primal noises escaped my throat, my body started to tremble, and my toes curled under almost uncomfortably as a fireball exploded inside of me, rushing to every surface, every nerve ending, every appendage like a speeding train, bursting from everywhere at once.

My guttural screams filled my ears, and I didn't care. Nothing had ever felt better than this. No orgasm I'd ever given myself could measure up, and nothing from Jeremy or anyone before him had ever come close.

He caressed me until my release was over and I opened my eyes.

Before me, was a rough-and-tousled-looking Leo, his shirt halfway unbuttoned, his jaw clenched, his eyes heavy with desire after giving me the screaming orgasm of a lifetime. It was possibly the sexiest view ever.

"*That* is now the hottest thing I've ever seen," he said, his voice gravelly.

CHAPTER SEVENTEEN

What does one say after having one's mind blown? Because "thank you" just seemed a little short.

As blood slowly reentered my brain, the checkmarks started making themselves apparent. As in—it was his turn. But when I reached for his zipper, he covered my hand with his own.

"Not tonight," he said, his breathing still labored.

"What?"

"Another time," he said.

I lifted an eyebrow, unable to decide if I should be confused or insulted. Me being me, panic took the lead.

"Hey, you don't have to make excuses," I said, pulling my dress back up to cover my breasts. "If you don't want to—"

"Oh, I very much want to," he said, catching my hands in his. Lowering one back to his bulging hard-on, he pressed my hand against it and held it there. "In case there's any doubt."

Desire churned low in my belly again. I may be satisfied, but I still hadn't seen the goods, and now that the window had been opened, it was on my agenda. And he felt so amazing.

"Then let me make you feel as good as I just did," I said, stroking him as I pressed a kiss against his throat.

He gave a moment's pause before cursing and pulling me back.

"Not tonight," he repeated, his voice strained. "This was for you."

"For me?"

"To show you that some men enjoy doing the work," he said, bringing my head down to his and lightly tasting my lips. *Oh. My. God.*

"Leo, you don't have to prove that," I said.

"I know I don't," he said. "But you don't understand how fucking beautiful that was to watch. To see you totally let go, and not care. That was worth giving up a hundred orgasms for."

"I don't think so," I said.

"Okay, maybe ten."

I laughed and kissed him again. "How about none, and you watch me ride your dick until you blow?"

His eyes closed, and I thought I had him.

"How about we wait until I have you warm and naked in my bed, wet and throbbing and begging me to fuck you?" he said. His eyes opened slowly, heavy with desire, and that was okay, because my power of speech was disintegrated. He lifted my hand to his lips and kissed it softly. "And then I will. Any way you want. Slow. Hard. Whatever will make you come apart like you just did."

I was there. The wet and throbbing was there. The naked could happen pretty quickly, and the begging wouldn't be a problem. Holy fuck.

It was the hottest, weirdest, twisted give and take. He was giving me this night of total abandon to show me how a guy can give, but taking back the reins in not letting me do him. And then telling me how our next time will be, but completely at my whim.

I should have been put off. I was absolutely turned on.

And there was a next time.

Sweet Jesus.

* * * *

My body wouldn't stop buzzing. All night. All morning. Getting ready to help out the diner at their Taste Test Fest booth at the Lucky Charm. Because—food. And because a tiny part of me hoped that Leo would show and he'd be nice and I'd be charming and Nick would realize that having his brother in his life was important.

It was a long shot. But to get back to the buzzing—I had something seriously bad going for someone I had no business being bad with. And my body couldn't wait for more.

In other words, I was being me. Doing what I wasn't supposed to do. Shocking. And I dressed cute in a black rhinestone-studded tank top with a matching painter's cap over a ponytail, clunky chunky wooden slip-on wedges, and four different mismatched bracelets up my left arm. And that part made me heady when I did it.

Gabi jogged over to me—like, literally jogged, sneakers and all—and stopped to grab hold of the booth like she might hurl.

"What are you doing?" I asked.

She held up a finger in lieu of words as she bent over and held her side.

"Don't puke on Nick's food," Lanie said, walking up with a huge hot tray of finger foods and wraps. "I'm fighting that already, and one of us is enough."

"Why are you running?" Allie asked, coming up behind Lanie with another tray. "I don't see any wild animals or gun-wielding psychopaths. That would be *my* only reason."

"Changing things up," she wheezed. "Health—feel—good."

"Yeah, that looks awesome," Lanie said, heading back to Nick's truck for more.

"Should you be carrying that stuff?" I said, following her.

"She's pregnant, not broken," Allie said, rolling her eyes with a grin as she twisted her dark hair up into a hair tie and handed me a pan of dessert samples and grabbed a meat tray. "Not that I haven't heard that ten times already this morning."

"Well, Nick has probably heard twice that," Lanie said. "So everyone should get the message," she added in a playful whisper.

"So, are you wishing for one or the other at this point?" I asked as we carried the loot to the booth.

Lanie shrugged. "Nick already has a grown daughter, so a son would be nice." She smiled to herself. "But having had neither, I'm good with either one."

"Daughters are awesome," Allie said. "But drama. Wish for a boy."

"I'm so happy for y'all," I said. "And Leo—"

I stopped, unsure what the boundaries were with Lanie.

"I know," she said, smoothing her shirt after she placed the tray. "That's a hot mess. I wish Nick would stop being so hardheaded about that."

"Leo is over the moon about the baby," I said. "And he wants his brother back so badly, but I don't know enough about what happened between them to have any answers."

"Girl, I'm married to one of them and I don't know much more," she said. "And most of that came from his ex-wife, so that tells you how closed off he is on this."

"Wow."

"All I know is that Leo was probably into some shady things, but it kept them in clothes and food," she said. "I think he disappeared around the time Nick found out that Tara was pregnant, or right after Addison was born—I'm not sure." She shook her head. "He doesn't talk about it, so I don't know if it was connected."

"Interesting," I said. "Leo did say that he let Nick down."

"It's so, so frustrating."

"Family means everything to him," I said, starting to hear myself.

"Are you getting to be friends, you and Nick's brother?" Allie asked. There was a knowing tone in her question, and my first response was to nix it.

"I guess," I said, averting my eyes. "Friends. Yeah."

Friends with benefits? No. That wasn't me. Then what the hell were we doing? And when did I become Leo's advocate with his family?

"I can tell," Lanie said. "And I'm glad. You're both new here, and it's nice to have that. He seems so much like Nick, too, it just breaks my heart that they aren't acting like brothers. This little person is going to need an uncle," she added, patting her belly. "Maybe we can keep working on them," she said, touching my arm and then pointing off in the distance. "And speaking of which, there's him and Addison."

She excused herself and wandered off to meet her husband and what looked to be a gorgeous female version of the McKane genes, and I turned to where Gabi was sitting in a folding chair gulping down water and stealing a miniature cream cheese wrap drizzled with strawberry remoulade.

"Hey, this is for customers," Allie said, picking another one up for herself and popping it into her mouth with a giggle. "God, that's good," she said around a mouthful.

"So good," Gabi agreed.

"This is a lot of food," I said.

"Well, the Blue Banana has been at the heart of Charmed for as long as anyone can remember," Allie said. "Certainly *my* whole lifetime. So what better way to showcase the Taste of Charmed—Taste Test Fest—whatever they're calling it now—"

"Aren't you the queen?" Gabi asked on a chuckle.

"Can you tell I don't check my e-mail?" she said under her breath. "But anyway, I thought it would be a great opportunity to sample some of Nick's newer dishes."

"Absolutely," I said. "So is the diner closed with him here?"

"Nah, we have the second string in play," she said on a laugh. "Which he's trained so well, it's hard to tell the difference. I'll head back in a bit, and he's coming in to close tonight, so they get to work on their own for a minute and he gets a break. Win-win."

Allie headed off to Nick-and-Lanie-land, and there was a cute, perky-looking blonde girl-woman darting her eyes between the food display and the back of Gabi's head.

"Hi," I said. "Are you looking for Gabi?" I said, pointing.

The girl looked like I might have just shot her, as she backed up a step and shook her high ponytail. Gabi turned around to see, and the look that washed over her told me all I needed to know. She turned back around without saying a word, but it wasn't about to be that simple. A tall man with thinning blonde hair and a bright red shirt walked up to join her, tapping something into his phone.

"Oh, man, stuffed peppers," he said. "I haven't had these in forever."

Gabi's eyes closed and she shook her head before scraping her chair around.

"That's because they give you the screaming shits," she said. "So go ahead, Bart, have a few. Have the whole pan."

The look on his face was priceless, as all the color from his shirt washed into his face.

"Gabs."

"Gabi," she corrected. "I don't have to put up with that horrid nickname anymore. What does he call you, Dixie? Dick?"

"Gabi, I don't want it to be like this between us," Dixie said, lowering her voice. "We were friends once."

"We—were not," Gabi said, standing. "I was your babysitter once. I pulled peas out of your nose more than once. I think I bought you your first bra. And I definitely got you the job with my husband. Friends?" She shook her head. "No, I'm pretty sure friends don't fuck their friends' husbands on their desks. I'm sure I heard that bullet point somewhere."

Dixie's pretty blue eyes filled up like she was the sweet innocent victim, and she walked away, hugging her arms to her chest.

Bart stayed and just looked at Gabi like he was so disappointed.

"Was that really necessary?" he asked.

"Are you really that stupid?" she countered.

He gave her one last look, glanced down at the peppers, and snatched one before walking off after Dixie.

"I hope it makes him squirt fire for a week," she said, landing back in her chair and turning it my way. Her eyes shut tight as she tapped a foot madly, her chin quivering.

I grabbed a napkin and pressed it into her hand, letting her squeeze mine discreetly where no one could see, till she got it under control.

"You okay?" I whispered finally.

Gabi took a deep breath and let it out slowly.

"I'm good," she said, blowing out a second breath. "I don't even *like* him anymore," she said. "Why do I still feel gutted every time I see them?"

"Because they hurt you," I said. "They did this, and had no consequences, and now they move on while you're still trying to glue your life back together."

She stared at me. "That's good."

I chuckled wearily. "Yeah, I'm great at figuring out other people's lives," I said. "Not so good at my own." Gabi took a long drink and peered at me over her water bottle. "Yes?"

"Speaking of," she said.

"We weren't," I said. "We were speaking of you."

"And now that's over, so it's your turn," she said.

"I really don't need a turn."

"You and Leo, now?" she began anyway, leaning back in her chair and kicking one ankle up on a knee. "You look adorable today. Have we progressed past the lap dance kiss?"

Visions of him in all black, sucking my nipple and fingering me to a mind-splitting orgasm floated across my head. And everything in me went hot.

"Why do you ask?" I said, picking up a to-go menu to fan myself.

Both eyebrows raised. "Oh, my."

"What the hell is wrong with me, Gabi?" I asked, closing my eyes.

"You mean besides dumping half a paycheck to keep a skank from groping your guy?" she asked.

My throat closed up. "He's not my guy."

"Did you consummate the purchase?" she whispered.

"No, but he consummated me," I said.

Her jaw dropped. "Shut up."

"And now I'm that girl," I said. "One toe-curling orgasm, and I'm acting like—like—"

"Like he's your guy," she finished.

I slapped a hand over my eyes. "I hate my life."

"He curled your toes?" she said. "You're my hero. I'm in awe."

He fucking curled everything. I blew out a breath.

"How's the business plan?"

"Are you kidding me?" she sputtered, leaning forward. "No, no, no, no, we aren't talking business plans right now."

"Yes, yes, we are," I said, widening my eyes as my scalp broke out in a sweat. "Because we have incoming."

"Shit, again?" she asked, looking around and landing on an approaching Nick and company. But I wasn't even talking about them. I was honed in on what was strolling up to my right.

Leo, Sully, and Carmen walked up to the booth, the guys heavily into conversation while Carmen's face lit up to see the desserts. All I could think of was that Nick and Leo were arriving at the same time. On Nick's turf again, sort of. And saying that's all I could think of was a boldfaced lie. Because the second his eyes landed on me, my composure shattered and splintered off into nineteen different directions of steamy what-the-fuckedness.

It wasn't going to stop there. Because in the next millisecond, my eyes automatically tuned in to the man coming up between them, still probably fifty yards out. I'd know him in a crowd even if I was struck with amnesia. He could dress exactly the same as everyone else, and yet would never fail to stand out as the cooler, shinier, richer, more together person than anyone else. With an expression on his face that said he was on a mission.

"Fuck," I whispered, feeling the familiar anxiety wind its cold tendrils around my neck and braid themselves through my shoulder muscles. He found me.

By some strange stretch of magic, Leo read my face, because he turned to follow my gaze, his expression changing as he saw Jeremy. His jaw muscles tightened.

"Uncle Leo!"

The squeal from Nick's daughter yanked me out of what was becoming a slow-motion montage. A fresh-faced young woman with all the best features of her father ran around to the other corner of the booth, winding through the growing crowd and literally stopping Jeremy's steps as she crossed in front of him to throw her arms around Leo. I instinctively folded my arms over my chest.

He said he'd *kept tabs*? He clearly kept more than that.

Leo laughed and hugged her back, but his eyes were distracted, panning from his brother to me and clearly wanting to look behind him before—

"Uncle Leo?" Jeremy said, stepping up to the booth, directly in front of me, a smile on his face as he watched them. "That's so domestic of you."

I frowned in confusion over the cold sweat taking over my skin. What the hell was he babbling about now?

"Jeremy, what are you doing here?" I asked quietly, but he wouldn't look my way, focusing instead on the two of them.

"Good to see you, baby," Leo said, kissing Addison's forehead and pulling her to his side, almost protectively. Carmen stroked her hair as if feeling the need to double-team it.

Nick came through the booth as the straightest route. He didn't look angry so much as bewildered.

"Addison," he said. "How do you—when did you meet Leo?"

"I don't know," she said, looking confused by the question. "Last year?"

"Six months ago," Leo supplied quietly.

She pointed at him playfully, looking like a pixie next to a giant. She was tall, but tiny in build.

"Evidently six months ago," she said, chuckling. "I was in on break and Mom and I saw him at the store. He came over for dinner."

Nick smiled tightly. "How nice that you told me."

She widened her eyes. "You tend to get a little tense on the subject."

Nick blew out a breath and looked at Leo. "Tara told you where I was."

"Was it a secret?" Leo asked.

"You didn't think that was worth mentioning?" Nick asked. "That you'd been back home and had dinner with my ex-wife and my daughter?"

"In the two almost-conversations we've had?" Leo said. "No. Didn't come up." He tugged Addison to his other side, farther away from Jeremy, who I noticed had been soaking the exchange up like a sponge. "How's school been?" he asked her.

Whew. I had to let out a breath. She was right. Every time the two of them shared air, the tension could be sliced open. I could just imagine the subject-matter attitude after years of no contact.

Plus, Jeremy wasn't helping. Nick might have no clue about who he was, but the vibes he put out were toxic. He wasn't even looking at me, but my blood pressure was spiking by the minute, just standing two feet from him.

"Awesome," Addison said, narrowing her eyes as she glanced back and forth between them. "Did I tell you about the student center? It's built around a natural amphitheater, so there's these natural rock stages and people just jump up there and do random shi—*stuff* when the mood strikes them."

Leo chuckled as he watched her, turning his back more and more to Jeremy, as though cutting him off from her. I couldn't figure that out. But possibly more important, Nick appeared to stand down. He backed up a step, let out a slow breath, and tapped on the table.

"Get you some food, Add," he said, and then looked at his brother as if he had to push a button to do it, but he did it. "You too, Leo. There's more than enough."

Wow.

That was a moment. I got goose bumps. I got goose bumps for my guy who wasn't my guy but fuck if it didn't feel eerily similar to what him being my guy would feel like. It was probably for Addison's sake, but the reason didn't matter. For this one little moment between them, there was peace in the valley.

"Hi," Lanie said, stepping up beside me and smiling at Jeremy. "Welcome to the Blue Banana Grille—outdoors! Help yourself to the samples."

Jeremy smiled at her and then finally at me, his eyes panning my appearance with the subtle flicker of disapproval that I would never miss.

"Micah, you've been here what—a week?" he said, his words slow and measured. My skin crawled at the lick of something sinister in his tone. "What do you recommend?"

"Oh, you know Micah?" Lanie asked.

Jeremy held out a hand. "I do. I'm the guy she screwed over to come here. Jeremy Blankenship, nice to meet you."

And just like that, the peace went *poof.*

CHAPTER EIGHTEEN

The smile froze on Lanie's face as Jeremy shook her hand, but her eyes went wary.

"I see," is all she said.

"Jeremy," I hissed.

Oh, my God, if I could have crawled under that table and disappeared into the pavement, I would have in a heartbeat. I was mortified.

No.

I was livid.

"Don't get me wrong," he was saying from somewhere in my blood-red haze, "I get wanting to come here." He made a show of looking around. "You've been wanting to ever since this thing popped up, haven't you, babe?"

"Please don't do this," I said under my breath. It felt like every possible heat molecule in the air joined up to hover over my skin. "Jeremy, let's walk off somewhere and talk, just me and you."

"No."

Leo's voice cut through the air, and Jeremy's head whipped to the side. "Excuse me?"

"She's not going anywhere alone with you."

Fuck, shit, hell, if I could have strangled Leo with a bacon wrap, I would have. My eyes filled with angry tears as the frustration rose to the surface. If my head could have erupted into flame, it would have.

Jeremy stared at Leo, his eyes going hard. He tossed a pepper into his mouth and nodded toward Nick as if Leo had vanished. "You must have been cooking your whole life. This is good stuff." He tilted his head a little. "Nah, you look like you did construction or something before this."

Nick's eyes narrowed. "You knew that before you got here. I worked for your dad, didn't I?"

Jeremy shrugged. "Lucky guess." He snagged another. "My girl loves food—I can see the appeal—but maybe your loser brother she's fucking on the side is the real reason she's still here."

It was like a wall of men shored up at once. Nick filled the space at my left, Sully loomed behind Jeremy, and Leo had Addison behind him and was nose to nose with Jeremy without me ever seeing him move.

"Sir, you need to leave," Nick said, his tone leaving no room for interpretation.

"And keep going," Leo said, his voice little more than a growl. "You have no business here."

"And you do?" Jeremy seethed, his lip curling. "Was it you on the bike? Was that your grand plan?"

Grand plan? What the hell was he talking about?

"It's over, man," Leo said. "She made her decision."

"Which *she* are you talking about?" Jeremy seethed.

"Walk away."

"Stop it," I said through my teeth.

Everything stopped as my words, laced with rage and hurt and mortification, sliced through the air. I was shaking, I was sweaty, and tears were streaking down my face.

"All of you, stop this," I said, my voice trembling with anger. "I'm right here. Nobody needs to talk for me or about me. I apologize that my business has just vomited all over yours, and that my *ex* has been so fucking rude, but I will deal with it." I sucked in a shaky breath, glaring at Jeremy. "How dare you come here and do this. You want to talk to me, you do it in private like a decent human being."

"You want to spout decency now?" he said, his voice rising as he came halfway over the table toward me, veins popping in his forehead. "With you spreading your legs for this piece of shit you barely know—"

A flash of motion at my left made me gasp as suddenly Nick had Jeremy by the front of his collar.

"You keep coming over this table, sir," Nick said in a low voice, "and you'll be in my world. I have the feeling that my brother won't hesitate to shove you the rest of the way."

"Nick," I heard Lanie and Allie say in unison.

My brain was shutting down. I couldn't process the embarrassment, the horror, the everything of it all. These people I'd barely gotten to know were swimming in a pool of my toxic waste, all because of my choices. I met Leo's eyes over Jeremy's form. He was glazed-eyed and primed and he couldn't see that that was exactly what I didn't need. I felt hands on me. Gabi gripping my hand. Lanie and Carmen with their hands on my back and shoulders. Telling me they had me. I was poisoning them and they had me. How was that right?

"This how you treat all your customers?" Jeremy said in a tight voice.

"Not usually," Nick said, his voice smooth. "But you bring out the love, what can I say." He set Jeremy back on his side of the table.

"You're going to regret that," Jeremy said to Nick before sneering down at me and turning it on Leo. Sniffing him. "You smell like you used to smoke," he said softly. "Nasty habit." He gave Leo a long look and turned to go, then glanced back. "Since you seem to like my worn-out leftovers, be my guest. I'm done with her."

The move was up and done before I could process the smacking sound. The sound of Leo's fist slamming into Jeremy's mouth.

"No!" I screamed, along with the various other shrieks and yelps and gasps from others.

Jeremy staggered, as Sully caught him and stood him upright with a look that dared him to so much as blink. He came up with a maniacal bloody grin and a chuckle to match.

"You've always been so easy," he whispered, laughing again as he shook Sully off and preened like a psychotic peacock. He winked and pointed as he walked off. "Be seeing you."

It was like a bad dream, as everyone turned to look at me. A bad dream that made no sense whatsoever. I put my hands to my face and shook my head.

"I'm so sorry," I said. "I'm—"

"Oh, my God, I'm so glad you dumped him," Gabi said. "What a tool."

Hot tears kept burning my eyes. "Y'all. I'm sorry."

"Why are you apologizing?" Leo said.

I stared at him through my tears. "Because he's not going to let this go. Why did you go all caveman and tell him he couldn't talk to me? Who appointed you my spokesperson?"

Leo stepped back as if I'd slapped him, and part of me was sorry for that in front of everyone, but damn it, he'd undone every ounce of personal progress I'd made with myself the last week.

"Are you fucking kidding me right now?" Leo asked.

I laid a hand on my chest and told myself to breathe. My heart was racing so fast, I could barely catch a breath.

"No, I'm not," I said, struggling to get the irritating tremor out of my voice. "Look, I appreciate the save-the-girl routine and all, but I don't need saving."

I closed my eyes and blew out a breath. "I realize that seems contrary to our short history, but I really don't need anyone fighting my battles or slaying my dragons, or punching out my ex because he insults me."

I was gulping for air, and I grabbed the table before I hyperventilated myself into passing out.

"He's a maniac, Micah. You let him talk to you that way?"

"There's no *letting* Jeremy Blankenship do anything," I said. "I can take his insults. What I *can't* take is someone ignoring me when I say to stay out of it and let me take care of my own damn business."

Leo narrowed his eyes at me like I was speaking Russian.

"I was helping you!" he said, every visible muscle taut and ready to spring, his eyes dark and angry.

"I didn't need that kind of help!" I cried. "It's not your fight!"

He chuckled bitterly and pointed at me.

"You're damn right about that."

I watched him turn and disappear into the growing crowd, tears still choking my breaths. Nick watched him as well, until he finally turned and held out a hand to Addison.

"Come back here with us, baby," he said, running his other hand over his face. "Get out of the crowd."

"What was that?" she asked, her face pale.

"That was the kind of man you don't want," I said, grabbing a napkin and patting at my face. "I'm sorry you had to see it."

"That was a blowhard," Carmen said. "His dad is just like him, just not as good looking to get away with it as often. Guys like that are all talk."

I shook my head slowly, blindly arranging things that didn't need arranging.

"I don't think so," I said softly. I wasn't even sure the thought had made it to my lips.

"Why?" Gabi asked.

"Because he didn't win," I said. "Jeremy always wins. He always has the last say."

"He didn't on your wedding day," Lanie said.

"Exactly," I said. "Which is why he was here. To put me in my place."

"And then my brother put him in his," Nick said. He frowned as though thinking hard. "I was a grunt on the crew, so I never met any of the owners, but I do remember when the company shut down. There was a fire or something."

"Jeremy's family home," I said.

Nick's eyes went far away. "Something's off about this."

"Maybe you should go check on Leo," Lanie said to her husband.

"It won't go well," he said, rubbing at his eyes.

"Do it *anyway*," she said. "He's your brother, Nick. Put this crap behind you and move on."

"I'll go," I said, breathing deeply and fanning myself with the napkin. "It's my fault Jeremy was here in the first place."

"Stop," Gabi said. "No."

I looked at her, wiping my eyes. "What?"

"Stop blaming yourself for what that Neanderthal says or does," she said. "You did the right thing. His choices are his."

"I second that," Carmen said.

Lanie raised a hand. "Ditto." She put a hand on her belly. "And I count for two votes."

* * * *

I walked to the florist shop with trepidation, not even knowing if that's where Leo went. This damn walking everywhere thing—he had a motorcycle and still walked just about anywhere, so there was nothing to look for.

It was a start, however. I went inside, and Drew was at the counter.

"Leo come in?" I asked.

"Boy, did he," she said. "All grunts and steam. Who pissed in his Cheerios?"

I sighed. "That would be me."

"Good luck with that."

I peered up the stairs. "Yeah."

I repeated those words to myself as my wooden wedges clomped up the stairs and down the hall and passed my door the four steps to stand in front of his. I would have thought he might have gone out to our roof spot—and I gritted my teeth that my head had just called it *our roof spot*—but his door was ajar. Like enough that I could see in.

And see everything.

Two big duffel bags sat askew, one spilling out onto the floor, one crumpled up against a wall, its contents falling out and scattered. The bag of motel shampoos was ripped open and the bottles were all over the living room. Was he living like that? Surely not. The man that wiped down a bathroom nearly to perfection after using it wouldn't live like—my heart jumped into my throat. Was he robbed?

I pushed open the door before clearheaded logic could tell me, *Hey, stupid, what if the crime is still happening?* But just as that thought could seep in, there he was. Sitting on his couch, leaned over with his elbows on his knees, staring at the floor. In front of him on the coffee table were the petrified cigarette and a lighter.

He glanced up at the sound, but then resumed his position when he saw it was me. That was fulfilling.

"Leo, what's going on?" I asked.

"Just go," he said, still facing the floor.

"What happened in here?" I asked, stepping inside.

"You listen well," he said under his breath.

"Yeah, about as well as you do," I said, my irritation simmering back at the surface. He looked up at me again as if he was measuring what it might involve to throw me out a window. "So deal with it and talk to me."

"Talk to you."

"That would be what I said."

He stood up. "You also basically just told me to go to hell out there, so what is it you're wanting me to *talk to you* about now?"

"Look, I'm sorry that Jeremy has it out for you because of me," I said. Leo raked his fingers through his hair with something that sounded like a growl and turned around as if he needed to keep his hands from throwing something. "And I know that you are prewired to go all alpha protector and all, but—"

"I am a man, Micah," he said, whirling back around.

"Fully clear on that," I said, hands on my hips.

"I don't have much," he said. "But what I have is important to me. All I can do is look out for the things I care about—the best way I can."

I had something ready to say but it died halfway to my mouth.

Did he just say that he cared about me?

Did he just—

He shook his head and walked across the room.

"My life has been simple," he said, grabbing a pen from a table and flicking it open and closed as he turned and headed back the opposite way. "Maybe not the happiest, maybe not the greatest, but that was okay." The floor ran out and back he went the other way again, flipping that pen over and under his fingers like a magician. "I made my bed a long time ago and I've had to live with it."

"Meaning?"

He stopped pacing and tossed the pen behind him, sending it clattering off into the kitchen. Okay. Maybe he did live like that.

"Meaning that you weren't in the plan."

CHAPTER NINETEEN

Was that—how—how was I to take that? I stood there and blinked and tried to process the million different ways that could go, because me being me, I was about to go south with it.

"I—didn't exactly *plan* for you, either, you know?" I said, folding my arms over my chest.

Those eyes that were destined to kill me landed with precise accuracy, stealing my breath.

"Meaning?" he asked.

"Mean—meaning that I have this special gift of falling for people who need to dictate my life, control everything I do, tell me what to say, what to do, what to—"

"I have no interest in any of those things," Leo said, walking slowly toward me. My words faltered and my heart sped up at every inch he came closer. "Zero. I know how important independence is." He stopped a foot from me. Touching distance if I wanted it to be. "What it means to have no one pulling your strings."

"Then what was that?" I said, pointing behind me. "Leo, I know you're a man, but that doesn't mean go charging forward, sword in hand, every time someone in your life has a problem."

"It does for me," he said under his breath. It was quiet but the meaning was deafeningly loud. My fingers itched to reach out, and I balled them into fists. I couldn't afford it. If I gave in—if I touched him, felt his heat, pulled him to me—my will would snap. "That doesn't take away your power, Micah. It doesn't lessen you. It just means I've got your damn back."

I could hear my breathing in my ears as his words sunk in.

"Why?" I whispered.

It was all I could muster. Why would he want my back? Why would he fight my fights? Why would he want all the drama that came with me, disguised as luggage but really filled with rocks?

He was shaking his head. "I don't know."

"Okay."

"Seriously," he said, lifting his hands as though to touch my face, but dropping them. Blowing out a breath. "You—are going to be the death of me."

My skin tingled at his closeness, at the intensity radiating off him in waves.

"That's not ominous at all," I managed.

"Everything about you is reason for me to leave," he said, his words so soft I wasn't sure he meant for them to be aloud.

I tore my eyes away from him to dart a quick glance around the mess of the room.

"Is that what you were doing?"

"For maybe a full minute," he said. "Before I couldn't go through with it and threw it all at the wall."

I blinked. "What stopped you?"

"Stupidity."

I chuckled, nervous laughter softening the edge. "Don't sugarcoat it."

"I'm not," he said, closing his eyes for a beat. "I don't do this. But you—" When his eyes opened, the half-second of vulnerability I saw there went straight to my heart. "You make me weak. You keep me off balance. And of all the damn people to—" He inhaled deeply and let it go.

"Care about?" I said. I actually said it.

Fuck a duck.

"Fall for?" he countered.

My words. Sweet God, I'd said that. My heart slammed so hard, I gasped.

An exhausted sigh escaped his throat, and he narrowed his eyes.

"Fucking death of me," he said, his voice thick.

"Ditto."

My hands won. Or one of them did. It landed on his arm, which spurred his to move up mine, which sent my other hand up his chest. He inhaled sharply and I couldn't stop there. All I could see was his mouth and I wanted it more than any logic could fight.

"Roman-off," he whispered as my hand wound up into his hair, his breath brushing my lips.

"Stop talking."

His lips claimed mine and my bones turned liquid under his hands. I melted into him, kissing Leo with every single fiber of my being. Soft, slow, wet, fast, needing, pulling all of him to me as tightly as I could, craving his body pressed against mine.

My hat went across the room as he pulled my ponytail free and ran a hand up into my hair, holding my head as he dove deeper into my mouth.

I was delirious with sensations, a moan escaping my throat as his other hand palmed my ass and traveled my thigh, tugging me hard against him as his tongue explored my mouth.

I needed skin. His untucked T-shirt was easy game as I slid my hands down his neck, down his chest, and underneath to the tightness of those abs.

He sucked in through his nose and growled as he tore his mouth from mine and dragged his kisses down my neck, whispering curses against my skin as I pulled his shirt up and forced him back as my mouth landed hot against his chest.

"Fuck," he whispered, his breathing ragged. He yanked his shirt over his head as I dragged my nails over his skin, kissing, tasting, nipping at his chest. "Micah—"

I was spun. In less than a second I was facing the door, and Leo's mouth was hot and wet on my neck, while his hands made quick discard of my tank top and bra.

"Oh, God," I breathed, as I closed my eyes against the dueling sensations of his tongue sucking, tasting my skin, his hands making love to my breasts, and then one of them sliding along my belly, down, down under my shorts, finding my wetness as his hard-on pressed against my bottom. "Oh, God, Leo, yes."

"Fuck, baby, I love how wet you get for me," he growled against my ear.

I was spiraling already, and I had to stop that. It was like being at the world's sexiest theme park, and there were too many rides left. I couldn't stop here again. It was his turn. I reached down and unzipped my shorts, letting him peel them off me, and then I turned back around and ran my fingers along the waistline of his jeans.

"Wet, throbbing, almost naked," I breathed, gripping the top front of his jeans and letting my fingers slide just below. "Put me in your bed and fulfill your promise, McKane."

The look in his eyes was a mix of amusement and primal need. He started walking backward, me holding on to his jeans and following, while he never took his eyes off mine. It was heady. It was terrifying. It was hot as fucking hell.

We paused short of his bed, and I popped the button, reaching for the zipper when his hand stopped me and then both hands cupped my face.

"Look at me," he said. "Micah—"

My head spun at the gear change. What just happened?

"What's wrong?"

A dozen expressions went across his face. "Be sure," he said finally.

Be sure?

If there was anything more certain in all of my lifetime, it was that I wanted to have sex with this man. And of all the thoughts that just ran through his eyes, that didn't feel like the question.

"I am," I said, running my hands up his arms, looking into eyes so dark and sincere that I felt it in the goose bumps on my back. There was something else in that look. Something troubled. "Are you?"

He sighed heavily. "So much," he said, leaning down to kiss me so softly and so thoroughly that my heart tightened in my chest. A burn started behind my eyes as he kissed me like that. It was—real. It was—"God, I want you so much," he said against my mouth. "But there are things—that you don't know—"

Something in me already knew that. Something was inherently present about that, and it was probably important and life altering and faith shattering, but I just couldn't. I couldn't let go of this moment and this man and go to the shattering place right now. It felt like it was now or never. And that right there should have sent me running.

For once, that wasn't even a consideration.

"Would it change my mind about being naked with you right now?" I asked, kissing him, eyes wide open. I needed to see his reaction. I needed the answer to be no.

He looked at me straight on, his hands traveling slowly down my arms. "It might," he said.

The words barely had sound attached to them, but they were mighty.

The burn that had touched my eyes flickered again, and I took a deep breath, blinking back tears. This could hurt me.

Now or never.

"Then don't tell me," I said softly. "All I need to know right now is if you want this," I said, pressing against him. Kissing his chin.

His fingers went up and fisted in my hair. "You have no idea," he said.

"Then show me," I said, unzipping his pants. He was commando. Sweet Jesus.

Everything that straining zipper had promised sprung free into my hands, and Leo swore as I stroked him against my stomach.

"Shit, Micah, get on the bed," he said through his teeth. "Please."

"Now who's begging?" I asked, lowering to my knees and trailing my tongue in a path, skipping the star and beginning again underneath. I kissed up the base, all the way to the end, as Leo grabbed my head with a moan and nearly lost his knees. "Like that?" I whispered against the head, before I took him into my mouth.

"Oh, fuck," he growled, grabbing on to a nearby dresser like a life support. "Mic—Jesus, that's—" His words left him as I made love to his dick with my mouth, sucking, stroking, licking, pulling him in for a taste and then taking all of him to the back of my throat in a rush. "Please, baby," he finally said, pulling me back to my feet. He was breathing heavily, and his eyes had gone wild. He kissed me, hard, picking me up and turning around to lay me on the bed.

"Tell me what you want," he said, lying me back and coming with me, holding himself up on arms that made me want to blow just touching them. He kissed me and then pulled back, kissed me again and pulled back.

"You," I said, pulling him down on top of me and rejoicing in the feel of his weight as I wrapped my legs around him.

Big arms wrapped around my body as we intertwined and he pulled my thighs tighter around him. It was sexy but also intimate. Primal. Familiar. Lovers wrapped up in each other like we'd been making love for years. Hands roaming, finding, pleasing. Mouths hungry and searching. Moving against each other in a mock fuck that had me shaking with need. Everything in my core was tuned to him. Nothing in my life had ever felt like this.

Because—

Falling.

No thought had ever rocked me more.

"Tell me what you want," I breathed, echoing his words. I held his face and looked into his eyes. "Tell me what you need."

"To bury myself in you," he said.

I felt every possible meaning of those words in my bones. All the things I didn't know were about to be buried inside me, too, and my heart wrapped around that. I wound my fingers into his hair, and in one tweak of an angle Leo moved the tiny string of my thong aside and sank into me.

"Oh!" I gasped, as every muscle in my body contracted around him, tensing and releasing as he filled every glorious space.

A breathy growl rumbled in his chest as he pushed inside, cursing into my hair, his fingers digging into my left thigh as he tugged it higher.

"God, you feel—*fuck*—" he grunted out through his teeth. He pulled out of me a little and thrust back in, both of us moaning in ecstasy as he bottomed out.

"Leo," I breathed, raking his back with my nails and then grabbing his ass. Oh, my God, his ass was fabulous, muscled, and delicious as he pumped into me, stretching me out, filling me up.

He lifted my legs higher, almost over his shoulders, pushing deeper and shutting his eyes as he swelled even bigger inside me. I closed mine, too, savoring the sensations. He felt amazing. I wasn't going to come like this. I couldn't remember the last time I had during actual sex. But he was huge and hitting everything, and I could enjoy the ride.

"Talk to me," he said, slowing his rhythm. My eyes popped open. "Tell me what feels good."

"It all feels good," I said, molesting the muscles rippling in his shoulders. He stopped moving. I frowned. "Wait. What are you doing?"

"Talk to me," he repeated. "Where's that woman who screamed up on the roof, riding my fingers?"

My inner muscles clenched at the memory, and he raised an eyebrow.

"There she is," he said, giving me a pump.

"Mmm," I said. "Quit stopping."

"Quit giving up," he said.

I gave him a look. "Anyone ever tell you that teaching during sex kills the mood?"

He dropped his head to nuzzle my neck, and started moving slowly again.

"Touch your breasts," he said against my ear, sending tingles down my neck. "Close your eyes if you need to, but touch them like you want me to." He moved his lips along my cheek and then backed up to sink deeply into me again, his pleasure stopping his words for a beat. "Teach *me*."

Warmth spread over my skin as I paused and watched him. Watched him just enjoying me. Being inside me, being with me, participating, talking, wanting me there fully engaged with him. It was like—going to Greece and finding out you know the language because you've always been Greek and didn't know it. And that was a horrible analogy, but I was just in awe.

I closed my eyes and let my hands move over my body, caressing my breasts, listening to his voice say naughty things to me as he moved steadily in and out of me. I pinched my nipples between my fingers and he growled as I tightened around him.

"Mmm, that's good," he said under his breath.

I let my eyes flutter open and meet his heated gaze as I rolled my nipples between my fingers and imagined him sucking them. Hard.

"Shit, you just got really wet, baby," he said, his jaws tight.

Holy hell, I needed to move. Things were getting maddening in there, and I needed to move on his dick. The way I needed. Now. It had been a long time.

"Leo," I breathed.

"Yes."

"Will you fuck me from behind?"

CHAPTER TWENTY

There was a half-second more of patient touch-yourself-and-I'll-wait Leo before his eyes went heavy with something much more feral.

"Grab the headboard," he said, his voice cracking.

He pulled out and I rolled over, looking over my shoulder at him as I wrapped my fingers around two wooden spokes on the headboard. He peeled my thong off and ran his hands over my ass as I arched for him, and he cursed under his breath.

"You are so beautiful," he whispered. "Hold on, baby."

Leo pushed back inside me, deeper, deeper, making me cry out as he plunged without mercy at a whole different angle. It was the best kind of pain as he dug his fingertips into the soft flesh of my hips, slamming deeply into me, and I found my rhythm, meeting him slam for slam.

It was liberating. It was freeing. I was cursing and begging him to keep going. To slap my ass, grab my hair. I didn't know who the living hell I was, but whoever I was channeling was the damn bomb.

"Micah," he roared. "I—"

It was happening. Something was happening. The pressure was building wayyyyyy off in Never Never Land, and I couldn't stop now. I couldn't feel my arms anymore. They were just a big giant burning sensation, pushing me back and forth, but I wanted it.

"Fuck me harder, Leo!" I cried as the build started in my toes, curling them under and almost cramping my calves. "Oh, God, please—don't stop!"

He was almost splitting me in half and I didn't care. I couldn't care. I couldn't breathe—that had gone by the wayside. I couldn't—all there was, was this phenomenal wave of holy fucking fuck—

Noises that sounded almost inhuman came from my throat as it crashed into me. Wave after wave beat into me and over me and through my bones as Leo continued his punishing pounding, and as my screams hit the downhill range, I felt him bow up like a beast.

My name never sounded so good as it did roaring from his mouth as he finally let his climax go. Again and again, he pounded his orgasm into me, finally ending with a shudder as he lay heaving against my back.

Slowly, we melted together into the bed, sweaty and limp, struggling to catch our breath. Leo rolled onto his back and held up a finger.

"Give me a sec," he managed.

I rolled over, too, drawing oxygen into my lungs. My body burned from every direction, inside and out. I felt like I'd been beaten, drawn, and quartered—or just truly and thoroughly sexed beyond imagination.

Never, ever had I experienced anything like that. I turned my head to peer at his profile, eyes closed, mouth open, pulling in air and probably listening to his heart still racing in his head. No one had ever been willing to work that hard for me—least of all, me.

"I'm sorry you had to run a marathon there," I breathed. "While climbing Mount Everest. And swimming the Atlantic."

He turned his head to me, eyebrows furrowed. "Are you kidding me?" he asked around breaths. "What are you sorry for?"

"That was a lot of—"

"If you say *work*, I'm going to pull your hair," he said. "Again." A chuckle wound its way out of my chest. "Micah, that was unbelievably hot."

"Even though you made yourself wait?"

He lifted a hand and ran a finger along my cheek.

"*Because* I did," he said. "Getting you there was erotic as hell," Leo said. "Watching you come undone." A lazy grin pulled at his mouth. "Watching you enjoy it a little rough."

Heat rushed to my face that had nothing to do with body temperature.

"Yeah, that was new," I said, smiling and looking away.

Leo pulled my chin back so that I faced him again. "Own it, Roman-off."

I chuckled. "I'll work on that." His expression was so soft, so relaxed and happy, that it took my breath away. "Tell me something," I whispered. "Something very few people know about you. Something you love."

"Lying in the grass, looking up at a clear sky," he said.

I smiled. "Really?"

"It's endless," he said. "Pure. Like an open road." His finger traced my bottom lip. "Your turn. What do you love?"

I closed my eyes. "Dirt."

He laughed, and I opened them. "Seriously! And rain. I love a soft rain."
"Have you ever made love in the rain?" he asked.
"I've never even been kissed in a sprinkle," I said. "It wasn't *practical.*"
Leo's brows furrowed. "That's sad."
"You have no idea."
We lay like that for a while, not talking anymore, my fingers loosely laced with his. Each lost in our own basking, our own recovery, our own thoughts.
Thoughts that were creeping in like vines, now that the horniness was sated. I turned his hand over to see his knuckles, which were starting to bruise.
"Do I need to go find you some ice and a towel?" I asked.
"I'm fine," he said.
"Oh, no," I said, kissing his knuckles softly. "You insisted when it was me."
His eyes went unreadable as he watched me do that, as if he was mesmerized. "And I will probably do that again the next time you punch someone," he said finally. "But I'm fine."
Of course my inner ridiculous girl heard "next time" like it was said through a megaphone and I had a squealy moment, but those *things* from before were swimming around us like sharks. It was time to dive in.
"Leo—"
"I told Nick I was working as a bodyguard, that I delivered papers, worked the late shift stacking lumber, that I had to haul potatoes—I really did have to haul potatoes for a while, but mostly I made up excuses for why I was always gone at night."
It was a giant info dump done all on one breath, and I didn't want to break his rhythm, but part of me was terrified. He wasn't just sharing; he was going to eventually get somewhere. And that somewhere was going to be relevant. I held on to his hand, feeling that keeping that connection was important.
"Nick was smart, though," Leo said. "Once he got old enough, he knew what I was doing."
"Which was?" I asked.
"Whatever I had to," he said. "Like I told you the other night. But—"
He stopped. Very much in the same place he had that night. I let the pause be a pause. Let him find his way through it. Suddenly, I was in no hurry.
"Nick got really distant and stayed pissed off at me most of the time, so I'd take off for a few days here and there. Maybe a week. Stay with a girl I was seeing at the time to *teach Nick a lesson.* But I got stupid," he added, his

voice little more than a whisper. "I got greedy. Blind. I stopped listening to myself. The girl had an abusive ex who I didn't know I was working with, and I should have. He spouted about her all the time. I should have clued in, but he was certifiable so I ignored him."

Leo sat up, letting go of me, and slid to lean back against the headboard. I followed suit, trying not to look nervous. Lying about jobs meant he had money he had to explain. Being gone at night meant it was secret and most likely illegal. *Will it make me not want to get naked with you? It might.*

"Nick also met a girl and got all wrapped up in that, got her pregnant, and came to me in a panic." He breathed in slowly. "And all I saw was an opportunity. I had a plan. I always had a fucking *plan*." Leo rubbed at his eyes and then down his face. "My brother—needed me. Put his pride and all his reservations about me aside, and came to me a scared seventeen-year-old kid needing a brother, needing advice, needing help from family, and all I could see was a girl from a wealthy family and the access we had that would make my psycho friends happy." Leo shrugged as if pushing away the memory. "Long story short, Nick threatened to turn me in if I went through with my plan, and we never talked again."

"Never?" I said. "Till now?"

"I left," he said, staring ahead as if he was watching the action in his head. "Addison was born, life went on. I wasn't there."

"What was the plan?" I asked, feeling brazen to ask that. He closed his eyes and I knew we were to the "getting there" part. "Or—why'd you leave?" I added quickly, suddenly not wanting to be there.

"It's the same answer."

It wasn't Leo's voice. I gasped loudly as he and I both jerked to the right toward the voice. The voice belonging to the man leaning casually against the open bedroom door.

"Jeremy!" I yelped, the word cracking like I was a prepubescent boy.

I grabbed a pillow to cover myself, while Leo vaulted over the bed in all his naked glory.

"What the fuck are you doing in my apartment?" he seethed, grabbing a notepad off the nightstand and rolling it. *Use what you have.* "Get the hell out of here."

"Your door was open," he said. "Shit's scattered all over the floor, looks like you were packing or something. Leaving again already? Oh—" he said, holding up a hand as Leo advanced on him. "I don't blame you for stopping to bang my fiancée first. She's a good fuck, isn't sh—"

Leo dropped the pad and his hands were on Jeremy's throat, pinning him to the door frame before the last word was out of his mouth.

"You miserable son-of-a-bitch," Leo growled. "How dare you."

Jeremy coughed and laughed in Leo's face, which made my skin cold. It was creepy and disturbing and—I was going to marry *that*? It was horrifying that he should see me naked with another man, just maybe an hour after accusing me of doing that very thing, but more horrific was the look in his eyes. Like he had checked out.

"Aw, did I insult your girlfriend, McKane?" he said, his voice strained. "Again? That's so cute."

The fact that he knew Leo's name triggered confusion. Should he know that? Had anyone ever said it?

"I should have—"

"Should have what?" Jeremy asked innocently. "Killed me? Turned me in?"

Killed? What movie was I watching?

"What?" I asked.

"Oh, that's right," Jeremy said, glancing at me before locking eyes with Leo. "You didn't get to finish telling her." In a surprisingly fast move of unexpected strength, he broke Leo's hold on his neck and shoved at him, his expression going dark. "Get off me," he seethed. "The smell of her on you is making me sick."

"Get out," Leo barked.

"Oh, I'm going," he said, turning my way to toss my shirt at me. His eyes went angry. "Your clothes evidently fell off in the living room. Believe me, I don't need to see more."

"Why are you even here?" I asked, yanking the tank top on. "What purpose could it possibly serve?"

He threw something else in my direction and I ducked as it landed on the bed with a jingle. My keys.

"My—my car?"

He looked at me with disgust, and I didn't even care. He brought my car. But—

"I filed for a transfer of title," he said. "It shouldn't take long. In the meantime, I want nothing of yours."

I snatched up the keys and hugged them to my chest before he might change his mind.

"Whatever the reason, thank you," I said.

"Don't thank me just yet," Jeremy said, turning to go, passing Leo—who had somehow miraculously found his jeans but never zipped them, standing there looking murderous and menacing. "Your fuck-buddy here still has a story to tell you." Jeremy grinned again, although his eyes were vacant. "Remember, McKane? About the old days, when you were fucking my girlfriend behind my back?" He did a head slap on his forehead. "Kind of like now?"

My blood felt like it ceased moving. Jeremy was the abusive ex. Leo— knew him. He—

"Andrea wasn't your girlfriend anymore, asshole," Leo said.

"Convenient memory," Jeremy said. "So did you forget about the rest, too? How we were going to rob your brother's girlfriend's family mansion, but you pussied out so we hit up my house while my parents were gone— and you wussed out *again* and threatened *me*, so—" He stared Leo down in an overly dramatic pose. "I'm sorry, did I end up telling it? Damn." He slapped him on the shoulder and Leo hit his hand away with his fist. "That's okay. You can tell her about setting my house on fire."

CHAPTER TWENTY-ONE

I felt like a useless doll on a shelf. Or on a bed. A shirt on my top half and a pillow covering the rest, sitting there staring at these two men like they were total strangers.

Because they were.

Who were these people in front of me? One who I was with for almost a decade and lived with and nearly married, telling me—and the other who I'd known for all of a week and somehow felt closer to than I'd ever felt for Jeremy, who had lied to me from the get-go. They knew each other. They'd—done horrible things together. Shared a woman. And Jeremy's house? The—the fire?

Leo?

"You know that's a fucking lie," Leo was saying from somewhere far, far away, bowing up.

I blinked in his direction and saw him towering several inches over Jeremy, looking beautiful with every muscle tight and angry, his jeans hanging loose and open on his hips. I'd just given myself to him heart, mind, body, and soul, and it was the most amazing and intimate thing I'd ever experienced. And now I felt completely violated. Because, yes, *heart* had really come to the party.

And now it pounded so hard and fast, I couldn't breathe deeply. The most fucked-up part? I didn't know who had betrayed me more. The gut-wrenching pain in my sternum gave me some idea, but I couldn't go there. My go-to fight-or-flight instinct couldn't even kick in, because who was I fighting? Who or what was I fleeing?

Both of them. This place. All of it. Scrambling out from under the sheet, I kept the pillow in front of me as I walked around the bed. Let them both watch my ass on my way out, because it was the last they'd see of it.

"I think your memory is fading, old man," Jeremy said.

"And yours is twisted, you psychopath," Leo seethed.

Get out. Leave. That's all that mattered. Survival mode was rising to the surface by leaps and bounds, and I refused to look at either of them as I passed.

Jeremy's hand clasped around my arm and pulled me tight to his side.

"Why?" he asked, his voice a whisper. "How could you just spread your legs for a lying lowlife criminal?" he said, close to my face.

I'd never truly been afraid of Jeremy. Intimidated by him, yes. But this—this was something very different. Actual physical need to escape his presence spread over my skin in a damp chill.

"I almost married one," I said, putting every ounce of repulsion I could muster into my words. "What's the fucking difference?"

Jeremy's eyes flashed with a split moment of hurt, and for that second I was glad. It was an awful thing to feel, but I didn't care. I yanked my arm free and kept walking before I could dare to look at Leo. I had so many thoughts I wanted to hurl in his direction, but I—I just couldn't look him in the eye and have it all confirmed.

My eyes burned with tears as I snatched clothes off the floor. The bra Leo had taken off me with the shirt. The shorts I'd let him peel down. The shoes I'd kicked off. My underwear was forever lost somewhere in his bed, but I wasn't going back in there.

Not ever.

"Look at you now," Jeremy said, coming up behind me. Cold chills went down my back as I wheeled around. "Picking up after yourself like a whore in heat."

"Fuck you," I hissed. "How—how can you be this person? I don't even know you."

His eyes panned me. "I could say the same about you."

"Get the fuck out of my apartment," Leo said, coming up behind him like an angry bear.

"Gladly," Jeremy said, with one last glare at me before walking out, the door still open behind him.

I stared at the empty doorway, at the mess around me, anything other than the man standing just two feet away.

"Micah."

No.

Hot tears spilled down my cheeks as the sound of Leo saying my name sent stabs of pain through my middle. Less than thirty minutes ago, he was whispering my name against my lips, against my skin, roaring it through a monster orgasm. Now—I headed for the door, taking the pillow with me, not caring that my ass was still bared.

"Micah, please," he said, closing the space behind me. "Let me explain."

"Stop—"

"You don't know all the—"

"And why is that?" I cried, spinning around. The stricken look on his face when he saw my tears nearly buckled my knees, but no. I would not be managed. Not anymore. "Granted, you tried to tell me before—" I clamped my lips together hard to stem the emotion threatening to swamp me. I swallowed and took a deep breath. "That's on me. I'll give you that. But you've had plenty of chances to tell me."

"I never did what he's accusing me—"

"Doesn't matter," I said, my voice shaking. "I don't care what you did or didn't do back then, Leo. I care that you looked me straight in the eye—more than once—and lied to me."

"Micah—"

"You saw him when we went to the house," I said. "He saw you. He even said something, and you denied it." Leo's troubled expression swam before me. "And how many times since?" I frowned as another thought—a horrible thought—an evil, hideous thought poked into my brain. "Or did you already know?" I asked on a whisper. "Did you know who I was when I got on your bike? When—"

"No," he said firmly.

I laughed as I blinked the tears free. "How would I know that? How do I know anything? How do I know you weren't there in town stalking him, or wanting to get back at him, and hey…there's his runaway bride… wouldn't she be *outstanding* in that capacity?"

Leo's eyes narrowed. "You think I'm that diabolical?"

I leaned in. "I have no idea," I said slowly.

The look that flashed over his face was pain. I'd struck a nerve. Well—I didn't need to care about that either, because every one of my damn nerves was shredded and left for dead.

"I never wanted to keep lying to you," he said.

"Was there a gun to your head?"

"He framed me, Micah," Leo said, his jaws twitching. "He and his cousin—" He blew out a frustrated breath and raked his hair back. "Yes,

I was an idiot and a criminal and greedy—all of that. I told you that. But *they* were fucking insane."

"I—I don't care, Leo," I said. I was shutting down. I could feel it.

"You have to care," he said, raising his voice. His hands went to hold my face but I pulled away. He blinked and met my eyes, and I saw defeat sink in as he recognized the pulling away in mine. "Okay. Well, let me just tell you this. I'm sorry you feel betrayed right now, but you should be thanking whatever instincts made you run. Because that guy at twenty-one did things to Andrea that would keep you up at night. And he set his own house on fire right in front of me, to prove a point."

"What?"

"With my lighter," he said. "And then threatened to frame Nick for it or hurt him or his—" He shook his head as if pushing that away. "Micah, I've lived every day since, trying to protect my brother by staying out of this shit's shadow. Because he's just crazy enough to follow through."

My head swam so fast, I thought I would be sick. I flashed to Jeremy's drunken mumble at Thatcher's.

When you take the girl, there has to be consequences.

I closed my eyes, feeling the hot tears streak down my face. What kind of person doesn't know who they live with? Who they share a bed with?

"When I saw him the other day, all that mattered was getting you away from him," Leo said. "I didn't want you all up in this."

"Once again," I said, feeling all the strength draining from my bones, "that's my job. Not yours."

"Why?" he said, shoving the word through his teeth. "Are you so fucking invincible that you can't use a little help? Why are you so stubborn?"

I tore my eyes from his and turned away. Focused on one step at a time as the heat from his gaze burned through my back. Or my bare ass. Whatever. It didn't matter anymore. It took me six steps to get to my door, a full minute to search for my door key in my wadded-up shorts, another ten seconds to nod blindly at Wanda as she stopped short coming down the hall with a fresh package of toilet paper.

"Are you okay, honey?" she asked, looking alarmed as her eyes panned my—um—appearance.

"I'm fine," I sniffed. "I'm sorry."

"Don't be sorry," she said, looking toward Leo's door. "Did he—"

"No," I said. "It's—" I shook my head and jabbed my key in the lock blindly. "It's just time for me to probably go back home." I drew a shaky breath as the lock finally gave way and I could turn the knob. "I think."

"Micah, honey," Wanda began.

"I'm sorry you had to see me like this," I said, attempting a smile as I shut the door behind me and turned the lock.

That click hit me like a wall, and with no one to hide it from, the flood took over. I sank to my knees, dropping everything in my arms except the pillow, and I let the sobs wrack my body as I cried into it.

* * * *

I hadn't cried yet. Not really. Not like that. Not a gut-twisting, from-the-soul, ugly crying till your eyes swell closed and you're choking on your own snot kind of cry. I'd never felt the need to. Not over Jeremy, not over the sad state of my life, my lack of a home or car—not anything really other than a few tears my first night in town.

I definitely made up for that.

Crying so hard that I passed out cold on the floor from exhaustion.

I guess I was due? Or could it be that being blatantly betrayed by a man I instantly—*instantly*—trusted and evidently fell for at a bungee-jumping-off-a-cliff degree hit me at every level.

The banging on the door pulled me out of it.

"Fuck!" I choked, my voice channeling a two-pack-a-day smoker.

I jolted up, not knowing what made me do the jolting, drool covering one cheek and my skull trying to revolt. Was I hung over? It certainly felt that way. My eyes wouldn't open. They were stuck, and rubbing them reminded me why.

I pried one golf-ball-sized eye open and blinked, looking down. I was sitting on the floor still naked from the waist down. I moaned and dove back into my pillow, feeling like a jilted teenager.

"Micah!" came a voice with the banging this time, making me jump again.

"Shit," I muttered, getting to my feet while holding my head. "Hang on," I croaked. "Have to find—there they are."

I pulled on my shorts and opened the door to Gabi, who stepped back a step.

"Ho—ly *shit*," she said.

"Whatever, come in," I said, turning back into the room and leaving the door open. "I have to find my eye drops. Give me a second."

"What happened to you?" she asked, following me to my bedroom.

"I had sex with Leo," I said, trying to clear the gravel out of my throat.

"And—he threw you out the window?" she asked.

"No, I just—" I stared at my bed. It looked like any other bed. It looked just like Leo's bed. They probably got them in a two-for-one sale. "Jeremy came—"

"While you were having sex?"

"After," I said. What was I doing? Oh yeah, eye drops. I pulled open a drawer where I kept bathroom things and half-heartedly rummaged. "But we were still naked, so it might as well have been. Hell, he could have been in the living room the whole time, for that matter."

"So—because—how did he get in?" she stammered.

"Leo's door was open."

Gabi blew out a breath. "Can you start at the beginning?"

I closed my swollen eyes. "Door was open when I got there, sex, talk, Jeremy, yelling." I took a shaky breath as I felt the emotion coming back on. "I left." Something odd caught my eye. No sunlight on the other side of the blinds. "It's dark?"

"Girl, it's after nine o'clock," Gabi said.

"What?"

"And I've been calling you for hours," she continued. "I didn't worry much about it until I talked to my mom and she said she saw you half naked and crying in the hallway and talking about leaving, so I drove over here as fast as I could."

I turned to look at her. She'd known me all of a week and was already a better friend than I'd probably ever had.

"Thank you," I said. "For checking on me. I—kind of had a meltdown and then I guess I fell asleep. Why were you calling earlier?"

"To tell you that that Mr. Bailey guy approved my business plan!" she said. "Sully told me at the booth after you left."

"I didn't even know you finished it," I said.

"Didn't want to jinx it," she said. "I had it done and e-mailed to Sully as fast as I could type. And evidently he sent it just as fast. So I'm going to rent the acreage, and he's funding my land preparation…but that's not the topic of discussion right now," she added, climbing on my bed and crossing her legs yoga style.

"Please, can it be?" I asked, sinking onto the bed. "My head is pounding."

"That's because you cried yourself dehydrated," she said, getting back up. She pointed at the bed. "Sit. All the way up there. In fact, lie down. I'm getting you some water and some aspirin. And then you're going to tell me what happened."

"I don't—"

"Sit."

I obeyed, turning to crawl up and lean against the headboard, pulling a pillow against my chest. When she returned and sat cross-legged facing me, I spilled it the best I could, crying again through some of it. Okay, most of it.

"So, he used to be a thief," Gabi said when I was done.

"That's all you got out of this?"

"I'm compartmentalizing," she said. "One thing at a time."

"Yes," I said, nodding. "But some of that was for survival."

"Robbing rich people's houses?"

"I said *some*," I said. "He also got caught up in the thrill of it, probably."

"So you're defending him."

I huffed out a breath. "No. I'm just—"

"You're just upset that he didn't tell you about his connection to Jeremy," she said.

"Yes!" I said. "Wouldn't you be?"

"Yes, but—"

"How can there be a *but* in that?" I asked. "How would you not feel completely—tricked or violated?"

"Because he'd only known you, what—a day and a half, maybe two, when we went to the house?" she said. "Seriously, would you have spilled all at that point if it were you? Or would you have just gotten the hell out of there?"

I inhaled in deeply and let it go, slowly, feeling the air leave my lungs. "And since then?"

She pulled her bottom lip through her teeth and looked at me as though gauging my reaction. "Since then, it's only been a week, babe. Maybe a heavy-duty, fast-moving week, but it sounds like when it became important, he tried."

Would it change my mind about being naked with you right now?
It might.

I clasped my fingers together so tightly that it hurt.

"Now *you're* defending him?"

She grimaced. "I'm sorry."

"Can we talk about the field, now?" I asked.

Gabi sighed. "Okay, but I'd rather do it when you're feeling better," she said. "And not in a cry-coma hangover."

"I'm fine," I said.

"Yeah," Gabi said. "You are just the poster child for fine right now."

Maybe not, but I needed distraction. "Field?"

She narrowed her eyes at me.

"Don't leave," she said. "Not yet, anyway. Think about it when you aren't distraught. What are your plans when your...honeymoon...is over?" she asked, cringing a little.

"Go back to work," I said, casting my eyes down. "I can't stay here across the hall from Leo, and I can't drive an hour back and forth every day, anyway. Why?"

"Because what if you had a job here?" she asked.

"In the florist shop?" I smiled. "Gabi, I love you, but I'd rather chop off my feet than work retail."

"Actually, I wanted to see what you thought about something," she said, pausing. I stared at her and gestured to keep going. I didn't have any witty banter left. "Like, maybe making the wildflower field a joint venture thing with Cherrydale Flower Farm, and you being my partner."

She covered her mouth with her hands like she couldn't believe what had just fallen out. I felt my jaw drop even before my brain could fully process what she'd just said. I was operating a little slowly, but invisible hands started pulling back the curtains.

"Say—what?"

"I know," she said, sitting up fully and pulling her legs under her like she needed to be taller. "We've known each other only a week, too. And I realize I just downplayed that, so this may not be the right tack, but I just can't help but think that we would be perfect running this together." She stopped for a breath, and my brain replayed it before she started again. Because—"I have the business knowledge, and you're like Mother Earth, and I'd have to talk to Drew and my parents about how we'd do it, I'm thinking no retail, just all wholesale to Grahams and any other florist, and you'd have to talk to your brother about percentage, and he might say no and they—"

"Yes."

She blinked. "What?"

"Absolutely."

Her eyes widened. "Are you serious?"

The sound of a siren whined in the background, barely noticeable.

"I mean, I'd have to talk to Thatcher," I said, already nodding. "And we'd—have a lot of hurdles. And work." My brain was checking off lists and making more at the same time. "But something—" My eyes filled with tears for only the sixty-seventh time today. "Something of our own, that we are passionate about. That—"

"No man, no *anything*—can take away," she finished.

The siren grew closer, and oddly sounded joined by a second one.

"That," I breathed.

Gabi's eyes misted over, too. She held up a fist for me to bump.

"That," she echoed.

I frowned as both sirens got really loud.

"Is that normal for here?" I asked. "That sounds really close."

"Not really," she said, getting up. "Let's see."

I slipped on my wooden clunkers and we walked downstairs. The smell, however, reached my nose before we ever even opened the door.

"Something's burn—" I began, and my words caught in my chest. Gabi's eyes met mine. "Oh, God, Gabi, something's burning."

CHAPTER TWENTY-TWO

The glow from the flames was easy to follow, not that two fire engines lit up like Christmas trees were difficult to see. Half a block down, I felt the smoky heat, and Gabi's gasp made my blood run cold.

"Micah," she breathed.

Gabi took off at a run, dodging the few people still in town that late who were congregating on the sidewalk.

"Oh, my God," I cried, yanking off the big stupid wedges and running after her, barefoot, with them in my hands.

The closer I got, hot gusts blew into my face, souring my stomach with each footfall. It couldn't be. Please God, please tell me he didn't…

I stopped short of the parking lot where firemen were throwing out barricades, and I sucked in a full gulp of singed air at the sight in front of me. The Blue Banana Grille was in flames. Mostly the roof, like a flambéed dessert, but it was licking down the sides. And indoors—the lights were still on inside, and all I could see was flame to one side and smoke and thick moving images. Women were screaming and crying as they stood huddled to the side as what I guessed were their men ran back inside. The smell was familiar, like I'd been there before, tasting the sour thickness of burned fabric.

An older woman was wailing. "My son! He's in the bathroom!"

I caught sight of Gabi running up to the building and gasped.

"Gabi!" I screamed, taking off toward her.

She didn't make it far, as one of the firemen looped her around the waist and lifted her off her feet.

"My friends are in there!" she shrieked.

Allie said she and Nick were closing tonight.

"Oh, my God," I cried. "We have to help them."

"Ma'am, we're working on it," he said, setting her down roughly. "I don't need you in there, too. We already have enough bystanders jumping in there. Let us—"

"They're the only ones doing anything!" Gabi yelled. "Where's the water? Put the fucker out!"

The front window shattered, making everyone scream and back up. I wheeled around to see what was probably volunteer or new firemen fumbling frantically to hook up a hose, most likely never having had to do this before. People were running everywhere. Two guys broke the lock on an ice machine and were throwing bags of ice inside the broken window. It was insane. It was chaos. And off on the other end of the parking lot, my eyes landed on a Harley, parked crooked, helmet lying upside down on the pavement a few yards away. As if he'd hit the ground running, throwing it aside.

Leo...

Enough bystanders.

Leo was in there. My chest tightened as I looked at the building, more engulfed by the minute, the inner lights flickering off. My already-swollen eyes burned and I couldn't breathe, and it suddenly had nothing to do with the heavy smoke.

Figures moved in and out of the smoky haze, a few more patrons running out, two waitresses helping an old man, shadows jumping in the blazing light, and two came farther out in our direction, emerging from the eerie cast.

"Leo?" I cried, moving forward.

"Ma'am!"

The figures stumbled closer, one holding up a smaller one, and I breathed a sigh of relief as I would recognize Leo anywhere, even blackened with soot, holding Allie around the waist as she coughed and struggled for breath.

"It's Leo and Allie!" I cried, pushing past the firemen and shoving off their grasp. Running to Allie, I put her other arm over my shoulder while Leo handed his side off to Gabi. "We've got you," I said.

"No!" she croaked, her voice all but gone as she coughed repeatedly and tried to talk. "Nick! He went after a disabled guy supposedly in the bathroom."

"I'll find him," Leo said, coughing, looking straight at me as we sat her on the ground. "Keep her here."

"Leo!" I called as he turned, but he never heard me. The fire was deafening enough, but the yelling and the water they finally figured out—it was impossible to hear anything.

I watched him run back in to the angry yelling of the fire chief, and then found the older woman again, on her knees in the parking lot crying as someone held her. Her whole life was in that building. As was Lanie's—oh, God, someone would have to—No, no, no, that wasn't going to happen. Because it couldn't. My heart clenched as I realized how much of me had just run into that building, too.

I shut my eyes, and suddenly realized why the smell was so familiar. It was the smell of my father. He did this. He ran into hell and saved people, and came home smelling of it with a smile on his face and peace on his mind. Willing to let my mother have whatever she wanted, because it was chump change compared to this.

Had she felt like this? Had she ever seen the man she loved engulfed in flame? Had she ever been so utterly paralyzed with—

There was a sizzling, sickening crack, as part of the roof collapsed.

"No!" I screamed, leaping to my feet. "No!"

Sparks shot off into the air like fireworks as the beams landed inside and the fire took off in a whole frenzy, feeding on new fuel. I felt the heat on my face, on my skin, on my bare feet against the hot concrete and debris as I ran. I heard Allie's distraught choked cries behind me, and the horrified voices behind her, but the only thing stopping me from reaching that door was a near-tackle by another semifamiliar body.

Strong arms scooped me up and ran back with me in the other direction before I even registered what was happening, setting me not just on my feet but in motion.

I wheeled around, stumbling next to Gabi, to see Bash Anderson glaring down at me.

"Leo's in there," I cried, my voice cracking as I tried to push forward, and he stopped me again. "And Nick."

"I know that," Bash said, hard emotion set in his jaw as he breathed heavily. "I just saw him save Allie's life. Believe me I know that." He knelt beside a sobbing Allie and pulled her into his arms, closing his eyes in silent relief. "But you going in there just makes it three instead of two."

Another beam fell, and everyone cried out. I turned and felt Gabi's arms around me as I sank to the ground with her, sobbing. We watched the beloved Blue Banana burn with two people we loved inside, water playing with the flames as firefighters rushed in. Everyone standing with me had years of history with this place. I didn't. But one of the two brothers inside that inferno had slammed my heart around and claimed it.

Tears poured down my face as I realized that. Even though I was still mad at him—

"You need to come out, Leo," I whispered through my tears, begging with my heart. "You need to come out so I can tell you—"

"There they are!" Bash yelled, crossing the space in seconds.

A firefighter was on one side of Nick and Leo was on the other, and between all of them they were carrying a young man in his late teens or early twenties. It was hard to tell who was holding who up, as it looked like the whole blackened, sooty group was about to crumble. Bash took the young man off their hands, adjusted his weight, and carried him straight to a paramedic, as his mother held his head and wept.

Nick and Leo both went to their knees as the firefighter helped guide them down, and another paramedic came running with oxygen. I was on my knees in front of Leo without any memory of getting there.

"I've got you," I said, wrapping my arms around his smoking torso as his chest heaved for clean air.

The paramedic strapped an oxygen mask on his face and told him to breathe deeply, and he did, never taking his bloodshot eyes off mine. Until he closed them and reached for my head, pulling it to his with one hand, the other still holding fast to his brother. Nick sucked in air from his mask and clapped his hand over Leo's.

For that one moment, everything was almost okay. It wouldn't be. It would never be okay again. But for one tiny speck of time, there was harmony.

"I love you," I whispered, closing my eyes.

* * * *

It was surreal.

Not what I said—although, yes, that was pretty far outside my wheelhouse. I didn't even know if he heard me, and I never opened my eyes to look. He didn't respond, and it didn't matter. Sixty seconds before that, I thought I'd never get the chance to say it to him, so being able to voice the words out loud, holding him close to me—that meant everything.

An hour later, we still sat on the ground in the parking lot, waiting to hear something from the fire marshall. It was early, but Nick and Allie were determined to find something out. Nick, Leo, and Allie all refused to go to the hospital after they breathed a little oxygen. Nick had a few minor burns on his arms, and Leo had one on his hand, but otherwise their only problem was exhaustion. And stubbornness. A lot of that.

I watched them all as they talked, as the girls cried together and watched the diner disappear in front of them. Allie looked haunted as she watched her life's work and her past fizzle into nothing, and Nick just looked lost. Lanie came for him, but ultimately had to go back home, the smoke hitting her nausea triggers. He mumbled that he'd be home later and just zoned out. It was meant to be his legacy. His future. I watched him—I watched all of them with a degree of separation, because no one was mentioning the obvious.

Only Leo and Gabi knew what I knew.

That I had caused this. I knew without a doubt who was responsible for this. I didn't have to hear it from officials. I brought him here. Then Jeremy seeing our chemistry, knowing it was Leo's bike I'd gotten on, and then ultimately finding us the way he did—that's what resulted in the charred remains of people's lives in front of us.

Leo was quiet, too, not looking up, just staring at some random point in front of him. I knew he was thinking some version of the same. And that this brief, fleeting moment of peace with his brother was about to be history.

"I did this," I said quietly, when there was a pause in the conversation. All heads turned to me. All except for Leo's, which started moving side to side. My stomach, my chest, my entire insides burned to match my eyes. "I did this," I repeated.

"What?" Allie said.

"This was—" I swallowed hard. "This was Jeremy," I managed. "I know it was."

"What?" Allie repeated, her voice still gravelly. "Why? What are you talking about?"

"He's done it before," Leo said, stone-faced. "Years ago."

"Years ago," Nick echoed. "Now what are *you* talking about?"

Leo rubbed at his face like he wished doing so would scrub it all away. All of it. Everything he didn't want to disclose right now.

"I'm not proud of some of the things I did when I was young, Nick," he said finally. "You know that. Or you should. But some of it I had to do for us."

"I know," Nick said.

"Not everything, though. Some of it was just really bad judgment," Leo said. "Greed. Hooking up with Jeremy's cousin, Roger, was one of them."

He had Nick's attention, as he sat forward. "Okay."

"Roger was a lunatic," Leo said. "But he got things done. He made us money."

"What kind of money?" Nick asked, his tone dead.

"Bought-you-a-truck kind of money," Leo said.

"That piece of shit?"

Leo looked at him like he wanted to punch him in the neck. "And then he brought Jeremy into the mix." His hand rested on my knee. "I never knew his name, I swear. I never heard it. I called him Cuz because Roger did, and honestly, I didn't even know *his* last name. It wasn't important at the time."

Leo lifted his hand, and I watched it leave, missing his touch instantly and feeling the hole already in my gut for everything I knew was coming.

"Long story short," he said, clearing his throat, "Roger wasn't the only lunatic. Jeremy went too far, and I wouldn't play, and he burned down his own parents' house in front of me."

"Oh, my God," Allie said under her breath, clapping a hand over her mouth.

"What the fuck?" Nick said, getting to his feet, spurring us all to follow. "Why don't I know this?"

Leo got up slowly and met Nick's eyes, so much like his own. "It's why I left," he said.

Nick shook his head and held out his arms. *"What's* why?"

"He used my lighter to do it," Leo said. "Without blinking an eye. It was the fucking freakiest, most psychotic thing I've ever seen in my life, even since. And he told me that if I still wanted to rat on him, he'd pin it on me, so when I told him I didn't care, he flipped it to you."

Nick stepped back. "Me."

"He said he'd hurt you. Or Tara. Or the—" Leo gritted his teeth. "Or the baby."

Nick looked ready to kill as every muscle in his body tightened, and he ran a hand over his face in a very Leo-like fashion. "You—"

"After what I saw, little brother," Leo said. "I didn't question it."

"So you left," Nick said, tight-jawed.

"That was the deal," Leo said.

"The *deal?*" Nick paced off, and turned back, chest to chest with Leo, who didn't budge, but also didn't bow back. "You put my baby girl at risk," he said, his voice shaking with anger.

Leo shook his head slowly. "I left my *life* so she wouldn't be," he said. "I left you. I walked away from *everything.*"

Nick paused, and his body visibly relaxed as his brain seemed to catch up with that.

"And now?"

"Now comes me," I said softly. "I'm such an awesome judge of character that I spent eight years of my life with someone who could do such a thing," I said, hearing my voice shake. "And never knew it."

"Except that you did," Gabi said. I met her smile through her tears she blinked free. "Something in you, an instinct, a vibe—something knew to get out."

I smiled back and whisked tears off my cheeks. "And I managed to hitch a random ride to Charmed with the one person who wanted nothing to do with Jeremy Blankenship," I said. "He wouldn't even have known that you were here," I said, looking at Leo, "if not for me."

"And then I yanked him across a table today," Nick said, closing his eyes and raking fingers through his soot-stuck hair. "He told me I'd regret it and I thought it was just hot air. You think he's so off his chain that he'd burn the diner to the ground over that?" he asked, his voice going gritty over the last words. "Fuck, this could have been our house."

"Yes," Leo said, before I could say anything. He was protecting me. "But he left Micah her car today, so he had a ride."

Nick met his gaze. "The cousin?"

"If I had to guess."

He continued to stare at Leo, hard. "Lanie—"

CHAPTER TWENTY-THREE

Nick ran for his truck, but it was blocked in by a fire truck. Leo was already on his bike, cranking up the motor when Nick turned his way.

"Come on!" Leo yelled over the deep rumble.

Without hesitation, Nick threw a leg over the seat and they were off. There was something beautiful in it. If the whole thing weren't so terrible.

"Let's go. My car's outside the shop," Gabi said, already running down the sidewalk.

"I need to stay," Allie said, touching Bash's arm. "But go. Help them."

He kissed her head. "I'll be back."

I felt frozen in place as he ran for his truck and Allie and I stood facing each other.

"I'm so sorry," I breathed.

She shook her head slightly, her eyes looking exhausted and sad, like all her tears were burned up, too. "It's not your fault, Micah." She hugged her arms over her chest and looked back at the smoldering remains of what was her whole life just two hours earlier. "Things happen—because that's what we're supposed to go through next. We have insurance. We'll survive. This was my dad's baby." She closed her eyes as words failed her. "I'm thankful that he has dementia right now. Is that a horrible thing to feel?"

"No," I whispered. "It's a love thing to feel."

Allie blinked two new tears free and whisked them away as she nodded toward where Gabi was already halfway down the street.

"Go. Make sure Lanie is okay."

I could find only one shoe, not that they'd served in that function, anyway. I grabbed it and ran to Gabi's car and jumped in.

"I saw your Mustang back there," she said.

"I haven't even looked," I said. "She must think I don't love her."

Gabi gave me the side eyeball. "You're one of those people, aren't you?"

I covered my face with my hands. "I don't know," I said, feeling the force of all my mistakes and sins descending on me with a fury. "I don't know who I am. I don't know anything anymore."

"Hey," Gabi said, grabbing my arm as she one-handed a turn. "Don't berate yourself. You are not at fault for what that asshole did."

"He burned down the diner," I said. "Destroyed people's livelihood." Tears choked my words. "Because he was mad at me. Mad at Leo. Who fucking does that?"

"His choice."

"But his choice could have been somewhere else!" I cried. "I could have gone to Denning, to Forest—hell, I could have gone to Egypt. I could have kept going," I said. "Grabbed a taxi like a normal person. *Not* climbed on a bike with a random stranger who just so happened to be the person he hates most."

Who I just told that I loved.

"And then you wouldn't have met me," she said. "And we wouldn't be starting a wildflower farm together."

I swallowed hard. How could I do that now? After—

"Oh, my God."

I sat forward and followed her gaze, the dread I'd become acquainted with washing over me like a thick mist. A dim lamplight upstairs was on—as if maybe Lanie was reading. The rest of the house was totally dark. Our headlights shown on the porch, as distorted shadows of Leo and Nick approached, and sitting up there like a king was Jeremy.

Casually rocking in a porch rocker.

"This nightmare won't die," I said under my breath.

"Come on."

I got out and walked across the gravel, not even caring about the pain on my bare feet. All I felt was hate. Mortification. Absolute repulsion for this person who somehow manipulated me into being what he wanted me to be all while completely disguising the monster he was. I knew he could be a narcissistic ass at times. I never imagined him capable of this. Not this.

Nick ran up to the porch and halted.

"What's that—" he said. "Why do I smell gasoline?" He took the stairs two at a time. "What the hell are you doing? Get off my property."

Jeremy held up a lighter and flicked it. It illuminated his face in the most unflattering of ways. Gone were the attractive face and pretty eyes.

The easy lazy grin that had won me over all those years ago. All that flame picked up was crazy. Bat-shit crazy.

"Back it up, baby brother," he said, sitting forward to lean on his elbows. "It'd be a shame to see this beautiful old house go up in flames like mine did." He took his finger off the lever as Nick backed down the steps. "With such a cheap little lighter, too. Leo, you should really invest in something sexy like one of those stainless-steel numbers with the special engravings." He wiggled the blue plastic. "These are boring."

I remembered seeing Leo's lighter on the coffee table next to the petrified cigarette. Jeremy was repeating history? Sweet Jesus, this needed to end.

"Stop it!"

Jeremy jerked toward my voice. "Of course you'd come with your new posse. I could have put money on it."

"What are you trying to prove?" I asked. "You destroy the diner, and now you're terrorizing a family? Who *are* you?"

"Something happened to the diner?" he asked nonchalantly. "That's a shame. First I heard of it." He made the sign of a cross on his chest with the lighter. "Swear to God."

"That's bullshit," Nick seethed.

"No," Leo said. "He wouldn't be here if he did it personally. He had his cousin do it. Where *is* good old Roger?"

"Can't say I know what you're talking about," Jeremy said, sitting back into the rocker again and rocking gently. "Haven't seen Roger in ages."

"My wife is upstairs," Nick said, hovering at the edge of the steps. "I realize that means nothing to you, since setting a restaurant on fire with people still inside doesn't faze you, but I'm telling you right now—you do this...you hurt one hair on her head, and you won't frame me for shit. I'll hang your ass personally."

"Wow, Leo," Jeremy said. "He turned out as mouthy as you are."

"You didn't answer my question," I said, walking across the grass, passing Leo, passing Nick, and walking up the steps. "What is your point here? What do you want?"

"Micah, stop!" Leo yelled behind me as Jeremy flicked the flame on again.

"He won't do it," I said, bluffing with every ounce of acting ability I had. Using my anger to fuel my courage. "He won't hurt me. And he sure as hell won't set himself on fire up here."

Jeremy's eyes panned my body. "Aren't you just a vision? At least you have pants on this time." One eyebrow raised. "Interesting barefoot-hick thing you have going on, though, sweetheart. Is that shoe special to you?"

I looked down, unaware I still had my wooden wedge in my hands. I could feel the gasoline on my tender, scraped-up feet. None of it made sense. It was like living in a surrealistic painting.

"Why are you doing this?" I asked.

"What do I have to lose, love?" he said calmly.

Too calmly. Possibly, I underestimated things.

"Why?" I said, my voice tremulous with rage.

Jeremy moved the lighter slowly, back and forth, watching the flame move sideways.

"Because he can't keep taking what's mine," he said, as if talking to himself.

"I didn't take anything," Leo said, one foot on the step next to his brother. "I didn't even know Andrea was your ex when we met."

"We were on a break," Jeremy said, looking up from the lighter. "She wasn't an *ex*."

"Well, evidently your idea of a break meant something else to her," Leo said. "Because she was done. And later when you threw a fit? She still wanted nothing to do with your lunatic ass."

"You want to play with me?" Jeremy said, lunging to his feet and grabbing my upper arm. "Because I may die up here, but I'll make sure you don't get this one, too."

"*This one?*" I said, pulling at my arm in vain. He wasn't letting go. "I'm not your spare change or your blow-up doll."

"You were mine," he said, holding the flame under my face. I could feel the heat licking my chin as I jerked my head away. "I loved you. And you broke me."

"I wasn't your anything," I spat. "I belong to me. And you don't love, Jeremy. You control. You manipulate."

Jeremy looked at me with an emptiness I'd never seen on him before, and I knew what he was about to do in the second that he did it. Everything slowed down, as though some invisible switch had been flipped. I felt his hand toss the lighter at the same time Nick and Leo jointly bull-rushed us. Leo yanked me around the waist and twisted me out and over the steps like some Olympic event, while Nick tried to bat away the lighter, missed, and tackled Jeremy with a roaring "*Noooo*" as they hit the porch decking.

I landed in a tumble in the grass as Leo went over the railing. And the lighter hit the gasoline-soaked deck with a—*pphmff.*

Like the kind that happens when flame hits water.

The fizzle made no sense. I could smell the gasoline. On the wood, on me, on everything. The shadow of Nick's head popped up looking curious, as Jeremy shoved him away.

"Hey, guys," said another voice from the right. "Did we miss the fun?"

It was Bash. Hell, I'd forgotten about Bash, as he strolled up with Lanie from around the side of the house.

Nick scrambled to his feet and pushed Jeremy to the side as he ran down to Lanie.

"So glad you check your texts," he said, pulling her into his arms and high-fiving Bash.

"Whoa," she said, coughing, reaching up on her tiptoes to kiss him. "You reek. Why do you smell like gas? Why does my porch smell like gas?" She turned to where Jeremy was staring at the lighter on the decking. "And what the hell are you doing?" she said, ironically echoing what Nick had said when he got there.

Leo picked himself up and made the steps in one leap, grabbing Jeremy by his shirt and yanking him down the steps, his face inches away.

"He's leaving," Leo growled.

"Fuck you," Jeremy said, struggling to get his feet under him.

"Get out," Leo said through his teeth. "Get out of this town, out of this state, even. I don't want to see you ever again. I don't want you around Micah ever—"

"Leo."

He turned to me with wild eyes I saw clearly in the headlights. "Oh, my God, Roman-off, you wear me out."

I walked up to Jeremy as Leo let him go with a shove, catching my shoe as Gabi tossed it to me from the bushes. The flicker of blue lights glowed through distant trees.

"*I* don't *ever* want to see you again, Jeremy Blankenship," I said. "For better or for worse—hopefully worse. Most definitely poorer. As long as we both shall live."

He grabbed my face and planted a hard kiss on my mouth as I yelped, shoving me back from it just as roughly.

"That's for not giving me the chance to kiss my bride," he sneered.

My left hand came up entirely on its own. The fact that it happened to be holding a five-pound wooden clog heel as it met with the side of his face and nose—well, that was just fortunate. *Use what you have.*

He dropped to his knees, howling and cursing.

"That's for trying to burn me alive, you son-of-a-bitch," I said, dropping the shoe next to his pathetic form as the police car pulled up. "Oh, so much for getting out of town. Good luck with that."

Leo leaned down and sniffed the porch, touching the wetness and sniffing it. "How did this not go up?" he asked.

"Aunt Ruby," Lanie said, crossing her arms over her chest.

"What?" Leo asked, turning around.

Lanie shrugged. "My aunt was—well, let's just say she still protects things around here." She threw a sideways glance at Nick. "I totally should have burned down the kitchen the other day and nothing happened. So... not letting the house go up in flames after being soaked in gasoline?" She nodded. "Not surprising."

Nick gave us a look that agreed. "I know it's crazy, but you really haven't seen crazy yet."

The policemen put Jeremy in the car and took our statements and, after what felt like ten hours, finally left with him. Nick and Leo looked at each other before he and Lanie left to go check on Allie, and there was something there. A beginning, maybe. There was hope.

I felt a hand on the back of my neck, and I turned into Leo's arms as he pulled me in. I couldn't remember ever feeling that safe. That content. Other than my brothers, no one had ever given me this sense of—peace. His hands were in my hair and around my back, holding me to him so tightly that my face was buried in the singed collar of his shirt. My nose inhaling soot and dried sweat and Leo. He had jumped up on that porch to save my life. He was taking care of me, and I should have been put off by that with my anti-help-Micah campaign, but he was—just being him. And in spite of myself, it felt damn good. I wrapped my arms around his torso and held him back just as tightly. I'd said words tonight. Big words. It didn't matter that he hadn't heard them, only that they'd come out of my mouth.

The tide had shifted. But this...this moment...this was all we could do with it. This memory would have to stick.

CHAPTER TWENTY-FOUR

Growing up on what was now Thatcher's porch, it always felt homey to me. More so than the house. Now every time I sat out on Thatcher's front porch the last few days, all I could see was Jeremy sitting in that rocker. Trying to end me, trying to hurt Leo by hurting his brother. Being responsible for all that destruction and pain. Over a woman. Two of them.

Damn him, he even stole my love of this porch.

Gabi had called every day for the past week, trying to talk me into coming back. Into "coming home," as she phrased it. It stabbed me in the heart every time she said that. Because I wanted it so badly.

I didn't want to be here, squatting in my brother's house, sleeping in my old room, glaring at the walls for the oppression hiding behind the wallpaper. It wasn't permanent, but I didn't know what was. Cherrydale had always been my hometown, but going to Charmed—that had been like nothing else. Not just because I found friends like Gabi and Lanie and Carmen and—other people. But because I found *me*. And that meant everything.

I wasn't sure I could be that person anywhere else, least of all the town where I learned how to bury it.

But my being in Charmed had hurt people. Indirectly, yes, but still very much real. Lives were damaged. Altered. Forever. Because I let *myself* be altered into someone I no longer knew in order not to see the monster in front of me.

"How can I ever trust myself again?" I said out loud.

"With closing doors?" Thatcher said through the open door behind me and to my left. "You can't. You're hopeless."

He handed me a hot, fresh cup of coffee, light brown from a spoon of hazelnut cream. I seldom took the time to make it that way for myself, but it was exactly how I liked it. And he knew that.

"Why can't all men be like you, Thatch?" I said, sipping and inhaling at the same time.

"I don't know," he said, sinking into the next chair with a sigh. "Ask Misty. I'm sure she has an opinion on that." He glanced my way and winked over his cup. "More than one, probably."

I gave him a sideways once-over. "Why are you this put-together first thing in the morning?"

It was the weekend, so he had on cargo shorts and topsiders, but with a nice pullover. He was shaved and smelled good and looked ready to go do something. It was seven o'clock. I was wrapped in an afghan in my worn-out, ratty tank top and shorts, with slipper socks on my feet and my hair pulled up on top of my head like a feather duster gone rogue. I *had* brushed my teeth and was feeling all on top of things before J. Crew here came strutting out.

"What? I get ready for the day," he said. "Then I'm more likely to actually do something than just lay around here eating chips and watching reruns."

I curled a lip at him. "You say that like it's a bad thing," I said. "Hey, did you look at that binder I gave you? About a plan for a wildflower farm in Charmed?"

Thatcher nodded over his coffee. "I did."

I waited with raised brows. "And?"

He gave me one of his studying looks, and I sighed and looked away.

"Don't put me under a microscope, Thatch," I said. "There's nothing to figure out. I just think that it's a great idea."

"Separate from both the flower farm and Graham's," he said.

"Yes," I affirmed. "But in a joint venture. Wholesale to florists, a deeper discount for Graham's since they'd be advertising it in the shop and pimping it as local and fresh, and a percentage of the profits come here in exchange for—well, essentially, me. And the use of some of our equipment."

"Initially funded by?" he asked.

I made a face. "Some rich old man in the woods?"

"Uh-huh," he said. "That sounds totally legit."

"I know, Thatch," I said. "But I—I really want to do this."

"Move back to Charmed?"

I grimaced. "Maybe just closer. Denning or Goldworth."

"And leave me?" he said.

"Not completely," I said. "I'd still put in some time here. But let's be real here. Roarke is two of me."

"Roarke is five of you," Thatcher said, ducking when I swung at him. "But I'd miss you. Nothing better than going out to the hothouses or a field over lunch to find my little sister elbow deep in the mud."

"I'd be sure to come do that every couple of weeks just for you," I said.

Thatcher grabbed my hand and kissed the back of it, looking down the street.

"If you need this, baby girl, I'm on board," he said.

Goose bumps went down my back, and sparks of excitement shot through my belly. This could happen. Something of my own—or *our* own— something I never imagined and never even dreamed up could happen, all because I'd lost my mind and ended up in Charmed and met Gabi.

I closed my eyes and savored it, listening to the early-morning sounds of the birds and soft wind blowing the leaves. Faraway noises of town life, and the deep rumble of a motorcycle as it grew louder.

My eyes popped open as it echoed nearer and nearer, my heart speeding up at the same ratio.

"Oh, shit," I said, as bike and rider rolled slowly into view, slowing more as he reached his destination.

"Someone you know?" Thatcher said, giving me a knowing look as he pushed to his feet.

"Oh, shit," I repeated, glancing down at myself. "Why does he always have to see me like this?"

Thatcher made a gesturing move down the front of himself.

"Ready for whatever the day brings," he said. "Just saying."

"Bite me, Thatch," I said, wrapping the blanket better around me. As bad as my hair was, I knew what it would do if I let it down, so I left it alone.

"Hey," he said, making me look up at him as I stood. "This time around, you don't *need* anyone, Micah. You're older and wiser."

"That supposed to be a pep talk, big brother?" I said under my breath as Leo dismounted his bike.

"That's supposed to tell you to quit second-guessing yourself," he said, heading for the door. "You did what you had to do to change your life. It might not have been pretty, but you did it." He gestured toward Leo with his chin. "And he's still circling. Trust your gut."

He went in and shut the door, just as Leo stopped at the steps, looking up at me. *Dear God, the way he looked at me.* My stomach tightened up in a ball and I gripped the nearest post.

"Hey," I said.

"Hey."

Just the sound of his voice sent my skin into *hello* mode. Standing there in worn jeans and a dark blue T-shirt, his hair a little messy from the helmet, he looked like fifty kinds of delicious. I licked my lips, just thinking of my hands in that hair and the taste of him. Those damn eyes—they were killing me—

Jesus, back it up, Micah.

"I'm sorry. I know it's early," Leo said, shoving his hands into his pockets.

I shook my head and leaned against the pole before I fell over. "I've been up."

"It's good to see you," he said, chuckling when I raised an eyebrow. "Yes, even looking like that." His eyes went serious and my heart squeezed. "Especially looking like that."

I'd left with very little more than I'd arrived with, minus the five-hundred-pound dress, and slipped out with no fanfare. In all the craziness of our week, we'd never exchanged numbers, so I left him an old-fashioned note under his door, telling him I was going home for a little bit and "needed to do some things." I signed it with "Roman-off," thinking that conveyed affection without saying it. And then obsessed over it since.

I thought it to be a good thing that there were no calls to wait for or phone stalking to do, but I found myself thinking of nothing else. Seeing him in front of me now—my breaths couldn't keep up with my heart rate.

"So—" I began, and then cleared my throat. "You found us. You on your way somewhere?"

"No," he said. "I just wanted to—" He blew out a breath, and the intensity in the air between us nearly choked mine clean out of me. "I wanted to tell you I'm moving into Carmen's rental house," he said. "I'm starting today. Should probably be done in about fifteen minutes," he added, making me laugh. "So—when you're done with your 'things,' you can come get your place back." A small grin pulled at his lips. "You'll have the bathroom to yourself."

"Well, until some freak moves in across the hall," I said on a chuckle and a too-high voice. "I don't know that I want to chance that."

I met his eyes and wished I could dig my fingernails into the wood. He'd driven all the way here to have this conversation, and he was going to have it.

"You aren't coming back?" he asked.

"I don't know," I said, the words hardly making sound.

"Micah."

"I'm not staying *here*," I said. "Gabi and I have a business thing we're gonna do, so I'll need to be closer than this, but—I don't know that I can be in Charmed."

"Because of me?" he asked, his brows furrowing.

"No," I said. "Yes." I rubbed at my face. "I can't face people there, Leo," I said.

"No one blames you, Micah," he said, stepping up one step. "If anything, it's attached to me, and I don't care. Nick and I are—we're getting better. They're building a new diner. Bash Anderson is being sworn in as mayor tonight and announcing it. Life's moving on."

Leo moved up another step closer and my eyes fluttered closed. I could feel his energy and it was intoxicating.

"And if it's about me—I'm sorry that I wasn't honest with you," he said. "Part of me went into protector mode—" He held up a hand as I opened my eyes. "I know. But I can't change that." He took a deep breath and let it go. "Another part said this was fucking real, and that scared me. Not too many things do that, Roman-off, but you scare the hell out of me."

"Back at you," I breathed.

"I've spent my entire adult life keeping people at bay," he said. "Not letting them in. Not investing in anything, because I was a walking lie." He shook his head slowly. "I'm done with that. Someone threatens my family now, my brother and I will kick their ass together." He stepped up one more, putting him face to face with me. I held my breath when he grabbed the front of my blanket and pulled me to him, his lips brushing my cheek. "I'm not walking away anymore. No more lies. No more secrets."

My mouth searched for him, and goose bumps covered my entire body when his lips covered mine. It was soft and wet and warm and everything I'd missed about Leo. How he could kiss me so lightly and yet put everything he felt into it. My eyes burned with tears as I kissed him back, and we parted. I wanted so badly to pull him back. To wrap myself up in him and kiss him for days.

"Whenever you make up your mind," he said, his voice raspy. One finger trailed my cheek and he backed down the steps. "You know where to find me."

"You're headed all the way back home now?" I called out when I found my voice again.

He straddled his bike and turned the key. "Unless you want to go for a ride."

More than anything I'd ever wanted in the entire world. More than my next breath, I wanted to go for a ride with him. But then what? We'd end up pulling over in Gladys Park, attacking each other behind a tree, and—yeah, I just needed to stay off that bike.

"Rain check," I said instead. Because—me.

Leo nodded and put his helmet on, and there for one moment before he slid the face shield down we were back there. We weren't Leo and Micah; we were a guy on a motorcycle at a stoplight and a spastic stressed-out girl on a sidewalk with a giant dress and a decision to make.

The seconds moved in slow motion, clicking in my head forever until he slid the shield down and broke the moment. Watching him back up and drive away was the hardest act of restraint and willpower I'd ever exercised. In my mind's eye, I ran after him till he stopped, got off, and kissed me into tomorrow.

"Reality sucks," I said, listening to the thrum of the Harley get farther away.

CHAPTER TWENTY-FIVE

All that day, I found things to keep me busy. I looked at Gabi's plan, played with some ideas, knocked around some names, made myself laugh on a few, paced the laundry room, and stalked the clock. At around four, I got antsy. And by five, I was dressed and ready to go and texting Gabi. If Thatcher had been around, he would have been proud. Or not really, considering he'd been there for around twelve hours already.

I had nowhere to go, actually, except the mayoral announcement at the Charmed pavilion, which Gabi told me started at six. So…if I were to go, then this would be the time. Theoretically.

I stared at my keys and told them to be strong. Stronger than me.

An hour later, I pulled into the park's parking lot and gazed upon the crowd mingling around the pavilion. If Leo was here, great. If he wasn't, well, I knew what was next but I wasn't going there yet. The last time I was there, I bought a man, went home, and got felt up on the balcony.

"Fight or flight," I said softly.

Once I got out and started walking, however, I knew something was off. People were dispersing. Several groups still hung out, talking and laughing, but some were passing me on the way to their cars.

"Micah!" Carmen called, waving at me from her little group.

My stomach came up in my throat as I scanned through Sully, Lanie, Bash, Allie, Nick, and a couple of other people for Leo, but he wasn't among them. I smiled anyway, hoping my disappointment wouldn't show.

"Don't you look adorable?" Lanie said. "I *love* that dress."

"Thank you," I said, doing a mock little curtsy. "It makes me feel pretty. And ordinary."

I hadn't dressed sexy. I wasn't going for that. I was comfortable in a soft blue sundress made of T-shirt material, and flip-flops. The one that had been in my honeymoon backpack. No diving cleavage, no bare back, just simple. My hair fell down around my shoulders, and I wore minimal makeup. I didn't want to stand out. I didn't want to make a show. I'd done enough of that.

"Oh, Micah," Carmen said. "You could never be ordinary."

"No, I'm really needing ordinary tonight," I said, to which she nodded.

"I hardly even notice you're here," she amended.

"Why, thank you," I said on a chuckle. "Did I miss it? Gabi said six."

"Oh, I'm sorry," Gabi said, rushing up behind me with a quick hug. "They started early because it's supposed to rain. I'm so sorry! I should have called you."

I looked around, feeling my buoyancy fall and all my insecurities come pouring back in. "No, it's okay," I said. "Congratulations, Bash!"

"Thank you," he said, beaming. "I mean, I was the only one running, so the win was kind of a token thing, but now I have to get my butt in gear."

I gave Nick a second glance, wishing I could just go back to my car and not be standing in front of these people I'd taken so much from. "How is everything?"

He looked down at me, eerily familiar dark eyes smiling. "Everything as in work? Or everything as in my brother?"

I felt my skin go warm as I smiled back. "Just everything."

"We're rebuilding the diner," Lanie said, eyes happy as she linked arms with a tired-looking but smiling Allie. "Insurance covered most of it, and I think a certain somebody in the woods is fronting the rest."

I narrowed my eyes. "That guy sure gets around for someone who hides in the woods."

"You have no idea," Sully said, rubbing at his eyes.

"I'm thinking of calling it the New Blue," Allie said. "The original name was a thing between my parents, and that would give it a modern twist."

"Allie, I'm so—"

"Don't," she said, laying a hand on my arm. Her eyes misted over, but there was warmth there. "It's not on you."

I swallowed hard and choked back the emotion that wanted to sink me. I blew out a slow breath instead.

"It's so good to see you," Lanie said, putting a hand on my arm next to Allie's. "We've missed you, Micah."

"I've missed y'all too," I said. "I didn't realize just how much till right now."

"Funny how one little week can get somebody all under your skin, isn't it?" Gabi said, widening her eyes to be cute.

"You're just not right," I said.

I know, she mouthed.

"But guess what?" I said. "My brother said yes to the proposal."

Her jaw dropped. "Oh, my God."

"Yep."

"We're doing this?" she breathed.

I laughed, realizing this was kind of like when I first got to town, committing to days. It was that moment.

"I think we are."

"What?" Lanie asked. "What are you doing?"

"Holy shit," Gabi gasped, fanning her face. "I'll tell you at Rojo's."

"We're gonna go get some dinner before the sky falls," Allie said. "Want to come?"

The thought of Rojo's made my skin flush all the way to my scalp, but Gabi laid a hand on my arm.

"Or since I heard one of the bartenders there mention that he's not working tonight because he took the night off to finish moving into his new rental house," she said, leaving the sentence hanging.

"At 1111 Erna Lane," Carmen added.

"You might not want to bother going to Rojo's," Gabi finished with a casual shrug. "I mean, I'll be there gushing about wildflowers and shit, but he'll be—moving heavy things around and flexing. Just saying."

* * * *

I pulled onto his street and slowed down, thinking maybe that would force my heart to do the same. Not even a little bit.

"Shit, Micah, having a heart attack in his driveway isn't sexy," I said under my breath. "Pull in. Stop the car. Remember the key. Dear God, what am I doing?"

I'd never chased a man before. Or—I wasn't chasing, was I? I was just—responding. To a conversation. With what? He said when I made up my mind. I hadn't made up my mind about anything. I was just here. Because evidently the Earth's magnetic force decided I needed to be, and Gabi mentioned flexing.

I was such a girl.

The little house was cute and it had a porch. I tried to focus on logistical things like that, but all my brain could see was Leo's eyes on me early

this morning, telling me the things he told me. Along with my own words
that night as I held him up after the fire. What was I going to say? *Hello?*
I still don't know where I'm landing, or if I can trust my own judgment
anymore, but I'm losing my damn mind over you?

My phone dinged with a text and I smiled when I read it.

I went by the house before Rojo's, Gabi texted. *Signed the divorce papers*
and dropped them at the post office. Chapter two begins. Thank you!!!

Exactly. Chapter friggin' two.

So proud of you, I texted back. *High-five to chapter two. And thank YOU.*

I got out and shut the door and made it to the steps before Leo opened
the door. My hands went on a full-out nervous flail, looking for somewhere
to land or something to grasp, finally deciding to clasp themselves in
front of me.

He had on a button-down white shirt and jeans, the sleeves rolled midway
up his forearms, and I had to lick my lips to remind myself I had lips.

"Roman-off," he said.

Fuck. How did he keep doing that to me, taking my knees out with the
first sound of his voice?

"Hey," I said, lifting my chin so I looked more confident than I felt.

He paused at the top of the stairs, the exact opposite of how we'd been
this morning, and my words froze in my chest. Not that I had any. But
what few there were—

"You want to come in?" he asked.

"No," I said. *Liar.* "I just—I just wanted, or needed, to tell you something,
and—well, you weren't at the thing." I pointed behind me like that nailed
it down.

"I was," he said. "But I left when Bash was done."

"Really cool, them rebuilding," I said.

"Yes, it is," he said. "Makes things right again. What did you need to
tell me?" he asked.

I closed my eyes. *I don't know. I don't know.*

Yes, you do.

"Yes."

The pitter-patter of tiny raindrops hit the ground around me and pinged
metallically against my car.

"Yes?" he said, stepping down a step. "Yes to what?"

Everything, I mouthed, the word not forming sound. "To you," I breathed,
backing up a step, feeling the rain on my face and not caring. "To us. To
stepping outside the box, to tr—" I blew out a slow breath on that one and
tried it again. "To trusting again. To—to—"

"Love?"

All the words fell out of my head. I swallowed hard.

"Yes."

Leo came down one more step and I backed up again. He followed.

"Are you sure?" he asked, his voice thick.

I laughed nervously. "Of anything else in the world? Of my life? Of where I'm living tomorrow?" I said, my breath coming in puffs. "No. But of you?" I drew in a shaky breath as raindrops stuck on my lashes. "Completely."

"That night," he said, walking out into the rain as slowly as I backed up, "did you—I mean, I've been telling myself I imagined—"

"I did."

My backside stopped against my car and he kept coming, until he was inches from my face.

"Please do it again."

My hands ran up his chest as his ran up my bare arms, taking the beaded raindrops with them.

"Leo," I whispered.

"Please."

"I love you," I said, as my eyes fluttered closed and I pulled his face to mine. "I love you."

His lips landed on mine and stayed, as he held my head and kept us there. When he broke the kiss, his eyes were raw with emotion as he tried to dial it back. Everything slammed against my heart with that look.

"You—you undo me," he said, his voice rough. "I've never loved anyone except my brother. Ever." He took a ragged breath and blinked several times. "Until now."

Hot tears fell from my eyes, mixing with the rain on my cheeks. We were a pair, the two of us. Afraid of love, afraid of trust, jumping in with both feet like a couple of lunatics.

"I love you, Micah," he said. "You make me crazy, but—"

"I get it," I said. "No one drives me crazier than you do."

"I don't know what I'm doing in the slightest," he said. "I'm probably gonna mess up."

I laughed and pulled his forehead to mine. "There's no *probably* to me messing up. You can count on it."

"But I'll never lie to you," he said, more seriously.

I looked in these eyes that turned my world upside down. That changed me in ways I never imagined were possible. Not to meld to him. To meld to myself.

"And I won't run," I said.

His hands smoothed back my wet hair and moved down my back to pull me tightly to him, as I wound mine into his hair so that our bodies fit.

"You're about to be kissed in the rain," Leo said against my lips. "Thoroughly and devilishly."

I smiled into his kiss. "I like devilishly."

"And there just might be something else in the rain to follow," he said, his hands moving seductively on my body.

"Yes," I purred, feeling like I'd never get enough of this man.

"Yes to that, too?" he asked, his mouth trailing down my neck.

"So, so, much yes to that," I said.

"I don't know my neighbors yet," he said against my skin, coming back to my mouth.

I grinned. "Love, let's give them something to talk about."

And now…
Read on for a preview of
the next Charmed in Texas Novel:
A CHARM LIKE YOU
by
Sharla Lovelace

Available December 2018, wherever ebooks are
sold.

CHAPTER ONE

I made a cursory sweep through the parking lot, then escaped out the side exit to circle the block so it wouldn't look like I needed to be there.

I didn't *need* it.

I just needed to *not* murder my ex-husband, and this was a means to that end—according to my mother.

Divorce.

A word so diabolical that it has group meetings to keep nice, normal people like me from becoming homicidal. Or at least that was my reason. I couldn't imagine why else anyone would want to spend a Thursday night listening to strangers whine about their lives. As I peered at the office building in front of me, windows glowing with warm light, that's what I pictured inside. Sad, depressed, bitter, whiney people.

That wasn't me.

There'd better be cookies.

"Well, this should be fun," I said under my breath as I turned off the ignition.

I dropped my keys into a big shoulder bag large enough to dive into or fake-pull important things out of if things got too hairy, and opened the door to the damp, chilly, January air. Was it my imagination, or was it colder here in Denning?

My little town of Charmed, Texas, may only be fifteen minutes down the highway, but it sure felt chillier here. Open. Exposed. Also, anonymous. I could have probably found a group there at home if I'd looked hard enough, but I'd much rather not sit around airing my dirty laundry to people I went to Kindergarten with. Or customers from my family's business, Graham's Florist. Or friends of my sister, or friends of the butcher's neighbor's cousin.

Charmed was gossip-heavy enough without adding my extracurricular activities.

I pulled my hoodie tighter around me and zipped it up, listening to the squeak of my sneakers on the wet pavement.

Yeah, I'd gone all out for this escapade. A t-shirt, jeans, a purple hoodie jacket I'd stolen from my sister because I loved the color, and sneakers that had probably seen better days since I started wearing them to cultivate my new wildflower field. I figured meeting up with bitter people required comfort, and besides, I wanted to blend. Like—into the furniture if I could at all help it.

There was a large darkish truck parked right at the building's entrance, still running with someone sitting at the wheel. Probably someone who came early to score a good parking spot, but knew he could wait till the last possible second and still score a cookie.

Just as I made it past his bumper, however, the engine cut and the driver door opened, blocking my path and sending a momentary shot of panic through my chest. Time slowed down and my steps halted as my eyes darted around in the dark for a graceful reroute. Lifetime movies and after-school specials ran through my mind on fast-forward. What kind of responsible female walked right up beside a stranger's vehicle like that? What was I thinking?

Over six feet of black boots, dark jeans, and a black leather jacket stepped out then, the man wearing them stopping at the sight of me twitching in indecision.

"Sorry," he said, glancing from the door to me. He moved out of the way quickly and shut his door so I could pass.

"No problem," I said, trying not to do a double-take as I gave him a polite smile on my way by.

Good God, if he *had* been out to kill me, I would have been easy prey, smiling like a smitten girl instead of keeping my guard up, or—hey, how about going another direction.

The man was hot, in that unassuming way some people have when they have no idea just how hot they are. Short brown hair and sharp, kind eyes registered with me in the few seconds we looked at each other, as well as the slight aroma of something woodsy. Like he'd sprayed one spritz of it that morning and it was still barely there. Or it was just soap and I was fantasizing way too much into it.

I fantasized a lot lately, since after ten years of marriage, six of which spent with my legs in the air trying to conceive before we found out we couldn't—or that *I* couldn't—my now-ex-husband left me for the twenty-two-year-old he was screwing at the office. A girl I'd babysat for when I was fifteen and she was a *toddler.* Missing signs like that clearly signified that my judgment was too flawed and damaged to trust myself with real people. I scooted past Hot Guy, shaking my head. *Get a grip, Gabi.* I stepped up onto the wooden walkway, and headed toward the door that sported Aspen Aldridge, Orthodontic Surgeon emblazoned on a sign. I felt his boots hit the wood a few steps behind me, and I refused to turn around and look paranoid. *Keep moving.* The door opened for me when I reached for the knob, as a stunning woman with short dark hair and a loose sexy pink sweater over perky braless boobs gave her apologies with a smile and a bigger one for my new shadow.

"Hi!" she said, casting her gaze past me to the golden boy back there. She dipped her head with a tilt and a husky chuckle. Seductress 101. Her big blue eyes shifted to me then as she probably realized the lump in front of him was breathing. "Hello!" she said, holding out a hand. "I'm Aspen! Welcome!"

"You're the doctor?" I asked, pointing at the sign.

"Guilty," she said, rolling her eyes and grinning.

"How are you tonight?" Hot Guy said from behind me, the deep rumble of his voice surprising me.

"I'm wonderful," she said, laying a hand against the swell of her breasts as if he'd just offered her the moon. My orthodontist never looked like her. Mine had pock marks on his face and chronic halitosis. I could imagine teenage boys all over Denning begging for braces and popping bands on purpose just to have the good doctor leaning in close and putting her fingers in their mouths.

"Hi," I said, holding out my hand. "I'm—"

"Nope," she said, *Gabi Graham* sticking in my throat as she stopped me with a hand up like a traffic cop. "No real names here."

I felt my eyebrows raise. "No—what?"

Aspen pointed to a table a few feet away where an elderly lady with a long white side-ponytail was arranging things. "Adelaide will show you. There are name tags and colored markers. We use pretend names to protect the innocent." She laughed at her own joke. "Seriously, it's just a way to be whoever you want for the night, so have fun with it."

I pointed to her nameplate on the door. "You don't play?"

She shrugged endearingly. "I used to, but once I started hosting...well, it's hard to be anonymous when you're hosting in your own office." She winked and laid a hand on Hot Guy's arm as she moved on. "Will you excuse me? I need to get something from my car."

I knew that was really flirt code for *hey big boy, can you come help me with your big strong muscles,* but he didn't seem to pick up on it. His expression said that he'd probably had a long day and wasn't in the mood to be a packhorse. I gave him a quick onceover when he turned his head, and I had to agree. He was too shiny to be a packhorse. In fact, as I glanced around the room at the three other men and possibly a dozen women—all looking like they were going out on the town afterward—I suddenly felt like a street urchin. Thank God I'd at least put on a face and didn't go with the hair-up-in-a-hat idea I'd originally planned.

"Um, I just remembered I have a thing," I said, turning back for the door.

"I don't think so," Hot Guy said, looping a finger in the hood of my hoodie.

"What the—"

"Don't leave me here with the vultures," he said under his breath, giving the material a gentle tug. "The newbie spotlight isn't as hot if it's spread out."

I blinked up at him. Was Hot Guy flirting with me? "You seem pretty able to hold your own. I think Dentist Barbie back there would probably hold your hand if you got scared."

"Hey, you two," said a loud, gruff voice suddenly at my right, making me jump.

"Shit," I muttered.

"Sorry," the sweet-looking white-ponytailed lady said, patting my arm as she worked at peeling a nametag sticker from its backing. "I have that affect. Welcome to life after signing *I don't.* We're a pretty friendly group, but a few really like to talk and they can get annoying. Are you big talkers?"

Both of us shook our heads as if on command.

"Now, you're welcome to share anything you want, or just listen, that's good too," she said. "I wish some people would just listen now and then." She cut her eyes toward a cluster of women probably in their forties who were dressed like they were twenty-one and club-hopping. "Aspen hosts us now, and she likes us to make up silly names instead of using our own." She slapped hers onto her shirt, patting it a couple of times. It said CHER.

"I thought she said you were Adelaide," I said.

"Not tonight," she said. "Tonight, I'm Cher."

I nodded. "Cool, can I be Madonna?"

Cher just looked at me. "No." Her eyes took me in, head to toe. "Lois Lane."

I coughed. "What? Do I look like a *Lois Lane* to you?"

"No, you look like you need a little boost," she said, turning around to grab a couple of tags and a marker. "And you?" she said, eyeing Hot Guy and scribbling onto another nametag. She peeled mine off and patted it onto my jacket, doing the same with his.

In all caps, his read *Clark Kent*.

"Really?" I said.

"All that perfection, but he's at a divorce group," she said. "So, pick your mask, but he's hiding something."

"He's—right here," Hot Guy—er—*Clark* said, holding up a finger. "Then again," he added, peeling the tag off his jacket. "He's not."

"Oh, no no no," I said softly, looping my arm through his as he turned on his heel, momentum pulling me with him a step as he headed for the door. "Vultures. Spotlights. Remember those?"

"You were leaving two seconds ago," he said.

"And now it's kind of a challenge, Superman," I said. "Come on, if I can be told I'm so homely I need a boost, then you can handle a little criticism."

"No criticism," *Cher* said. "I'm just saying if anyone says they wouldn't like to see Superman here with a little scruff, shirt sleeves up, and faded jeans, they're lying."

There were no words as Superman and I stood there gaping at her.

"Anyway, there's cookies if you hurry," *Cher* said in a loud whisper, backhanding me in the arm.

I spurred back into movement, holding up a hand. "And there's cookies."

"But you have to hurry," she repeated. "I brought them, but people are going to scavenge them quickly. Aspen only brings healthy shit."

"Seriously?" I said. "To a divorce group crowd? Shouldn't it be like brownies and ice cream and—"

"An ice cream bar," Superman said. "With glasses and root beer so people can make—"

"Oh my God, ice cream floats," I said. "My best friend makes me one every time I'm having a horrible day. Can you imagine how mellow everyone would be at this if they got to slurp on an ice cream float while they sit there?"

A low, rumbling laugh made his eyes crinkle at the corners, and the sight made my insides go all warm. In the light of the room, he had morphed from just simply hot to drop dead scorching. Short, no-nonsense hair, eyes that flickered between light brown and hazel. Chiseled everything and clean shaven, not one wrinkle in the black button-down shirt he wore when he slid the jacket off, evidently giving in to stay. I felt the group sigh of every woman in the room, and on that point I was actually on their side. Whoever he was, he was beautiful.

"Does sound like a good idea," *Cher* said. "When Aspen took over hosting a couple of months ago, it went from donuts and cookies to fruit and vegetable trays."

I turned to see Aspen come back in toting a large fresh fruit tray, stunning in all the vibrant colors. The fruit, not Aspen, although she ran a close second.

"That's awful," I mumbled under my breath. "I mean, it's pretty, but you can't eat pretty."

"That needs to be on a bumper sticker," he said, attempting to reapply the nametag to his shirt.

"No," I said, pulling it off. "It's all mangled. Let's do a new one." I grabbed a blank tag. "Are you sure you want to stick with Clark?"

"It wasn't my idea," he said. "Kathy Bates over there nailed it on me with her hidden mallet."

I laughed and covered my mouth. "She is scary."

"You have a better idea?" he asked. "Go for it."

"Elmer Fudd?"

"Really?"

"Popeye?"

He gave a slow grin. "Only if you're Olive."

Little tingles shot to my belly.

Nope. There would be no tingles tonight. I may be off men for the next ten years, but I wasn't off sex, and I didn't need to be tingling toward anything naked with a man from a divorce group meeting that I might have to face again. That was not only baggage meeting baggage, but the Titanic meeting the iceberg.

"Oh, I'm nobody's *Olive*," I said. "I'm not even crazy about being anyone's *Lois*. I'd rather be a Jane Doe and be on my own."

"Please," he said. "You're about as Jane Doe as I am." His gaze slid over me quickly. "And she called *me* out for hiding. You should have gone for Wonder Woman."

I frowned. "You think I'm hiding? Dude, you don't even know me."

Two palms went up. "No, I don't. So, let's just go back to where this was easy. Make me *Clark Kent* again, and let's eat."

"Works for me," I said, feeling some of the flirty fun fizzle away as I wrote up the new tag.

Hiding, my ass.

I slapped it against his chest, and patted it for good measure, completely ignoring the heat coming through the fabric.

He looked down and then at me. "You okay?"

"I'm awesome," I said, flashing a smile that felt about as genuine as most of the boobs in this room.

"Did you completely miss the Wonder Woman comment?" he asked.

I blinked up at him. Yeah, I kinda had.

Still.

"Come on. *Lois* needs a cookie."

He sighed heavily and walked to the cookie tray that four other people had already descended upon, ignoring the brightly colored fruit, and scooped up four. Pressing a chocolate chip cookie into my hand, he shoved a snickerdoodle one into my mouth.

"Let's sit down before we get trampled," he said, heading to a fold-out chair.

Nothing makes you feel hotter than being left standing there with a cookie hanging out of your mouth. I bit it off and held the rest as I followed him, slowing my steps. Irritation sat on my skin like something sour, and that front door still called to me. Hot Guy sat, leaning forward on his knees, eating a cookie absently as if his mind was already somewhere else. I could walk right out that door before he even had a chance to get up and stop me. If he even really cared to.

It was now or never.

About the Author

Photo Credit: Leo Weeks Photographers

Sharla Lovelace is the bestselling, award-winning author of sexy small-town love stories. Being a Texas girl through and through, she's proud to say she lives in Southeast Texas with her retired husband, a tricked-out golf cart, and two crazy dogs. Among her work is the bestselling novel *Don't Let Go*, the exciting Heart Of The Storm series, and the fun and sexy new Charmed in Texas series.

For more about Sharla's books, visit www.sharlalovelace.com, and keep up with all her new book releases easily by subscribing to her newsletter. She loves keeping up with her readers, and you can connect with her on Facebook, Twitter, and Instagram at @sharlalovelace.

Printed in the United States
by Baker & Taylor Publisher Services